THE FIRST AFFAIR

THE FIRST AFFAIR

A Novel

EMMA McLAUGHLIN
and
NICOLA KRAUS

ATRIA BOOKS

New York   London   Toronto   Sydney   New Delhi

ATRIA BOOKS

A Division of Simon & Schuster, Inc.
1230 Avenue of the Americas
New York, NY 10020

First Atria Books hardcover edition August 2013

ATRIA BOOKS and colophon are trademarks of Simon & Schuster, Inc.

For information about special discounts for bulk purchases, please contact Simon & Schuster Special Sales at 1-866-506-1949 or business@simonandschuster.com.

The Simon & Schuster Speakers Bureau can bring authors to your live event. For more information or to book an event contact the Simon & Schuster Speakers Bureau at 1-866-248-3049 or visit our website at www.simonspeakers.com.

Manufactured in the United States of America

10 9 8 7 6 5 4 3 2 1

Library of Congress Cataloging-in-Publication Data

McLaughlin, Emma.
   The first affair : a novel / Emma McLaughlin and Nicola Kraus. — First Atria books hardcover edition.
      pages   cm
   (ebook) 1. Adultery—Fiction. I. Title.
   PS3613.C575M35   2013
   813'.6—dc23

                                          2013009368

ISBN 978-1-4516-4342-8
ISBN 978-1-4516-4344-2 (ebook)

To the unforgiven girls

"How do you do that while raising children and being a husband and leading a party and running a country and traveling the world, pursuing a vision of democracy? You build walls, you compartmentalize, you make sure that no one ever knows you completely."
—Mimi Alford, teenage mistress of JFK

THE FIRST AFFAIR

Prologue

It was graduation weekend, long after midnight. Parents had been packed off to their motels, or talked into making the drive home alone with U-Hauls affixed to their tails. The air had chilled and there was a fire in the hearth of that sagging house, which someone else rented the year before and someone would rent the year after, the unchanging backdrop to an unchanging drama. Of course we wanted to think our year was different, our heartbreaks, our pregnancy scares, our Fs in organic chem, but they weren't. There was nothing unprecedented about us. Even the enormity of graduating into the worst job market anyone could remember was being played out before fireplaces just like that one on campuses across the country.

We shared beers and bongs, and random liqueurs bogarted at Christmas, looking at each other with affection intensified by a calcifying nostalgia. Someone in our group within the group placed a bottle down on the sticky wood floor and gave it a spin. Just truth or drink. Because by this point we'd made out with whoever we were going to; no point forcing the issue.

My best friend, Lena, her ticket to LAX on her folded quilt upstairs, laughed and nudged me into the impromptu circle, curious to see what I'd finally disclose at the zero hour. She kept stroking her newly straightened hair that made her look like Jennifer Hudson's younger sister, a preparatory step for the financial job she was about to start on the other side of the country.

What would I do without her?

I looked over and saw Mark still trying to get closure with his ex-boyfriend. Ashley was trying 'shrooms, because if not then—

when? And the bottle had slowed in front of Willow, who was telling the story of her first penis. Something about a dropped suit at summer camp—more innocent than her interrogator was hoping, but, hey, she answered the question. That was the only rule.

I saw the time on a phone vibrating its way under the sunken couch and my chest pleated in. The hours were dwindling. I knew I would stay up until Lena and I shared a cab to the train station. This would all be over and my internship would begin and I wasn't ready. I dropped my head on my freckled arms, my ginger ponytail flopping like a cast anchor. I wanted one more day on a meal plan. One more class to walk to. One more free movie.

I looked up. The bottle pointed at me. "Jamie," Mateo prompted, rubbing his curls off his forehead still covered by a smattering of acne.

"Yep."

"Oh, shit, she's giving me one of those Jamie smiles. Uh-uh, I'm not letting you off. Lena." Mateo looked to where she stood behind me. "Anything left you want to know?"

"What'd she get on her Spanish final, did she let that skinny guy from sophomore year sleep in my bed, and *where* are my red shoes?"

I laughed as Mateo shook off her suggestions. "Okay, Jamie, for a shot of Patrón and the last Mallomar. First time you gave a—"

Before the media thought they knew everything about me, before a bunch of lawyers at the Office of the Independent Counsel tried to know everything about me, before one man *did* know everything about me, I was a girl with secrets.

Part I

Chapter One

June 11

When I arrived at the White House the President was our shared responsibility, beyond also being the adjective attached to everything in the building. The Rutland administration. The Rutland agenda. The Rutland luncheon. He was the word in every fifth sentence, a ubiquitous stamped signature, a photograph over the royal-blue carpet on the way to the staff entrance. Under normal circumstances he would never even have known my name, but I unwittingly entered the White House at a time when we collectively sidestepped normal as a nation.

As a Vassar poli-sci major, my ambition had been for a job in urban development—before my scope rapidly widened to include anything without a name tag. My wealthier classmates had staved off the demoralizing hunt with grad school applications, but my debt already verged on not-get-out-of-bed paralyzing, so I applied for summer internships, the longest of long shots being for the White House. As much as I couldn't afford it, I prayed the unsalaried credential might be the key line item to differentiate my résumé. I'd heard that was especially true at Starbucks.

I'll never know for certain, but I assume it was the recommendation from Lena's mom, Gail, a major political fundraiser, that tipped the scales. Whatever it was, one day I was resigned to moving home and picking up shifts at Chili's, and the next I was sprung via Amtrak from Poughkeepsie to the West Wing.

I was assigned to the Department of Scheduling and Advance. Our mandate—which became my word of the day: my mandate, his mandate, their mandate—was to ensure that the President, the First Lady, and the traveling circus that is the press corps all got where they were supposed to go, be it New Delhi or Foggy Bottom.

The day this story starts, really starts, began with an absolutely insane marathon-length meeting. I'd been there only three weeks and was still getting used to the formalities; that morning the paid employees got to sit in cushy ergonomic swivel chairs around the conference table, while the junior staffers camped on the hard folding chairs behind them. And then there was us, the interns, standing pressed against the wall, with our practiced look of aggressive gratitude. I was wearing the black pumps I'd gotten at DSW that I thought epitomized the job, but of course were knockoffs of knockoffs and could only have been comfortable if I'd had Barbie feet. We'd been standing for maybe two hours by this point and I decided to surreptitiously slip a foot out and rest it on the floor.

To my right, Perfect Brooke sighed in slicing disapproval. If the interns had broken into a dance routine, Perfect Brooke would have led it. It would be the most boring dance routine you've ever sat through, but the show would be a hit anyway because that's how Brooke's life worked.

I'd naively thought this was going to be like the first days of college, where you form a ragtag clique with some kids on your dorm floor and go to the cafeteria together. Not that you'd hit it off with everyone, but usually there'd be at least one keeper and eventually you'd build a posse. After growing up just outside Chicago, being in a city like D.C. felt energizingly familiar, but my casual suggestions to Yelp a cool bar were met with suspicion. There was this slim hope hovering in the air that someone might be offered a permanent position at the end of the ten weeks, and my fellow interns were ready to club each other with their binders to get one. (It was basically a dowdily dressed version of the Hunger Games.) So, from what I could tell, the other interns went back to their Airbnb sublets, rubbed themselves with the *Financial Times*, and listened to NPR until they climaxed.

Leaving me to subsist on a constant stream of texts from my college friends, who'd scattered to take refuge in their C and D plans, while I spent *way* too much time in my own head. Hence, as the meeting entered its third hour, I was focused on my feet, on a potential job I was waiting to hear about, on Perfect Brooke's derision—oh, and that I needed to pee. Badly.

Just to remind you, Congress was digging in against passing the President's budget because they were still pissy about losing the election four years earlier. So America had been operating for months on a "continuing resolution," not dissimilar, I thought, to the credit card making it possible for me to be there. It was set to expire in two days if his demands for social service funding weren't met, which would effectively bring the government to a screeching halt.

A President and First Lady's schedules are need-a-new-definition-for-it tight on a normal day, so the prospect of being up to a week behind had thrown us all into a wrestling match with the space-time continuum. "What are we telling the Prime Minister?" one of the staffers, whose name I could never remember, asked insistently as he squinted at the dry-erase board. It was a heated land grab for every minute—and it had come down to a standoff over Uruguay.

"What are we telling the Prime Minister?" the department head, Margaret, repeated blankly, a marker hanging limply at her side, the aroma of which was making all of us ever so slightly high.

"Yes," the staffer repeated. "Am I removing POTUS from the teachers' union on June twenty-second so they can meet?"

"The teachers' union luncheon," another staffer growled, tugging at his loosened tie, "is attended by four *hundred* members. Citizens of the United States. Registered voters. It cannot be moved for bullshit face time with Uruguay. Stop asking, Gerry."

I reminded myself that Bushy Eyebrows was Gerry.

"Great!" Gerry threw up his arms, flashing dampened Oxford pits to the room. "I'll just tell the Prime Minister of Uruguay that Chris thinks his country is bullshit."

"It's an election year, Gerry," Margaret, whom I'd come to regard as imperturbable, reminded him with straining calm. But, capitulating, she put out a hand surgeon-style and the staffer closest gave her a fresh napkin to replace the saturated eraser. She wiped out the work of the last hour, eliciting frantic keyboard taps from those who'd yet to finish their transcription and a groan from everyone else. Except me; I was savoring a tiny prickle of pride because I'd brought that napkin. That napkin had no idea when it was stuffed in the metal dispenser at Capitol Bakery that morning that it was destined for greatness. I had grabbed a stack when I abandoned the coffee I was about to treat myself to in favor of two dozen oven-fresh sticky buns, which I ran in to work in hopes of making the day feel a little less cage-matchy—only to find the meeting that had been threatening for days was kicking off. So my buns were congealing into hardened globs in the kitchenette, but my napkins were there—they were helping.

"Okay. Potential government furlough scenario. Starting back at day one." Really? Surely I couldn't be the only one who had to chug a liter of water after commuting in the 95-degree heat. There had to be others desperate for a bathroom break.

The D.C. humidity and I were introduced when I stepped off the train with my life folded into two bulging suitcases. It's what floating in the Dead Sea might feel like—if instead of floating you were trying to walk to the opposite shore. With luggage. It's not as if Chicago doesn't have heat waves, but at least there the lake air keeps things moving. In grade school we learned the capital was born on swampland, but hoofing it in your one Ann Taylor Loft suit is something else entirely. I spent a full five minutes a day admiring that the founding folks didn't just say fuck it. Not that it wasn't an *enormous* privilege just to be able to stand against that wall. It was. Huge. It was just hard to keep the wide-eyed expression of appreciation in place when one had to pee oh so badly. Brooke was probably wearing a catheter.

"Don't you have to pee?" I whispered to Brooke.

She shot me another disapproving look. In retrospect, it would have taken more than a sticky bun to win over Brooke. Maybe if I'd spiked it with something—Xanax? Celexa? What's the one that makes you a nice person?

I chewed the inside of my mouth and shifted my attention from the web of abdominal pain to the job offer I'd been waiting on from the Los Angeles City Planning Commission, an email that could already have been on the phone I had to leave at my desk. It was possible, as I stood there, that I already possessed an actual job with health insurance and everything. Which meant a place with Lena in L.A. And a paycheck. I was going to kiss that check and make a copy, frame that, and then cash the check and buy myself a proper bottle of wine.

Gail's pied-à-terre, which I was staying in, with its White House view and uniformed doormen, was full of proper bottles of wine. The kind sommeliers study. I perpetually felt like I was failing it when I sat on its custom carpet and played omgpop or reheated a frozen burrito in its chef-grade oven. Weeks prior, I could have thrown back my shower curtain to find seriously anything—a hook-up, a moonshine contraption, a performance art rehearsal. Now I knew what awaited me—a wall of showerheads I couldn't figure out and a shelf of Chanel products for the rare occasions when Gail swung through. I should explain that Gail still credits me with saving Lena's life when Health Services misdiagnosed her appendicitis sophomore year. Lena's never been entirely sure whether Gail was more thankful that I got her to St. Francis in time or that I took notes for all her classes.

Margaret threw her hands up. "We're now just repeating options we ruled out an hour ago." No one denied it. "Okay, lunch break." I attempted the most dignified version of scrambling over everyone I could muster.

Peeing crossed off, I swung by the kitchen to reheat my goodwill tour. "Pecan bun?" I pimped, and a passing staffer nabbed one. "Thanks," he said, blowing the heat off as he chewed. I held one out to Brooke, but she looked as if I'd taken it to the bathroom with me.

"Allergic to nuts?" I determinedly offered her the opportunity to soften her rudeness.

"No." She covered the papers she'd just started to work from as if I might have wanted to filch her tedious assignment over my own tedious assignment.

"Oh my God, I'm so hungry I could eat your brain zombie-style. Seriously, cut your head open with this pen so I can eat it." A slight brunette appeared, arms full, carrying a massive patent-leather tote she could easily have climbed inside of. She dropped her iPad and binder on Brooke's desk to grab a bun as I took in her statement bangs, python-print wrap dress, and open-toed wedges. Definitely not one of ours. "It's just wrong that these things have, like, a stick of butter in them."

"A stick?" I asked. "No. Maybe half." She wasn't much older than us.

"Two halves," she said as a man in a tight suit approached us and she scooped up her things with her forearms, licking a caramel string off her finger.

"Rachelle." He literally snapped for her.

"Thank you," she said to me. "You're a genius. An evil genius." I watched her leave, feeling like I'd just missed the last van pulling out for senior week.

Brooke picked up her brown leather bag. "Do you want to come?" she asked with a resignation that implied I was clinging to her ankles.

But maybe this was the moment. Maybe a friendship was about to form. Maybe outside this building Brooke became someone else entirely. "Uh, sure."

I followed her brisk stride while I fruitlessly checked emails on my phone. I told myself it was okay. It was barely past ten on the West Coast; plenty of day left there to hire me.

I asked Brooke if she knew who Rachelle was here with.

"Some PR group getting footage for the campaign," she answered as she walked.

"Funny, the thing she said about eating my brain," I offered.

"I can see why you'd think so."

Getting to like you, getting to hope you like me . . . "So, where are we going?"

"To buy lunch."

"I have a peanut butter sandwich in my purse."

She didn't respond as we exited into the flattening heat. Everyone had initially assumed from Gail's address that I was a fellow trust-funder, but the logo on my dad's polo was definitely *not* a pony. As I was unable to share a favorite Hampton, memories of trips to Europe, or any opinion on my mother's personal shopper's taste, it became rapidly apparent we wouldn't be exchanging friendship bracelets.

"Gross," Brooke muttered, pulling her starched blouse away from her chest. I realized she was wearing The Shirt. It had an extra button between the cleavage and collar, designed for D.C. women to achieve neutral modesty on the four-inch drop from uptight to whore. I'd been debating sucking it up and buying one.

Brooke informed me that she had to get cash and, letting go of any hopes of banter, I followed her into the ATM while composing a text to my similarly inaccessible sister asking her advice about the purchase. Erica, whose Titian hair magically stays pin straight while the curl of mine is more reliable than a barometer. Whose nose is the thinner, perkier version. Who's an inch taller, a size four to my six, and whose pores, even through adolescence, were never visible. She grabbed all the good genes and I got the leftovers. Four years older, Erica lived in Manhattan, where she continued to evade my lifelong attempts at preemptive consultation. Her opinions about my choices *after* the fact, however, flew like sniper fire. At our grandmother's suggestion, around fourth grade, I was signed up for an Irish clog-dancing class, which I loved. The pageantry, hair ribbons, and rhythms were a revelation. But I was all of five minutes into rehearsing in our bedroom when Erica decreed that either the clogs went or I did. I gave it my best, slapping my bunny socks on the hardwood, but Saturday's practice always found me queasily unsure of what I would produce once wearing the actual shoes. Needless to say, I quickly retired and was back to watching Nickelodeon with the sound down.

I imagined her reading my inquiry between stock trades, or whatever it was she actually did as an analyst. I'm certain that my missive was two sentences and three exclamation marks too many, that I re-read it twice, and added a "you rock!" before hitting Send.

"Drugstore." Brooke's bag hit my arm as she pushed out the door on what was passing for our lunch date. Three weeks earlier, I had not had to trail people.

I texted Lena while I waited. *"Nostalgic for shower vomit this morning."*

"Nostalgic for finals—3 term papers in 48 hrs—didn't know how easy I had it." She bemoaned the brutal pace of her new position at a wealth management firm in Beverly Hills.

Brooke signaled from the long line that I should go next door to the deli and start on that long line.

"*When you get a minute (hahaha),*" I typed as I walked, "*find out how I can turn the AC down from your mom?*"

"*That shit is set at freeze. Menopause, bitch.*"

"*Aw, menopause—we DO have things to look forward to!*"

"*Don't believe you,*" she responded as I went inside the deli. "*Am going to die at this conference table.*"

"*No word on job yet. Getting worried.*"

The phone went quiet and I knew she had to jump.

I glazed over at the TV above the beer fridge—in D.C. even the delis are tuned to CNN. The blandly attractive face of Brianne Rice came onscreen. I was a freshman when she'd come forward claiming that the President had made "sexual overtures" at her when he was the junior senator from Pennsylvania. Her accusations drove what was pretty universally considered to be one of those Swift Boat smear campaigns that inevitably come up during an election.

Lena and I had debated the veracity and relevance of that claim over French toast sticks. I remember wondering if Brianne was telling the truth, and then being fairly sure she wasn't, and then it didn't matter. While it was hard to imagine that our President, whom *People* had dubbed "Dreamy-in-Chief," would make a rebuffed pass at anyone, more germane to everyone was that his wife was beloved. While public opinion of him vehemently split the country, it was universally agreed that Susan Rutland was a First Lady who, in her spirit and style, elevated us. It was inconceivable that she didn't captivate his heart as she did the world's.

I tried to hear what was happening as I watched footage of the Supreme Court, which is never very exciting footage. Rutland's legal team had kept the case at bay by claiming that, as a sitting President, he couldn't be sued. In breaking news, the Supreme Court had agreed to hear their argument, which made the heads of those in line tilt up.

But suddenly someone else pulled my attention. "This place is packed," a boy with both the tan and air of one who'd just hopped down from a lifeguard chair addressed me. "What's the deal? Are their Doritos a particularly good vintage?"

"It's a convenience thing," I answered, lifting my restricted intern pass, which I wore on a lanyard as if it granted me backstage access to Adam Levine, though all it really allowed me was to follow a tight route from security to my desk. "Like the restaurants on the turnpike."

"Sorry, but if that's a dig at Arby's we might have to take this outside."

"Sir." I put a hand to my heart. "What girl wouldn't pay a toll to get a meal from under a heat lamp?"

He grinned. I guessed he was on vacation or en route to one. Perhaps down to the Carolina beaches. I'd heard some people our age were actually doing these things. Backpacking around Europe, sitting on docks, drinking at lunch. The door opened again and Brooke pushed in with a blast of the summer I'd never have again. "Why's everyone here?" she asked with annoyance, cutting in front of us.

"Sorry," I mouthed to him as she grabbed a diet something from the case.

His warm breath was unexpectedly at my ear. "I just heard about this jazz thing in the park tonight. You know about it?"

I nodded. "I'm not let out of my cage very often, but yes, I do."

The harried lady at the register beckoned and I stepped up to get an iced coffee while Brooke curated her chopped salad. When I glanced back, my eyes met the boy's as they telegraphed his interest. I had no idea how to parlay this into anything. On a small campus, parlaying had been unnecessary. An awkward coffeehouse introduction could be followed by a mailbox run-in followed by the eventual beer-goggled hook-up. Restricted geography was on my side. But now I realized I'd have only one-shot chances with people, and the prospect that I might end up living alone with cats seemed very real. He finished paying and, to my total surprise, handed me the ripped-off top of his résumé. *Oh, so that's what we do now.*

I surreptitiously read his scrawl as Brooke positioned her salad in her tote. *"Concert starts @ 7. Meet me at the south entrance?"* I flipped it over to see his name, Josh Wright, cell phone, and email in a sturdy, masculine font.

As we stepped outside, I smiled down the straw into my iced coffee, thinking of Josh. Jazz in the park with Josh. "You don't have a boyfriend," Brooke stated as she slid her Wayfarers down off headband duty.

"No, no I do not." Brooke mentioned *her* boyfriend with a frequency that rivaled our fellow intern Todd's ability to work having been a Senate page into any conversation. The boyfriend's name was Bentley. Bentley was doing some business thing in London. Bentley was playing some sport thing in a league. I imagined Bentley wearing The Shirt and pearls, his big feet stretching the elasticized backs of Brooke's Tory Burches.

I took a long slurp, thinking of the intermittent string of discarded flannel shirts on the floor of my dorm room. "Nothing serious. Not since high school." The guys at Vassar had been so repulsively tentative: perpetually half-high, too in love with their film projects—their *vision*—to really come for anyone in a grand romantic gesture kind of way.

Not like my first boyfriend. In junior high I'd started studying every afternoon at the Naperville town library to avoid Erica, and I had a crush on Mike Harnet from the first time I saw him in the stacks. He had moved with his family to New Orleans from Norway because his dad was a musician. I loved how he spoke—his English was pretty perfect, but his inflection was highly formal, and it made me think of Tolkien and wizards and fairies. He had a mop of short black hair, a still-pink scar on his temple from dueling a playground slide, a braces-free smile, and a declared mission to determine a favorite book in every single section. One rainy day when I got up from my spot, I returned to find a Post-it left on my science textbook. He'd written, "*?*" When I looked up, he was watching me from between the stacks. We stared at each other like that for a moment, suspended. Then I marched down the deserted aisle and thrust the square of yellow paper at him, feigning annoyance. Mike lifted his finger, then slowly circled it as if about to land anywhere on me. A foreign heat popped open in my chest and radiated downward. *Oh my God,* I thought. *Oh my God.* He leaned in very slowly until the warmth of his chapped lips landed on mine.

That was our first kiss.

So I worried. In the years that followed, I worried that I was incapable of feeling something for someone who didn't know how to initiate.

We followed the shade of the awnings, passing the frame store with that ubiquitous dorm-room poster of the woman applying lipstick while the shirtless guy watches. "I miss that." I gestured with the tip of my straw.

"What?"

"You know, The Look."

"What?"

"How he looks at her. Appraises her. That thing where you can see it in their eyes—they're in."

"Right. Okay, Jamie." I did not picture Bentley giving Brooke The Look. "Can I offer you feedback?"

"Sure!" I said automatically as if she'd offered me ice cream.

"I just think you should . . ." She turned her wrist, her thin Cartier bracelets staggered on her arm hairs. "Be beige."

"Beige."

She nodded as though she'd cleared her conscience and continued across the street. I took a long drag of my straw. *What?* "Sorry, just to clarify."

"Yes?"

"Beige is . . . ?"

She let out a how-do-we-solve-a-problem-like-Maria sigh as we arrived back at security. She unrolled her sleeves and closed her ninety-dollar button. "Being *charming*," she said the word derisively, "doesn't inspire confidence. We just thought you should know, okay?" She gave me a flat smile and went through the screener. *We?* I stood there with my face beating. I did not get that place. At all. I tugged out my phone as she walked off, willing it to beam me out of there—I *just* needed that job to come through.

For the remainder of that afternoon I still didn't get any word, but I did manage to book multiple hotel-room blocks, schedule a magnitude of press-corps bus charters, and locate the largest dining room in

Skokie that had a "homey feel" while seating nine hundred some-odd people. And furtively search everything about the adorable Josh Wright all the way back to his fourth-grade intramural soccer photo. Here's what I knew: (A) always adorable, (B) possessed over a thousand Facebook friends, including the handful we had in common, and (C) was from—wait for it—*Los Angeles.*

Finally I was there, having the kind of night I thought life after college was going to be full of. I was a girl working for free right in the heart of it all, reclining on the grass as the waning sun streaked the sky orange. "If the intern program needed a brochure, the cover should be a picture of us here, now," I said to Josh as I took another sip of wine he had the class to bring to the concert with two plastic cups.

"I don't think they're pitching a lifestyle." He smiled and leaned back on his elbows.

"Come on, hovering-with-the-hope-of-getting-chosen is totally a lifestyle."

"In L.A., too," he said. "My dad once got handed a head shot while having his teeth cleaned."

"Sorry, I meant to say homely hovering."

"We have homely. Despite the mayor's best efforts, we even have old people and the disabled." He tipped his head to my shoulder. "So I'm sure I can find some homely for you when you come out." I suddenly remembered that I hadn't checked my email since I ran out to meet him. I sat forward to root in my bag and realized I'd left my phone in my desk.

He slid his from his pocket. "It's a little after nine."

"When's end of business out there?"

"Now-ish. This doesn't have to end. Come on." He grinned. "I'll walk you back."

We strolled beneath the magnolias as he told me about Wesleyan. We compared if-I-don't-get-off-campus-I'll-shoot-someone trips into the city. We laughed about his roommate's obese pet rabbit who hated him and waited every night for him to get into bed before leaping onto his head. We lamented over job searches—his just passing the one-year mark. "Well," I said, slowing as we approached the guard booth. "You can wait here—I'll text you if I get stuck—"

"I'll come in with you."

"Yeah, right." I grinned.

"But you work there."

"Not really. I mean, I definitely don't have clearance to bring anyone in—I could meet you at a bar. Or if anyone needs me to do anything and it takes me more than twenty minutes, we could meet up near your hotel?"

He tipped back on his heels. "Okay. I was kinda thinking . . . I don't really have a hotel, actually, not in the budget—Dad's getting a little uptight with the bankrolling at this point. My flight's first thing. I was just gonna wander, but, wow, it's so humid—and the mosquitoes. How about I wait at your place?" He leaned in to kiss me.

I stepped back. "Um . . ."

"Come on, Jamie."

"I'm staying at a friend's mom's place, so I can't—"

"Oh. I get it. Well, maybe we can meet up later," he said, looking up and down the block, so abruptly over me. "Which way is the Metro?"

I pointed, suddenly not feeling like an object of desire so much as an easy mark. Like Homeaway.com crossed with Nerve.

He didn't even wave as he walked away.

Inside, the vapors of wine turning rancid in my mouth, I strode quickly to my desk, where my phone was vibrating in the drawer.

"Mom?" I answered, voice loud in the near-empty office.

"Hey, you have to resend me that email about visiting you for the Fourth." She sounded distracted. I pictured her at the old computer in the living room, the phone clamped to her shoulder as she slit the day's mail from its envelopes, heels slipped off and knee-highs soon to follow.

"Okay." I put in my headphones so I could check for the job offer while talking. *Please let this day be erased by this email*, I thought. *Save me, save me, save me . . .*

"The thing is, we weren't sure how Erica was going to get to you from the airport."

"She can take the Metro, it's super easy. Or there're buses. And there's always a cab." Gmail downloaded.

"It might not be a good weekend for her to get away, with her work."

"You two could always come without her." I knew the answer to that one.

"We'd like to see her, too," she reminded me.

"Of course, great." And there it was. From the City of Los Angeles, as if the whole population had weighed in on me. I clicked it open, my eyes darting to read that they were reluctant to inform me . . . at this time . . . they would keep my application on file . . . if.

If.

"Everything good with you, bug?"

"Yes, great. You guys okay?"

"Yup, all good," she said, and then I heard the soundtrack of whatever my dad was watching recede. "So get this," she continued in a hushed voice, and I knew she'd stepped onto the top of the basement stairs. "Baker announced he's retiring this fall."

"So that's good, right?"

"Good?" Her voice rose, and I could see her dropping her head against the phone the way she does when she's reached the day's end.

"Because he'll finally be gone," I reasoned. Ten years ago Chip Baker, coach of Chicago U's football team, fired Dad when he tumbled off the wagon in the preseason.

"Well, sure. But first he'll be everywhere. You know how this town feels about him. Your father hurled the remote at the screen. Oh, there's Erica calling me back. So, if she's a go we'll see you on the third?"

"Can't wait. And let me know if there's anything special you guys want to do while you're—"

"Great. Love you." She hung up. I sat at my desk, now hoping I would be spotted and pulled in to do something—urgently—that I could accomplish—brilliantly—and reclaim this incredibly crappy day.

I was brought back by a text from Erica responding to my shirt question, hours later. *"No."*

An empty apartment waited. The anesthetizing whir of its appliances. Too many more days with Brooke and her "people." Followed by Chili's. And my parents.

A headache from the cheap wine building, I tugged my ponytail out of its elastic band and walked quickly down the empty carpeted hall, shaking out my hair. I dropped my head back, letting out a breath to the dentil molding high above. *Fuck. Fuck!* This was so not how this was supposed to go. I should have applied to more places, sucked it up and moved home, saved the money that could have put me closer to escape than defeat, been more beige. Suddenly two Secret Service men emerged from the opposite office, passing swiftly. And then, just like that, there was the President, so much taller than me, the solid warmth of a muscular arm grazing me as he strode past in a white dress shirt. His sandy-blond hair glinting in the lamplight, a hint of spiced deodorant in his wake. The magnitude of it spun me around.

Between two ficus trees potted in Ming bowls, twisting to gaze over his shoulder, this happened and I know it with absolute certainty. At that jet lag of an age, in that drought of a time, on a day when being called inconsequential would have been a promotion, the most powerful man in the world gave me The Look.

And I was the only one who saw it.

Chapter Two

June 14

You often hear newly engaged people say with a bemused, grateful look on their faces: if I hadn't missed my usual bus, if I hadn't gotten the address of the bar wrong, if I hadn't gone to that party I *really* didn't want to go to, then I never would have . . . But for that second encounter to occur, the universe didn't just manifest a measly spilled drink or stalled subway.

Sometime after midnight, a text came in from Margaret confirming what CNN was already saying. No last-minute budget compromise had been arrived at. The U.S. government was shut down. I clicked around the channels, seeing the same banner passing beneath every sitcom rerun: *All non-essential federal employees are required to stay home.* Meaning all *non*-employees would be essential.

The next morning, I stepped out into a rushless rush hour. In the schoolyards, parents dressed in sweats were milling instead of dashing off. There was no line at Starbucks. But the drugstore was already completely out of laundry detergent, which tells you all you need to know. Washington standard is to work seven days a week until you have an embolism, but for once the salons were going to be packed. And the vets. And the mechanics. Long-overdue thank-you notes would be written *and* mailed.

I rounded the corner to Pennsylvania and, even with a few blocks to go, could already see the news vans. The correspondents were trying to summarize the situation for the treadmill crowd: the President wasn't backing down and the Senate Majority Leader was being a dick, more focused on breeding miniature Pomeranians—his honest-to-God hobby—than on bipartisan resolution. He had a tiny one the size of a furry clementine, named Ronald, that he carried to work with him, like Elle Woods. While voting aggressively against gay marriage. So there was that.

The interns filed inside the eerily empty building, half buzzing with conjecture about what might happen to or for us, the other half struck apprehensively silent as if this had all been an elaborate plot to harvest our organs for aging congressmen.

Brooke, nostrils flared, strode in with what I'd call a Jonestown level of purpose. Headband unprecedentedly left home, she was letting the river run.

"Okay, guys." Margaret emerged from her office, clapping. Everyone was instantly rapt. "Triage time. For the duration of the furlough, all interns are going to be moved . . ." She paused, and we all visibly leaned in. "Upstairs." She dropped the last word like the Christmas stocking full of bearer bonds she knew it was.

We had been given a hasty tour through the executive offices the first day, mostly, it seemed, so we'd know the fire exits. A hand had been tossed in the direction of the Oval Office. But now we were going *upstairs*.

Brooke turned to me as we all scrambled to grab our possessions. "I am going to kill this."

I believed her.

The interns were pooled into one very determined, inappropriately euphoric, workforce of people who wanted to kill it. But what became quickly apparent is that few had the clerical skills to do so. While they could prepare an opinion for a senator or make Graydon Carter a dinner reservation, they were lost when it came to anything that could be farmed out to a highly trained hamster. And I was suddenly grateful for every vacation I ended up monotonously filing by my mother's side at her insurance firm while my friends were candle dipping. And these guys were learning semaphore.

We were set up in the pen down the long corridor from the Oval Office, where the President was on the phone trying to use back channels to get the Senate Majority Leader and his little dog to return to budget negotiations. It wasn't going well. We knew this because every time the door opened we could hear distinct—and gratifying— swearing. If you've ever sat around calling your elected representatives fucking assholes, imagine hearing the President do it.

At noon a few of the interns were dispatched to get subs, then at seven they ran out again for pizzas. We took turns keeping the coffee fresh and the water cooler full. By eleven, Margaret said anyone who wanted to leave, could. No one did.

Around midnight I hung up with the Director of the Office of Management and Budget, who had given me twenty-step instructions to a two-step task he obviously would have preferred just doing himself. It was like explaining putting on pants to an alien. I scrolled through the late-edition headlines, trying to get some sense of where this was going and paused on a small article, a human-interest link from the *Chicago Tribune*. A patron had commissioned a bronze statue of Baker that would be placed in Lincoln Park on my dad's jogging route. I reached for my phone.

"Good morning," he greeted me brightly, as he always did when I called home after midnight. I love his voice, the hint of an Irish accent from his childhood before his family moved to the South Side. I had always liked talking to him when Mom and Erica were in bed because he seemed to appreciate the company. The only time he slept well, Mom says, was when he drank. "What are you doing?"

"Still at work," I answered quietly.

"Ma says they called you guys in."

"Yep. I'm down the hall from the Oval Office. Not too shabby." I tilted my head down as Todd glanced over, his nostrils dancing disdainfully.

"Eh, Rutland picks and flicks like the rest of us."

"You don't know that," I said, smiling. "Bluebirds might bring him a silk handkerchief, or North Korean children—we don't know what secrets this guy keeps."

Dad laughed.

"I just saw about the statue," I said.

He paused for a second, probably taking a swig from his O'Doul's.

"You know, Jamie, it may just be my age, enlarged prostate or what-not, but I can't get through my run anymore without needing to take a big piss. I'd not been sure where to go—the men's rooms are a little sketchy at that hour and the woods can be buggy. So they've just done me a favor."

"Okay then, so long as you're taking it in stride."

"Love ya, kid."

"You too, Dad." I hung up, smiling.

I have no idea when I eventually got home or what time I got back in the next day—in my mind, I passed through Gail's apartment as if on a conveyor belt, swapping out clothes and swiping on deodorant. The news channels were already saying that the presidential bid of the presumptive Republican nominee, John Partridge, had gone from dubious to posing a tight race.

Anxious, we tucked our heads and hit our piles. Just before lunch the political media film crew came back. The tan man in the tight-fitting suit stalked around with the tip of his rimless glasses between his lips and then jumped on Brooke's desk. Rachelle, the girl who'd wanted to eat my brain, arrived, carrying coffee in one hand and a half-eaten apple in the other. She registered our confusion.

"Hi. Okay, so Geoffrey, here, is setting the camera angles. We want to show that you guys are all still hard at work." She tried to keep her eyes on him as she brought us up to speed, the shifting making her look even more nervous. "This isn't a vacay."

Without actually acknowledging her, Geoffrey gestured for the apple and took a bite. "You," he said, mouth full.

"Me?" I pointed at my chest.

"Switch with him," he ordered. "That's an Asian cluster."

"We don't want this to look like a cafeteria," Rachelle explained as Geoffrey thrust the core at her.

"Thank you," Rachelle said to me as I moved while seemingly weighing whether he wanted her to keep it. "That's great."

"It'll do," Geoffrey conceded. "Your hair works for me—natural?"

I nodded over the twenty or so people between us, feeling my face turn the same red as they commenced filming. "*Don't* look at us," Geoffrey said sharply. "Busy! Busy! Busy! And serious."

"Like you're at a very busy funeral," Rachelle offered. A few awkward minutes passed while I stared meaningfully at the work of the guy whose desk I had taken.

"Fuck!" Our faces flew to Geoffrey as his darkened over the coffee. "This is . . . skim."

Rachelle winced. "I'm so sorry—"

"Cut!" He summarily dropped the cup in Brooke's trash, sending liquid sloshing onto the side of her desk. "Just fucking cut. You and you and you—Lucy!" Geoffrey pointed at me.

"This way, please," Rachelle implored us, looking miserable.

Having no idea what was happening, we trailed Geoffrey and the cameras.

"How's it going?" I asked her tentatively.

"I'm thriving on this," she muttered.

"Really? He seems like kind of a . . ."

"He is. It's my mantra. 'I'm thriving on this.' But I'll be on the verge of convincing myself and then he opens his mouth."

"Plus you have that lovely apple core there."

"I shall sleep with it under my pillow." She gave me a sidelong smile.

"Now stay," Geoffrey instructed as we were rounded into the Oval's reception area. Pick the most intimidating thing you have ever done in your life. Go ahead. I'll wait. Now multiply that by ten.

The Deputy Chief of Staff came out of the office. She was in a twill pantsuit and sneakers, literally ready to run to the Hill at a moment's notice. "Oh great, perfect timing," she said to Geoffrey. "Let's get that youth footage—show this as a vibrant, *young* administration and that what Partridge makes up for in seniority he lacks in having any fucking idea what's going on." I was starting to wonder if this was some kind of election-year tic, everyone overcaffeinatedly narrating their purpose.

She pushed the door open and the President stood from behind his carved desk. For us. For a split second, I imagined he did a little double-take at seeing me again. But I couldn't swear to it. We shuffled in, past the eagle seal in the carpet. *Holy shit.* That was all I could think. *Holy shit.*

"Hi, guys," he welcomed us casually, hands resting on the hips of his trousers. "Where do you want me?"

"Oh, that's just fine, Mr. President," Geoffrey said, unctuousness replacing his irritation. "If you could just sit there? And work, perhaps. Maybe they can huddle—or take turns passing you things. It's just B-roll, so there's no sound."

"No problem." He reseated himself and picked up his tortoise-shell frames.

"If you wouldn't mind, sir, might I suggest no glasses?"

"Makes me look my age, huh?" Rutland smiled. "I don't usually have a huddle of interns around my desk. What should I . . ."

Geoffrey snapped his fingers in my direction.

"Jamie," I said in response.

"Jamie, can you hand him a folder?"

The deputy materialized a folder as the camera started recording. I crossed to the President's desk. We made eye contact as I handed it off—his were so much greener than in the pictures. The side I'd held had a visible damp handprint.

"So, sorry." Geoffrey shook his head. "It looks like she's serving you—"

"A subpoena," Rutland joked presciently. Yes, really.

"I was going to say a steak. Why doesn't she come around the desk and you could show her something?"

"As if I care about young people understanding things?" Rutland added dryly. As directed, I stepped closer while he opened the file and leaned down to point something out on the blank paper.

"Sir, I'm sorry, sir, your, uh, hair," Rachelle entreated. Geoffrey cut his eyes at her, but she was right to say something. It had flopped in his face like those pictures from his college days. He puffed his lower lip to blow it up. I noticed he had little freckles along his lip line that must always be airbrushed in photos. His skin was handsomely sun-lined, as though he'd spent a lot of time outdoors doing wholesome things in his almost fifty years. Like his was a life well lived.

"Perfect, let's keep moving, shall we?" Geoffrey cooed. Rutland leaned forward and the crest of thick blond hair flopped again, revealing a few silver strands. "Sir." Rutland puffed harder.

"Don't you use hairspray?" I asked. The two guys from Stanford stepped back as if I'd farted out my mouth.

Rutland put down the folder and looked me square in the face. "The second you start wearing spray you have relinquished your humanity. I wear foundation for the cameras, sure. I've even been known to powder. But I draw the line at spray." How could I not have smiled?

"Cut," Geoffrey trilled.

"I think we got it," Rachelle added.

"Have we?" Geoffrey said as if amused, but causing Rachelle to gulp as though later he'd be shouting that question with a raised wire hanger. "Thank you, sir, we appreciate your time. As my lovely assistant has so astutely noted, we're all set."

Rachelle backed the interns out of the room, bobbing like a pack of grateful Mitsubishi executives.

The President smiled and the door shut. And that could have been it. The story I tell my grandkids. But spilled drinks and stalled subways . . .

By the third day I had lost a disgusting amount of sleep, but I'd met Rachelle, a potential friend, and had a great anecdote to reenact as soon as I was with actual human beings and not the Orcs I shared an office with.

The fed-up mood of the nation was impossible to ignore. Partridge gave a speech, the thrust of which asked, *Does Rutland hate America?* "Commanding words from the Republican nominee," Wolf Blitzer commented in the nightly recap. "Yes," the correspondent agreed. "Whatever else comes out of this budget standoff, I think we can agree Governor Partridge seems to be experiencing real personal growth."

I snorted my cold coffee. "Oh good," I said, grabbing a napkin. "Silver lining found." The Orcs looked at me strangely. "I mean, c'mon, it'd be *such* a shame to shut down the whole U.S. government if Partridge wasn't going to get to grow as a person. Maybe he'll make a vision board? Or refinish a bureau."

"That isn't funny," Brooke reprimanded.

But she was contradicted by a deep guffaw from behind us and all turned to see the President holding his sides, his shirttails untucked. Everyone leapt up. "Thanks, Jamie, I needed that." We all startled at my name. Then I remembered I'd told him over the sweaty folder. And he was a politician. "Sit, sit—it's the middle of the night." He waved us down, but nobody moved. There was silence where there'd been breathing. "How are you guys holding up?"

No one knew who was supposed to answer.

"Great, sir." Todd actually swung his fist in the air, adding, "It's a pleasure to serve."

"Is it?" Rutland asked wryly, but his gaze returned to me.

"The pizza's not bad," I said with the hint of a shrug.

Rutland walked over to the pile of boxes. He pulled out a long-cold slice and, for want of a napkin, slid it onto a piece of stationery. He leaned on a desk and we watched him take a bite, his eyes closing for a moment as he chewed, his exhaustion evident. "We really appreciate you all being here. You're making it possible for us to hold their feet to the fire." On the screen over his head the ticker read, *Rutland one-term President?* "National Parks were closed today, passport applications went unprocessed, veterans went unserviced, the CDC was shut down." His chewing slowed. "Gutting Medicaid isn't an option—this all can't have been for nothing." He gestured in a way that seemed to encompass not just the shutdown, but his administration. "Well, thanks for dinner. And the hard work. I'm heading to the residence," he said as if someone might ask *us* for the President's whereabouts. He walked to the doorway, eighty or so sets of eyes on his back. "Gonna try to grab an hour of sleep. I suggest you all do the same." He stopped and turned, his gaze locked on me for a second.

I knew I should say "Sir" and nod, but I just smiled. Like I was at a party we might leave together.

I dropped back in my chair and plunged my attention to the columns of numbers, aware of the eyes on me, the flush creeping up my neck. Flipping the folder closed, I reached for the next one, sensing the snide thought bubbles popping up around me. I heard my phone buzz in my bag, and, grateful for the activity, checked it.

"Hey James. Recently moved to NJ. Trying to resist the impulse to get big hair or start crime cartel. Hope all's good in your world. MH." I stared at the initials. Mike Harnet. On a normal day—not that I knew a normal day, having been cannon-shot from college into the White House, but I believe on a normal day—I would have contemplated what this meant and how to respond for minimally an eternity. If he had texted me even a month earlier, I might have finally broken down and told Lena about him so she could analyze his every possible meaning. But the text had arrived at that moment when, for the first time in a long time, a new Look had fritzed my brain.

Mike Harnet is someone you think you know a lot about. I know a lot about him now, too. But then I just thought of Mike as someone I was long out of touch with, and, with everything else going on, I did what had heretofore seemed impossible: I forgot about it.

By the fourth day of the furlough it seemed like every hair in the city had been trimmed, every dog groomed, every hedge manicured— people here, across the country, and in unstable economies around the world were ready for this to be *over*. Germany said something that roughly translated to "Get your shit together." Standard and Poor's threatened to downgrade U.S. credit, and by nightfall, Rutland's approval rating had plummeted.

Meanwhile, on what felt at the time to be the cringingly trivial front, I had run out of clean clothes. So I borrowed a blouse from Gail's closet and threw on my uncomfortable-but-clean H&M hookup bra that I had optimistically brought to D.C. because, well, I didn't picture Todd and his ilk being the norm here.

Todd, whose face was permanently pink from rubbing it to stay awake. As my mascara (mandatory for redheads) prohibited me from doing the same, I instead pushed my index fingers into my temples and blinked up at the fluorescents until a white buzz brought me back. I'd stopped trying to make Margaret love me. I was just trying to survive without making the type of clerical error that would cause a butterfly effect to unknown people in unknown parts of the world years from now.

Rutland, reelection and legacy slipping away, had taken to lapping our bullpen in jeans and a faded polo, eyes on his loafers, motioning us down each time he passed, but we popped up anyway, like we were doing the wave. Brooke permanently hovered over her chair. She probably played a sport.

Sometimes Rutland would walk and talk with his Chief of Staff, Amar Singh, tossing a softball between them. It was something to see Rutland up close, presidential uniform abandoned, a ketchup spot on his shirt from lunch, hair unruly, and caring so deeply about incomprehensible numbers that to him were a line of too-real people that stretched from the Pacific to the edge of his desk. And it occurred to me that, on one level, he was exactly who you'd want doing this job, while on the other, he was so not cut out for it. My grandmother would have said, "He'd give away his last potato," and not as a compliment. It was actually her gravest insult, thrown my way most memorably in fifth grade when I let the neighbors think I broke their garden gnome so Erica wouldn't get grounded right before the Spring Dance.

As they walked, they agonizingly agreed on the points of capitulation they would reapproach the Majority Leader with in the morning, each one a social-service bloodletting. My stomach burning, I stole another of Todd's TUMS.

Sometime close to midnight Margaret dropped a fresh stack on my stacks, this one bound in a distinctive red rubber band. "Jamie, run this to the Chief of Staff's office. We needed these signed off on two hours ago. Don't stop walking until you've put them in Singh's hand—even if you have to push into the men's room to do it."

His assistant's chair was unoccupied. Emboldened by Margaret's instructions, I knocked and pushed Singh's office door farther open. The dimly lit room was packed with briefing reports, stacked waist-high from the floor, and on one wall was a framed silk illustration of that blue elephant, the one with all those arms and the kind eyes. Beside it, the door leading to the series of private rooms that connected Singh's office to the Oval was open and I thought I heard footsteps. I walked quickly through, stepping out of the light, and felt for the switch. The chandelier revealed that I was in the executive dining room. The door across the room slammed shut. Admittedly it was a childlike instinct that propelled me the length of the polished table toward the crystal knob, hand outstretched, like the famous fictional girls I grew up reading about. The ones who sought a garden, a city, a rabbit—or a man. On the long list of prohibitions I carry now, I would never open a slammed door. But then, I think it was the slammed door that drew me the hardest.

Unable to see, I heard it first. His breathing. Tight and irregular. A wheeze—like dying. "Sir?" I don't know how I knew that the form standing in the shadow outside the sliver of light was him, and not Singh, but I did.

"Shut the door," he spoke on the inhale.

"It's Jamie, the intern from Scheduling, and—"

"I know."

"Do you need me to call someone?"

"Shut the door."

I did, stepping in, and not out as he maybe—probably—meant, confining us in the windowless black. I had no idea what room we were in. "Do you need an inhaler?" I asked. I felt the darkness move and moved toward it. "Sir?"

"No."

I took another step. I could smell him now, the vestiges of cologne, a faint sweat. I felt a hand brush my leg and dropped the papers. I reached out and he clasped it, hard enough to hurt.

"Sir? Are you having a panic attack?" I knew what that was. "Sir?"

"Greg."

"Greg." The syllable. Technically a correction. But also an invitation, one he would explain months later, that allowed me to say, "Breathe. Through your nose." I felt him buck. "I know. It feels like you'll die. Like you won't be able to draw enough air in, but it'll actually force everything to calm. Trust me." I took an exaggerated breath through my nostrils, adding my other hand to his. "Greg?" I heard him try, his fingers crushing mine. "That's good," I whispered.

"That's good. You're doing good." His grip relaxed, his breathing slowed.

It took me a few moments of us standing like that—in the perfect darkness—to realize he was crying.

"It's okay," I said, like I would to a little boy, though I didn't really know that it was. Or probably knew that we weren't anywhere in the vicinity. "It's okay."

His hand pulled slowly into himself, not letting mine go. I took a step, permitting my body to make contact with his.

Then, sensing a second tacit invitation, I allowed my head to tip, coming to rest against his chest, the worn cotton of his shirt damp from his perspiration. We stood like that, breathing in tandem, the world outside on pause. His other arm wrapped around me. I knew his face was tilting down and I let mine tilt up. When his lips contacted mine they were wet and salty.

I was so outside myself. I wanted to tell him to stop so I could catch up enough to actually be there in his kiss, but I also knew once he stopped that this moment—this astonishing moment—would become a strange shard in my past.

"Fruity." He pulled away to murmur his first word in the after of whatever this was.

"TUMS."

"The Binaca of Washington."

"My grandfather used Binaca," I said, immediately cringing.

We heard the phone ring on the other side of the wall. "Shit." He abruptly stepped back, leaving me off-balance, a chair-rail molding hitting my hip. "I have to . . ."

"Of course."

He opened the other door, and I could see a slice of the eagle's wing in the Oval Office carpet. We squinted. "You can . . ." He indicated the door I had come in.

"Okay."

"Okay." He nodded, and then it was dark once more.

I didn't linger. I returned straight to his private dining room, glancing briefly in a sterling candelabra to smooth my hair before shutting the light off. Then, instead of barreling back into Singh's office, I took the door that opened onto the public hallway that ran parallel to the private rooms I'd just invaded.

Brooke was approaching, her arms piled with briefs.

We both froze. Her expression was inscrutable.

Stalled subways, spilled drinks, a few extra seconds fixing my hair—what would it have taken?

The papers. "Shit," I said out loud.

Suddenly I heard footsteps pounding behind us in the hallway. Rutland overtook us, striding a few feet on to Singh's returned assistant, tossing the binder with the red rubber band inside—"Have him sign off on these and get 'em to Margaret ASAP." He pivoted and walked right past as if I were invisible.

I watched Brooke look from his departing back to me, the way something in a terrarium snaps down its furry meal, as she processed that the President was finishing the errand I'd been tasked.

I found control of my feet and walked back to the pen.

That night none of us went home.

I kept my face away from Brooke's, glued to numbers I couldn't make sense of, names that blurred, my mind stuck as I found myself gripping my own hand under the desk to understand the pressure of his fingers. Trying to pinpoint where his terror had led him to kiss me like I was a sip of water in sun-blasted sand. I felt the nuclear sensation of, if only for a few heartbeats, being the answer for the man to whom the world looked for answers. As I sat there, the very high of his need was key-cutting into my brain.

Just past dawn I was taking another swig of tepid coffee as someone called at the TV, "Turn that up!" It would be the clip eventually viewed over seventy million times on YouTube, but that was the first time anyone saw it: the Majority Leader giving that impromptu interview to a fan with a cell phone. Unlike Rutland, he looked like he'd just strolled off the fairway. "It doesn't surprise me that he's made us wait a week," he blustered, even though *he* was the one refusing to come to the table, buoyed by the rising tide of popular sentiment. "And he should be forced to wait *another* week," he said in a hairpin turn of logic toward the truth of his own inaction. "It would serve him right. He's inconsiderate. He once forced me to leave Air Force

One by the back door. We never got a thank-you note for that copy of *Moby-Dick* we gave his son, and he has *never* invited me to Camp David. He's just rude."

We all know what happened next. Public opinion whiplashed so fast even Fox couldn't spin it. And to this day you can't Google him without getting a picture of his head on a baby's body.

I snuck out so I could be at Ann Taylor when they opened. I charged one perfectly cut suit and a blouse with darts. I vowed to get a really great haircut and new makeup. Because I was following the evaporating trail of a cigarette down the street that I wanted to inhale again.

I walked back through security, thinking I looked like a high-powered attorney, my old suit and Gail's blouse balled in my bag.

"There she is," Brooke said flatly.

"Here I am," I replied brightly. "I had a job interview," I added to explain my makeover.

"So you didn't hear?" she asked as I realized she was clearing the administrative drifts on her desk into a box.

"Hear what?"

"All right then," Margaret said, making her way through the room, collecting the all-access passes from the interns. "Back to the basement."

I looked up at CNN's confirming ticker—and just like that, it was over.

Chapter Three

June 24

I wasn't going to tell. Ever. I had decided minutes after the fur-lough ended, when I abruptly knew for certain that this was a con-tained experience, that I was going to keep an unmade promise to an absent man. There was no way for me to let him know that he didn't need to be afraid of my telling, but he didn't. Because I couldn't imagine disrespecting the searing memory of his lips searching out mine that lit something deep inside me every time I replayed it. Each day my silence would build his trust. Then years from now he would pause somewhere, reading in a beach chair or rising in a ski lift, and think, *wow, that Jamie, I could really rely on her. I wish I'd let her in more. I needed her and she was perfect.*

And I felt important.

But then Lena came to visit a week later and I grossly underesti-mated the friendship deprivation tank that I'd been living in. Add the lubrication of a split bottle of white at the Indian place and, well—it popped out while we were standing in the midst of a throng of Adams Morgan bar-hoppers. Her frozen yogurt dripped onto her knuckles as she just stood there, slack-jawed. We stared at each other with wide, inebriated eyes. "Holy shit." She dropped her voice while the suited revelers parted to pass us on the sidewalk. "You're being serious right now."

I wiped my napkin across her fingers, wishing I could suck the last few seconds back. "Let's ditch these and see if we can get one of those guys to buy us a drink?" I proposed, a technique I'd used in the past to move the conversation off things I suddenly regretted bringing up, like my dad punching a wall parents' weekend.

"Nuh-uh." Lena withdrew her hand. "No way are we just returning to our evening." Spotting a garbage can, she grabbed my cone and tossed it along with hers while I flashed to coming upon Greg, the sound of his labored breath. She turned back to me. "How?"

I shook my head as the mental sparkler I'd burned to the point of dust reignited. "I don't even know." The strip was at full throttle. It was the last place to be having this conversation that I never should have started. Girls burst from the bar behind us on the pulse of a throbbing bass. Giggling, they attempted to ballast each other.

"You did—*that*—and you didn't tell me for a *week*?" Lena crossed her arms while I rubbed my sticky skin with sticky napkins. "I've been talking so much about my middle-school crush's best friend hugging me at a bar that I'm actually *hoarse* and you've been sitting on *this*."

"I'm sorry!"

"I feel like we're going to be all face-lifted in our rocking chairs and you're going to, I don't know, slip in that you had a kid I never heard about."

"God." I shuddered. "No. I only want the kids you will hear about."

"I'm being serious."

"Lena."

"No, you do this all the time. I tell you everything, every fucking thing."

"I tell—"

"No, you talk and you're the one with all the funny stories and everyone thinks you put it all out there, but then there are certain things where you do this weird look-over-here—when it comes to family—guys—and I've been thinking about it—"

"You've been thinking about it?"

"Don't you trust me?" Her brown eyes searched mine. This was the last thing I wanted. It was, in retrospect, an unfortunate moment for Lena to hit her wall. I told her that I did trust her, because I did—because she was my most important person—and then I had to prove it.

"We ended up in the private hallway that connects the Oval Office to his dining room and he kissed me."

"Holy. Shit." She lifted her hands to her cheeks.

"Yeah."

"Holy. Shit."

I nodded, the wine swinging my head into a deeper dip.

"We need to—I don't know what—get more drinks. And candy."

I pulled her in for a hug and begged her to just come live with me and follow me around everywhere. "Please? We're rent-free, and I'll pay you in cheap Indian food."

"One, nothing is free when it comes to my mother, and, b, stop stalling." She weaved her arm though mine to direct us toward the nearest liquor store, our flip-flops flapping in unison.

The next morning we were too hung over to venture out and made do pillaging Gail's frozen flax waffles while I helped Lena play through whether this was the right moment to quit smoking. (It wasn't.) We camped with the balcony doors open, the frigid and humid air canceling each other out. "You know this makes us bad people, right?" Lena called from the kitchen.

I reminded her that I'd once embarrassingly insisted we not only compost in our dorm room, but use one roll of toilet paper for a week. "I think our carbon footprint can sustain a little wasted AC."

"Jamie?" She came to the doorway, finishing off a spoonful of peanut butter.

"Yeah?" I asked from the couch.

"You hooked up with the President of the United States."

"Kissed. 'Hooked up' is an exaggeration."

"The President of the United States knows that you taste—"

"Don't."

"Fruity."

"Ugh." I dropped my face into my magazine until I heard her resume foraging in the fridge. This was the only detail I had given her beyond the kiss, and while I didn't love myself for it, I felt I had told her only the part of what transpired that was mine. Nonetheless, I was relieved to hear her phone from the bedroom. "Is that Kelly Clarkson? Someone's calling you!"

"*Shitshitshit.*" She careened past me and answered in the grown-up register previously reserved for professors.

"What? Oh my God, what's wrong?" I asked when she reappeared.

"The Tuesday client meeting got bumped up and they want me to come in right fucking now."

"'They'?"

"*She* wants me to come in."

"Does your boss know you're on the other side of the country?"

Lena shook her head. "It doesn't matter."

"But we had the rest of the day!" I felt a childish sense of panic.

"Jamie, seriously?"

"What? I'm just—"

"This is my job." She crossed her arms.

"I know."

"I mean—"

"What?" I said quickly, but we both knew the thoughts that hung between us. That I didn't have a job being the kindest. That I made out with my boss's boss's boss, the harshest.

"Nothing, just—I need to check flights. I'm sorry."

I tagged along to National because my revised plan of reading *Gone Girl* and changing toenail polish could accommodate the scheduling addition. Slithering her suitcase at full speed around the dawdlers, dressed in the Escada suit she'd wear directly from the airport to the office, Lena looked like she'd fly the plane herself if they let her. Jogging alongside her, dressed in the sweater hoodie and cutoffs that I would wear directly back to an empty apartment, I looked like her assistant. At best.

With a few minutes to spare before she passed through security, we found chairs across from the monitors. I sipped from my water bottle and we reminisced about when we had everything we needed within a two-block radius—food, post office, library. How an ID swipe granted us access to all of it.

She pointed to where my phone lit up beside me with a text from Mike's number. As this was the last moment I wanted to finally tell her about him, I dropped it in my bag. It had been over between us for so long by college that I'd never mentioned him and as I sat there, I acknowledged to myself that Lena was right. When people talked about high school, about firsts, I'd found it was easier to say nothing at all.

On the TV overhead, Mrs. Rutland was doing jumping jacks with a group of elementary school students—throwing herself into it until she was flushed and perspiring, with seemingly no consideration to vanity, which only made her more beautiful. A boy who had lost fifty pounds on her Fit for Life program beamed, leaning against her as she put her arm around him.

My face dropped to my Tretorns as awkwardness settled over us. "I mean, not that it matters," I said quietly as the broadcast moved on, "because this would *never* happen again in a million years, but maybe they have an arrangement?"

"You're part of an arrangement?" she repeated.

"No, Lena, I'm not *part* of anything."

"I always think how many wives would be surprised to find out they're in *arrangements*." The same sourness permeated her that did whenever she referenced her father.

"Lena, this isn't—I'm not going to break up a—I'm not going to *marry* him. Jesus."

"So that's that, then?" She sought confirmation.

"Look, the planets aligned and a rock star grabbed me for five minutes in heaven—two minutes! It's not like we're having a thing. I couldn't even make a thing happen if I wanted to," I tried to reassure her, despite the fact that, in total honesty, I wanted to. "Nobody can get to that man who isn't supposed to. I mean, unless he takes to wandering the basement or hanging in the staff ladies' room."

"So if he was, you'd do it again?"

I stared at her. "This is a pointless conversation." I stood up, wishing I were wearing pants. "And I'm sure you have to go."

Lena pulled out her driver's license, looking down longer than necessary, and I feared my disclosure had stained something between us. "In the morning now I walk out to the kitchen and it's my mom and I'm like, 'You're not my friend. Where'd my friends go?' I'm a total bitch, but I can't help myself, I just miss you so fucking much."

"Me, too," I said over the swelling in my throat, as I was gripped by What Ifs. What if I got stuck on the East Coast or, worse, back home, and couldn't afford to visit her? What if her job took off and she got even busier, if that were possible, and made all new friends, and our lives diverged into the high-flying money manager and the barista? Was this just—it?

"*Something* will come through." We hugged as I struggled against tears and she told me there was no one else like me.

"You, neither." I forced myself to let her go.

Back on the metro, so palpably without her, I tried to pull myself together but couldn't. Memories tumbled, making me alternately smile and tear up. The time Lena called a dorm meeting because someone had taken a shit in the middle of the student lounge and she grilled us like Hercule Poirot. The time she put my grandmother's silk scarf over the lamp for hook-up ambience and burned a hole right through it. The Ferragamo one she bought me couldn't really replace the sentimental value, but I never told her. I knew she felt awful. Then I was thinking about my grandmother and family—and suddenly I remembered Mike's text.

Given what you know about him, it's probably impossible for you to understand why I responded. But I can only tell you the story as it happened, and with Lena's plane taking her farther from me by the minute, I felt a desperate need for unvarnished connection. Mike had always known what to say to calm my panic. In fact, he'd been the one to help me through my first attack. It was a summer weekend after sixth grade. The firehouse carnival. The plan had been to "run into each other" and do one ride together. Instead, Erica had shown up with a tongue pierce. More than a few beers down Dad had gone ballistic, and as soon as Mike saw the state I was in he turned in a way that encouraged me to follow. There behind the tents he squeezed my palm and told me to breathe through my nose. The colored lights were blurred by the hazy heat and the thumping house music amplified my heart. I remember that he finally started dancing goofily until I was laughing. He looked so relieved, and it was only then that I realized how much I must have scared him.

"*Hey there. I just graduated, actually. Interning at the White House. Glad to hear all is well. Take care. JM."* Feeling the phantom flutter in my pained chest, I stared at my phone and wondered, would that be it?

"Which house is that?" pinged right back. Followed by, *"Really proud of you, James. Not surprised at all."*

I smiled and wiped my cheeks. *"Just dropped my best friend at the airport,"* I replied. *"Lonely."*

"In a room full of people," he responded as the clouds shifted outside the curved glass. *"I'm lonely, too."*

I managed to leave it at that.

I was pulling my ticket out to exit the station when I discovered Rachelle's card in my bag and sent her a text at the first glimpse of sky. She texted back, *"Drinks, pronto,"* and sent me the address of a restaurant by the water where she knew the bartender. When I arrived, an older crowd was finishing a late brunch, and I apologized for my appearance.

"Please." She dismissed me, looping her thin arm through mine to weave me around the umbrellaed tables. Rachelle, looking like an MTV stylist had dressed her to deejay a military lunch, was wearing a khaki romper with gold buttons and matching platform espadrilles. "I'm so happy to be out of my apartment I could scream," she said conspiratorially. "My roommate, who, like, subsists on spray margarine, is doing her calorie splurge tonight and won't stop talking about what she's going to order in. It's disgusting."

I commented that this explained her wealth of knowledge about sticky buns.

"Oh, no. Everyone knows that." She looked genuinely concerned. "Don't they?"

"I didn't," I admitted as I hopped on a bar stool.

"My first job was at Cinnabon at the Tucson mall. I smelled like cinnamon for the entire summer." I loved how she talked, like she was gargling her words at the back of her throat. "Which is a turn-on for guys, that's a fact. Not that I wanted to turn on a single one of my customers." She shuddered before trotting to the other end of the bar where the waitresses were placing their orders. It felt so good to have somewhere to be. She returned with two glasses of something orange. "Sex on the Beach. I know it's cheesy, but I have to order that when it's summer and I am nowhere near sex or a beach."

"Oh God, I thought it was just me." I sipped from the stirrer straw. "I imagined the program would be packed with cute smart guys."

"Oh honey, Josh Lyman is a myth. I'm sure there is some cute lurking here somewhere, but it's like a treasure hunt." She pulled the potato chips over to us. "It's so good to talk about something other than how many points are in pad Thai, you have no idea."

We covered what brought us there, our impressions of it, and how not there we wanted to be. "I keep wondering if I had more than five dollars a day to spend if I'd be experiencing a whole different city," I mused. "If I wasn't one trip to the library away from being asked out by Artie with the candy-cane-striped walker—"

"You wouldn't, I can tell you." She waved her short red nails. "This August marks year five for me. Jewish is Georgetown's idea of diversity. I cannot *believe* I haven't gotten a job in New York yet—when I graduated I was so convinced, I actually put a deposit down on a place in Greenpoint. Everyone cool from boarding school and college is there. I see the parties on Facebook and the nights out and I'm still going to the same lame bars—only I'm not, because I have no one to go with—it's like I totally got left behind. I thought I'd meet people at work, but they're old and they suck."

"Yeah, your boss is—"

"The love child of Kim Jong Il and Leona Helmsley. He's imperious and condescending and there's just no winning with him. And political PR is just lame." She finished her drink. "I wanted to be in entertainment. I grew up near Canyon Ranch. All those celebrities coming and going, the private planes, the limos with the tinted windows."

"It sounds glamorous."

She snorted. "It was glamorous-adjacent."

We shared our first impressions of each other. "You seemed very, um . . ."

"Un-D.C.?" she offered hopefully.

I put my finger to my nose.

"Lucy, that's the nicest thing you could say to me. Okay, so what's with that Brooke girl? We hate her. And we need another round. Don't move."

A bomb couldn't have moved me. After the discomfort that had tinged my weekend, it was delicious to be seen with fresh eyes. When she returned, Rachelle told me with great intensity, "Rachensity" as I would come to call it, about her soul mate in the form of Matt McGeehan. "Matt was a year ahead of me at the school my parents shipped me off to so they could finish their lovely divorce without worrying about accidentally decapitating me with a flying plate or something. He was just—*it*. He was in *Godspell*—I think he had, like, one line, but he opened his mouth and I was just done for." The planets had shifted because he'd recently friended Rachelle and they'd begun a flirtation. "And . . . he's moving to New York. It's going to happen, right?"

I wanted nothing more than for that to be true for her. "Emphatically *yes*."

Her hands crossed over her chest before clenching mine. "You'll totally find a job, too. No doubt. Just take it on like a rattlesnake on fire."

The next morning I emerged from Gail's apartment with my eye sockets aching from the night's snake-on-fire LinkedIn/Monster/craigslist binge. In the light of day, nude modeling probably didn't require a pros-and-cons spreadsheet.

Margaret had left a Post-it on my desk, *"See me,"* and I immediately freaked, running through all the tasks I'd been assigned the previous week. I had quadruple-checked the hotel reservations, emailed the confirmation numbers, gotten kosher meals arranged for the *Hasidic Times* reporters—

"So, Jamie . . ." Margaret looked up from behind her buried desk.
"Yes!"

She nodded as if trying to remember what I was doing there. At least my offense or oversight wasn't blinding. "Yes," she repeated, lifting a finger in the air to detain me while she jogged her memory.

"For you." She swiped a laminated ID from her stack of folders. "To ferry communications. Requested by the Oval Office."

I looked down at the words "Full Access" and heard my pulse swoosh in my ears. *Why, how?!*

She repositioned her mouse. "Okay?" she asked the screen.

"Yes."

"Oh, Jamie," she said sharply.

I turned back in the doorway, a cold heat breaking—did she know? "Yes?"

"We may have a position opening up and I wanted to gauge your interest in staying on after."

"A paying position?" I asked stupidly, dumbfounded.

"Until the revolution."

"Um, yes. Of course. Yes!"

"Great." She returned to her email. "We'll talk more. I have this fire to put out."

Back at my desk, the plastic card clutched between my sweating hands, I felt like an invisible chorus was hitting its high note. A job. An actual *job*. Okay, not in urban development, and not in L.A., with Lena. But still, a *job*. And in a year—or maybe two—I could be positioned to really move to L.A. properly. Get a used car and a mattress filled with more than air. I had to get it, I *had* to.

I stared at the pass—he'd requested this? He'd requested *me*? The sparkler ignited—the heat of his grip, his fingers spreading across my back—*waitwaitWAIT*. I was misreading it. I had to be. An intern in each department must be given a pass to make deliveries. This was totally standard and I was getting all worked up over—

"What. Is. That?" Brooke looked down with crossed arms.

"It's a—"

"I know what it is. Why do you have it?" She snatched it.

"What does she have?" Todd bounded over with an exuberance not usually seen in anyone past puberty. "We get all-access? Hey, John?" Todd leaned over John's computer. "Sorry, man. But we get all-access now?"

John thought for a moment as we all waited breathlessly. "Grab me a Coke, Todd." Dismissing him, he pulled two dollars from his wallet.

Brooke slung the pass back to me. "This is fucking bullshit," she muttered. Ignoring her sucked-in cheeks, I looked toward Margaret's office, expecting her to emerge momentarily with an errand.

Nothing.

I went to the ladies' room and gave my armpits a splash-down with paper towels and industrial pink hand soap. I chewed gum, pushing it over every tooth. I looked around the tiled room as if there might be a round brush and hairspray hiding somewhere.

For the rest of the day I whipped my head up every time Margaret came out, the other interns whipping theirs to me in turn. I typed things, scheduled things, emailed things. At eight o'clock, I raced home. I waxed things, bleached things, polished things. I tried on every combination of everything I'd brought to D.C. My finger hung suspended over a billion dollars in lingerie charges. I managed not to succumb, if only because it would cost another billion dollars in shipping. I woke up an hour early to blow out my hair.

And then I waited. For three straight days, I was Saturday-night-ready for twelve hours at a stretch.

And here's what I learned about a suit that Fits You Perfectly: what at first zip feels like a reassuring sense of having your curves hugged morphs, on day four, into the suffocating feeling that you're rolling in on yourself. I was no longer marveling at how this skirt showed my thighs so much as staving off grabbing a plastic knife from the kitchenette and hacking at the center seam until I popped open like a pack of Pillsbury crescent rolls.

And I was hungry—from being too nervous waiting for the pending nothing to eat. And tired—from levitating over my mattress waiting for the pending nothing to sleep. And then Margaret sent me on a delivery!!! "To the WHC office to get an approval form stamped." (Opposite of exclamation marks.)

I took the folder, reminding myself not to hang my head. I felt like an asshole. An asshole whose cheap, scratchy lace underwear had just chafed its way into a thorn crown of humiliation. I went upstairs to the appointed destination, two long hallways from the President, each urn and guard and grown-up I passed underscoring my naïveté. As soon as I made the delivery I went to the nearest ladies' room, tugged off the assaulting thong, and shoved it deep into the garbage. I was done.

"Jamie." Gerry pointed me to Margaret's door as soon as I returned to my desk. I looked at him questioningly, but he was back to his phone call.

"Oval Office." She handed another file off. I stood there dumbly. "Jamie?"

"Yes, sorry. Yes." I took it and turned back to the stairs, one heel in front of the other, my mind blasted quiet. I arrived at his secretary's desk, the imposing everything around us making me feel like I had imagined that he had kissed me when I was just two rooms away. Had I? I mutely lifted the file to her.

She smiled over her bifocals. "You can go ahead in, dear."

I managed a nod and walked past her to the open mahogany door. The midday sun was streaming through the windows. His desk chair was empty. "Ah, Margaret sent you." I turned to see him coming from his washroom, his white sleeves rolled, the light catching the blond hairs on his forearms.

"Yes, I . . ." I raised the folder in front of my chest.

"Why don't you have a seat? Save you a round trip." He took it from me—inches away—and then leaned back against the edge of his desk, sliding on his glasses. It was impossible to reconcile that this man, at utter elegant ease here, had been hunched over and shaking. I perched on one of the two blue silk settees that faced each other. I was maybe five feet from him. He gazed at the documents. I crossed my legs, quickly wiped my palms on my skirt, and then clasped my hands.

I remember thinking that I should say something, but the First Dog spoke instead, growling to himself as he rolled over in his executive dog bed. "My cousin had a Portuguese water dog when we were kids." My voice was too loud.

"Oh?"

"They have insane energy."

"Yes." He took off his glasses.

"Did you know—I'm sure you know, but trainers recommend they wear these weighted jackets and carry bricks or bags of flour when they go for walks in order to tire them out." Maybe, given the panic attack, he had blacked out the entire encounter. "I guess they're bred to be seriously hardworking." Maybe he didn't even remember it. Maybe ferrying this folder was just a general request that happened to fall to me.

"Sadly, no fish to herd into nets here."

"Isn't that crazy? Herding fish into nets. How would that work, really? Do they bark at the water? It sounds like a synonym for a Sisyphean task." *Why am I talking about this?*

"I wanted to pass healthcare reform, but that would be like herding fish into nets!" he said gamely.

"See?"

He smiled. It was a specific, rope-line smile. I crossed my legs tighter.

"I'm going to be a few minutes." He glanced at the open door to his secretary's office.

"No problem—I mean, of course."

"Do you want something while you wait?" His eyes held mine. My mouth went dry. He cleared his throat, laying the file on his desk. "Water, or a soda?"

"Yes, a Coke," I managed. "Please."

He walked behind my couch through the doorway to the room where we had kissed and I tightened one palm on the other as the grandfather clock ticked. The dog snored. It was taking a while, longer than it would take to go to a refrigerator and pull out a can. I turned and was totally unprepared to see him standing in the door frame, his expression serious, set on me. He took a beckoning step back, his fingers at his sides, twitching as if he wore a holstered gun.

I could see his secretary at her desk, but he remained intent, so I crossed the carpet. He stepped against the wall, indicating I should pass, and I realized what we had been in the last time was actually a short hallway with four doors—one to the Oval Office, one to the dining room, one to his study, and the last one, toward which he was directing me, to a dim, windowless powder room. Within a breath he was behind me. I could feel him standing there, his frame creating a shadow from the hall light. I started to turn but he said, "Please," so simply that I froze. We stood like that for a few seconds, maybe longer.

"Are you okay?" I asked, not daring to move my head. "How have you been?"

"No." His voice was low. He stepped closer. Right behind me, touching. And again, I felt surprised by the firmness of his frame, the flesh-and-bloodness of him. I didn't lean back, didn't move, didn't know the extent of what his "please" was requesting. I thought I could feel his heart through my back—could feel him bend to my hair and the warmth of his breath as he inhaled me.

"I want you," I heard myself tell both of us the truth, "I do."

His forearm circled my waist and his mouth was on my neck as I felt myself tilted forward against the marble vanity. My palms braced on the cold stone as he pressed himself against the back of my legs, his hands roving down to the hem of my skirt, tugging it up. I tilted my head back, twisting to find his lips as he made contact with where I'd been waiting for days. At the discovery that there was no fabric to delay him he moaned into my mouth, slumping forward. I reached down to caress him through his trousers and he gripped my hair, a second from coming, I knew—but he pulled my hand away. Our eyes caught in the mirror as he slid one hand into my bra, the other inside me until I couldn't not—not—his palm flew over my mouth as I shuddered. I dropped to my forearms from the relief.

I turned around to finish reciprocating, but he stopped my hand and shook his head, both of us panting, our foreheads dropping together as he gathered my face into the deepest kiss.

The bathroom door was still open beside us. Trembling, he tugged down my skirt and nodded me out. I stood in the shadows of the silent hall, my breath returning. I didn't know where I was supposed to wait or for how long. There were pictures along the wall in gilded frames and I forced my dilated pupils to zero in on one. He was in shorts and a Nantucket T-shirt, sitting on a porch. And he was laughing. Really laughing. Susan, her tan dark against a pale yellow bathing suit, lay with her feet in his lap and he was tickling her, the space between them soft and familiar, not hard and panting. There was nothing about that captured moment—which, judging from Susan's haircut, was not long ago—that I could convince myself looked remotely arranged. It looked real, like love.

Which meant this was . . . what?

The toilet flushed and he emerged, wiping his bangs back. He looked at me as if he knew me and pulled me into a tight hug, but my eyes were locked on the picture, trying to analyze which of these two embraces was real. He brushed the hair off my face before going to the small bar in his private study to get me a Coke. Weaving his fingers through mine, the feeling of his wedding band intruding between my knuckles, he led me out of the shadows and then released my hand as we stepped into the sun.

"Great, thanks for waiting." He circled his desk for the manila folder, extending it for me to come and take.

"Okay, thank you." I turned away with it; the dog stirred.

"Jamie."

I pivoted.

"You can take your soda." He motioned for me to flip the tab.

That night, Lena's IMs pinged with the speed of Morse code as I pushed my toes against the sharp sisal rug, where I'd slid to charge my laptop in the nearby outlet. *"It's bad, right?"* I typed, my hair almost dry from the shower I'd sat in trying to make sense of the afternoon. *"He's really married."*

"And you don't want to be the porn he can't risk downloading," she typed back.

I dismissed it as a mischaracterization based on what I had shared, or rather not shared, about our first kiss. But if I was honest with myself about it, we hadn't held each other or even really talked. This was undeniably—*"He's really married."* I gripped my forehead.

A moment later she responded. *"I'm choosing to take comfort in that, you know, as a citizen."*

"I just wish it had been bad. Or awkward. Or a letdown. It was so— there's some connection here that is just, well, as you have identified, base. Which is why I will heretofore deliver papers in not just panties, but a snow-suit. Hemmed in razor wire."

"So back up—they might offer you a job? Will you take it? I'm not saying pleasenopleasenopleaseno. Except that I am."

"There's no way it's going to happen. The competition is beyond fierce. I mean even if it does—and it's such a long shot—I don't think I should stay here, do you?"

"Agreed. I think nude modeling might be the healthier choice."

"Thanks, Mom." I hit Send and was startled by the sound of the landline in Gail's room. My parents were the only ones I'd given the number to. I jogged down the hall.

"Jamie?" The voice hit me like cardiac paddles.

"Yes?"

"It's Greg. Rutland," he added his last name to clarify.

"Hi." I glanced at the digital clock. Two fifteen in the morning. Was this a booty call? Did I care?

"Am I—I didn't wake you?" he asked.

"No, no, I was just, um, chatting with a friend. How did you find this—"

"Getting your file took a level of strategizing that put my efforts in the Middle East to shame."

"I don't know how I should feel about that."

"I was gunning for flattered."

"Accomplished." Smiling, I sunk down onto the crisp duvet, so far beyond flattered. Wooed. To put this in context: at Vassar, if a guy held the cafeteria door for you, he'd consider himself Lord Byron.

"I didn't know if you'd answer, or this Gail—"

"No, she's—I'm just using her apartment for the internship. I'm alone."

"It isn't Gail Robinson, the RNC fundraiser?"

I cringed. "She's really a nice person."

"She's brilliant," he conceded. "Partridge's best asset."

"Well, I kind of saved her daughter's life, so she's overlooking my politics," I said quickly, trying to tacitly communicate that the thing we were tacitly not acknowledging was explicitly safe with me. "I mean, she's never here. And that's—she's not here. So, um, yes." I waited. Was it the right answer?

"Look." I heard him blow out. "I'm sorry about today and also the, uh, other day. That's why I called, to tell you that."

"Oh. Okay." Neither booty call nor flattery—I was, apparently, being triaged.

"I didn't intend to—I wasn't planning," he continued.

"Okay."

"I don't seem to be able to think clearly around you."

"Ditto."

Then he laughed the same deep laugh he had that first night in the bullpen, and I realized that was something the public didn't know about him—what he sounded like when he cracked up. "So what brought you to the White House?" I was unsure why he wanted to keep talking, but it felt like an opportunity.

"Tell me you're not calling me to poll?"

He laughed again. "I want to know."

"Well." I shrugged as if he could see me. "I had a complex strategy my generation is really perfecting. First I applied for every job in America. Then I applied for every internship."

"So it wasn't me," he joked.

I rested my other hand on my stomach. "You've been an unexpected bonus."

"Funny, that's just what the Majority Leader calls me."

I laughed. "It's really mind-boggling that anyone takes him seriously." Through the opening in the closet door I saw the shelf of Gail's wigs. "Can I ask you something?"

"Shoot."

I almost brought up the panic attacks, but I lost my nerve. "Do you ever just want to throw your hands up?"

"Go back to waiting tables?"

I smiled. "I mean, just lose it. How do you keep slogging through when everything you try to do is flat-out lied about? I mean, when Pence got up on the House floor and said that ninety percent of Planned Parenthood's budget goes to abortions, how did you not immediately run to the Rose Garden to say, 'Are you fucking kidding me?'"

"It's tempting."

"Or when Republicans now accuse you of being a socialist when you're just trying to keep the funding for the programs *they* started? Their selective memory is astonishing."

"Yeah, well, those people have given me more than a few gray hairs." He sidestepped the question. "I have advisors saying I should color it . . ."

"No."

"You don't think?"

I realized he genuinely wanted to know. "It's undignified. Presidents go gray."

"That's me, Mr. Dignified." He cleared his throat. I flashed to the picture of him tickling Susan like they were everyday people. I knew I should bring her up, remind us of her realness—if only so he could tell me what I was missing, what the public didn't know that would somehow make this okay. Dignified.

I bought myself a second. "Even when eating pizza off a memo, hard to pull off."

Running through every possible comment or question I could phrase, I realized that my broaching her was the equivalent of dousing the conversation with a fire hose. And, much as it shamed me, I couldn't risk it. "Where are you right now?"

"In my study. On the couch with a million pages of briefs that need to be read before sunup."

"Anything interesting?"

"Depends on your definition. And how much you like numbers." Another sigh. "If an issue makes it to my desk it has no solution. I'm asked to make the shit calls where someone gets fucked." It was the honest version of his stump speech.

"I'm so sorry. But you seem to be handling it—I mean you—"

"Right," he said quietly.

"No one could breathe under that kind of pressure."

"I sense you could handle it." It felt like he'd just bestowed his strongest compliment.

"Well, thanks, but it's understandable is all I'm saying." I wanted to find an implicit way to reassure him.

"I doubt that. People don't like to picture their leaders poleaxed."

"Does it happen often?" I dared.

"More than it should, which is not at all. Tell me something about you. About Jamie from Illinois."

"Um . . ." I thought. "Okay, my cousin's dog, the one I told you about today?"

"Yes."

"Well, she was a ridiculously beautiful dog, calendar-worthy. But total Cujo. She'd dig up crap from the backyard and then run with it. But not, like, bones. She found this rusty pickax and would growl terrifyingly if we went to take it away from her. All the fur around her muzzle turned orange. And she'd race through the backyard and we'd sit with our legs up under us at the picnic table so she wouldn't take off a limb as she passed."

He laughed again. "Family picnics, I never had that. Must've been nice."

"Hm," I said, hearing how it sounded up against my memories that weren't. Then I thought of his mother making stuffing with Kathie Lee and Hoda. She seemed like someone who had picnics—I was surprised to hear otherwise. And in this tenuous space between us, it felt weirdly inappropriate for me to follow up.

"Are you close to them?" he asked—because he could follow up.

"Um . . . well, they're coming for the Fourth, so . . ."

"You didn't answer the question, says the man who knows how not to answer a question."

I mustered a small laugh.

"They'll be proud of you, I'm sure," he said gently.

"I hope so. They haven't visited me since freshman year, so . . . yeah."

"Back to this dog," he swiftly offered, seemingly sensing my discomfort. "Sounds like a candidate for a watch list."

"Or to be unloaded on unsuspecting cousins," I countered.

"Ah, smart."

"See, impossible decision made."

"Yes, Afghanistan is just like that."

"That's really why I brought it up." Tumbling downhill in the rhythm of our banter, I fully flirted. "Aren't you taking notes?"

"I want to call you again." My breath caught.

"Okay," I said into the dark.

"I've laughed more in a few minutes with you than I have since the correspondents' dinner. I want to think of you sleeping peacefully while I sit here and sort through this shit-mess."

"Then think of it," I said, wanting peace for him, too. Not knowing how to say that without sounding ridiculous. Not wanting him to go. Afraid he'd want to call me again but never would. Afraid I hadn't said enough—or too much—to get him to reach out.

"Good night, Jamie."

"Good night, Greg."

It had begun.

Chapter Four

July 3

I spent the next week or so hovering in this new idea of myself, like a downtrodden, oh, I don't know, intern, who had just discovered her superhero alter ego but couldn't tell anyone. I walked the streets in my new suit, looking like any other office drone, and the people I passed on the concrete had no idea I was the balm craved by the man in charge of it all. Eager for confirmation that I hadn't hallucinated the whole thing, I bought an extension cord and slept with the phone by my head.

I tried to focus on work, on submitting my résumé, on my parents' pending visit and not letting ludicrous daydreams like being the next Carla Bruni creep in. I actually tuned in on myself having a heated debate about whether I would stick with American designers or dare to go foreign like Jackie.

The Friday of my family's arrival we were slammed. With the campaign at full throttle, everyone was trying to figure out how to compete with Partridge, who had nothing better to do than cross and recross swing states, eating corn dogs and telling factory workers who his leveraged buyouts had put out of business that he was the only man who could find them new jobs. Meanwhile, Rutland was hampered by this little country he had to run, so it was our department's job to coordinate with the campaign to make his routine public appearances double as election opportunities. Of course July Fourth weekend was identified as the prime occasion to score patriotic points, and I think the DNC would have shot him out of a cannon if they thought he could stick the landing.

Between the logistical details of essentially staging a giant pep rally on the grounds and all the President's extra travel, the atmosphere in our office had the tension of a timed chess match. In the midst of this, Margaret's secretary got a summer flu and I was pulled in to assist (read: hold binders and hand over Post-its) at a meeting among her; Abigail Stroud, the First Lady's Chief of Staff; and Max Fishman, the head of the campaign to maximize—

"Love." Which, believe it or not, was the Secret Service's code name for FLOTUS. "Susan needs to be on the ground every day from now until November sixth," Max said insistently, bordering on angrily.

Abigail, who was six feet in flats, leaned toward—and over—Max. "Look, Susan wants another four years of this as much as the next person," she said in a weary way that made it sound like the next person was a Republican. "But you know the deal."

"I don't care," Max said, red rising from his collar like a cartoon of a boiler. "She makes people fall in love with him, and we *need* that right now. Thanks to that furlough, we're behind in the polls, behind in fundraising, and what we have is a wife with an eighty percent approval rating."

"This is Adam's senior year, and Susan's made it clear she isn't going to run herself into the ground making up for Greg's mistakes. *This*"—Abigail circled her hands at the building around us—"will be over one way or another. She'll honor the agreed-upon number of public hours per week—that's *it*."

After they left I asked Margaret about Abigail, who seemed like the last person someone as genteel as Susan would want as her representative.

"Oh no, it's the opposite. Someone like Susan *needs* a bulldog like Abigail to advocate for her."

"Isn't that the President's job?"

She didn't answer.

I met my family at the airport because it was only my dad's third time flying. He couldn't get over how much smaller the seats were than on his last trip. "I had my knees under my chin, my feet in the lap of the couple in front of us, and my head resting on the baby behind us. Mind you, it was a very comfortable baby."

The first time he flew, he was a six-year-old moving to America. The second was to visit me Freshman Weekend. My parents hadn't been in my dorm an hour when the call came in from the San Francisco police—after so many near misses, Erica had inevitably been in a car accident. Only it turned out what actually happened was that she was so wasted, she got out of the car on a hill without putting it into park and it rolled through someone's fence and pitched into their hot tub. Which probably would have been a civil matter if she hadn't punched the cop who arrived at the scene.

They spent the rest of the weekend on the phone, missing everything, and Gail discreetly stepped in to be my surrogate. I remember trailing Lena along the Sunday brunch buffet at the inn where Gail was staying, praying the lump in my throat wouldn't give way to tears over the Canadian bacon. Erica got sober shortly thereafter. Honestly when it came to my graduation and Dad begged off, I was relieved.

"All right, Dad, you're going to want to stay straight on the Potomac River Freeway," I instructed from the passenger seat of the rental he'd insisted on despite my explanation of the Metro. I looked over to make sure he'd heard me and realized he was wearing the Izod that Erica and I gave him for Christmas. Meaning that Erica gave me her Amex and I signed the card from both of us.

"This is absurd," Erica grumbled from the backseat, where she was emailing with her office. "We're so close, we could've walked. Why'd we wait in line an hour to rent a car?" I was mystified, too—mostly by the expense, but I think the idea of having the car for the weekend gave him a base, like a snail's shell.

"Take the ramp toward Rock Creek Parkway." I gestured at the sign.

"And why didn't you just get the GPS?" Erica added.

"It was thirty-five extra dollars a day," Dad answered, "which means something to some people." And we were off.

"D.C. isn't really a walking city," Mom added brightly, patting Erica's knee from where she sat beside her in the backseat. I don't re-member when she started sitting with Erica—possibly before I was born—but they both said the passenger seat made them queasy.

"Mom, when were you in D.C.?" I asked.

"Oh, you just hear that."

"Another left on Virginia and here we are!" I announced as we pulled into the circular drive.

"Well, isn't this fancy," Dad said.

"I hate these postwar apartment buildings." Erica unbuckled her-self.

"Doesn't it feel claustrophobic?" Mom asked as we got out. "Being squashed in by so many people?"

"No more than your office does," I answered. Mom worked in the city for Midwest Mutual, where she'd been the assistant to one mid-level manager but eventually served seven of them, making their days go smoother. Watching her, the fatigue, the need to vent at night what she'd kept herself from snapping all day, made me want to grow up to have an assistant, not be one.

"Dad, follow the driveway around to the garage—Gail has a space assigned to her apartment. It's 8K."

"Got it."

"I didn't think of that," Mom considered as Erica unloaded the bags.

"You hair looks nice," I complimented Mom as we walked to the brass elevator bank. She had darkened it from her usual box red.

"I don't know who I think I'm fooling with all these freckles, but what if I was a brunette for a bit? I could wear pink." She gestured to her cardigan.

"I have a standing appointment every three months for lasering," Erica responded as the door opened. "I am going out like Nicole Kidman."

I looked at my very speckled arm.

"Well, some guys think they're cute." Mom wrapped her own speckled arms around our waists and squeezed us. "And they'll want to kiss every one."

Erica wriggled out of Mom's embrace. "My head hasn't fully

cleared from the flight." The wheels of their overnight bags made a soft purr against the tan carpet. As I pulled out my keys, I watched my sister do this thing she does, her eyes dropping momentarily to the middle-distance as she performs what I think of as a full-body inventory. It's always followed by a pronouncement. "I need coffee." Like that.

I can't imagine being so in tune with myself. At that moment I needed a job—and occasionally I remembered to floss. I could have lived on Frosted Mini-Wheats until someone was actually trailing behind me with a hacksaw, begging to take my diabetic leg.

Stepping inside, my eyes landed on the annoyingly steady red light of the answering machine. Not that he'd have left a message. But then it didn't occur to me that he ever would have called in the first place. Or bent me over a sink.

"Okay!" Snapping myself back to the present, I started talking with the animation of a campus tour guide. "This is the place!" I actually walked backward across the living room, arms outstretched. While I objectively knew I was just borrowing Gail's high-thread-count life, I was still proud of where I'd momentarily landed. "Isn't it amazing?" I pulled back the drapes to reveal the White House, my money shot.

Erica threw her palm against the glare. "I'm seriously getting a headache."

"How about some water, hon?" Mom asked. "Jamie, can you get her water?"

"I, um, of course." I turned to the kitchen, but Erica helped herself to one of Gail's Fijis from the glass-front mini-fridge. She sat on the couch, placing her manicured fingers to her temple. Her sleeves dropped back and I noticed she really didn't have freckles anymore.

Mom sat beside her, face drawn in concern. "Can I get you anything?" she asked.

"Ma, I'm fine, I don't need anything. I just need coffee, and could you—" Erica's arm thrust out.

I leapt to redraw the curtain, the room dimming.

"Fucking asshole!" Dad blew in, slamming the door. "The parking guy was a total prick. Why are we sitting in the dark?"

"I'm so sorry," I said. "What happened?"

"If I ask you where the spot is, obviously I don't know." My father jabbed his fingers repeatedly between his chest and the floor. "If I knew, I wouldn't need to fucking ask now, would I?"

Erica kept her head tucked to her knees.

"Would you like a drink?" I offered.

"Always." His usual line.

"I got your favorite!" I pulled out a liter of Irish lemon soda I'd tracked down at a gourmet store in Georgetown.

"Oh." His face fell. "Doctor said I'm not supposed to have anything acidy anymore. Just the whiskey." He winked. I poured him a water.

"So you guys are sleeping in Gail's room, and I thought Erica could share the guest room with me—"

"That's a lot," Erica interrupted.

"Okay." I regrouped. "Why don't you take my room and I can sleep out here."

"No, I'll sleep on the couch. It's fine." She looked up. "Just with you breathing and everything." She hunched her shoulders and flexed her palms. "I'm not good with people in my space." She volunteered this less like an embarrassing shortcoming and more like an affirmation at a self-awareness retreat. This was another thing I always forgot she did—these pronouncements of her self-defined limitations as if they were assets in her catalog description.

"No, sure." My phone buzzed. Bushy Eyebrows summoning me. "I'm so sorry to leave you guys, but I need to be back by the four o'clock meeting. You can order a cab to the restaurant if you don't want to drive again. Um, I thought you might be tired from the trip—"

"Great." Without letting me finish, Dad crossed the hallway to Gail's room. "Here?"

"Yes."

He kicked his shoes off and sort of dove onto the bed.

I turned to Mom and Erica. "So I made a reservation at Grafiato at eight. It's supposed to be amazing, all small plates. Rachelle wants to join us—you guys are going to love her—"

"I thought it was just going to be the four of us," Mom said.

"She has to work tonight—she won't stay long." I wanted them to see my whole life here, meet my friend. "And then I thought—the weather's supposed to be nice—we could take a stroll to the Lincoln Memorial."

"Sounds great." Mom stood, ready to nap herself. "Um." She leaned into me. "It's not too pricey, is it? Because the tickets were a fortune."

"My treat!" I said, instead of mentioning how frequently she shuttled to see Erica.

She smiled, pivoting between us. "My girls," she said warmly, some memory playing behind her eyes. "I love it when we're all together." She kissed my forehead and then retreated to the bedroom. I watched her slip off her pants and fold them neatly over Gail's vanity chair before closing the door.

"Do you want to nap too?" I asked Erica.

There was the inventory, followed by a tiny head shake before she looked at me with a hint of a smile, relaxing a bit as my parents drifted off. She pulled out her laptop. "I'm going to work. We'll see you at eight—if Dad and I haven't killed each other. If it's just me and Mom at the table, that's your cue to take the car from the valet and dump it in the Potomac."

"Got it."

Embarrassed that I was the only intern who took my dinner break to break for dinner, I nonetheless enjoyed Rachelle going toe-to-toe with Dad. "I'm sorry, I studied Irish literature in college and it was the most depressing thing I have *ever* read." She touched my dad's arm. "You do know what Greek gods are capable of, right? Turning people into trees, moving the seasons, spitting souls out of hell?" She explained to the rest of us, "Irish gods are all scrabbling over one potato. It's like they never got the playbook. No one tapped them on the shoulder and said, 'You can make more potatoes.' It is the most pathetically depressing mythology you will ever read. I think in one story someone invents an umbrella and then it has a hole in it."

Dad laughed until he had to dry his eyes with his napkin. Erica finished her dinner, then mine, then Mom's.

———

"Rachelle's a spitfire," Dad said as we approached the steps to the Memorial, Mom and Erica a few paces behind us.

"I'm so glad you guys like her. It's taken me a few weeks to find someone to hang out with."

"Everyone's——?" Dad tipped his nose up with his finger.

"Yup. And it's not just the money stuff—they're snobby in a way I never encountered at school. Lena could forget sometimes, like she'd ask why I didn't replace my phone when I dropped it, or something, but she's never snobby. Here it's like someone fired a gun and they're scrambling to find the connections they'll need to get where they want to go and they decided on the first day I'm not it."

"Fuck 'em."

Smiling, I gazed up before we started to climb. "I don't care if you wear Confederate underpants, I dare you not to find something moving about Lincoln lit up at night."

"Agreed."

It passed through my head that I should tell that to Greg if he ever did call me again—

"It's disgustingly humid." Erica interrupted my thoughts, tugging her pale blue blouse away from her chest. "Do we have to be climbing steps?"

"I know." I sighed in commiseration. "I've given up trying to get my hair straight." Of course, Erica's had only flattened farther to her head. It was lank, sure, but at least it wasn't conspiring to resemble cotton candy when she wasn't looking.

"I thought night might be better," she continued. "It's not. People say New York's humid, but it's not *this* bad." Or she'd already have had legions of coping strategies. "And Peter has good air-conditioning at the loft." My parents' ears visibly pricked up at the mention of her boyfriend. All we knew was that they'd met in the program, he came from money, and he worked in real estate development. "This is disgusting."

"Bug, my feet are starting to blister." Mom touched my arm apologetically and I saw she was wearing the slingbacks she bought for my cousin's wedding that had never fit properly.

"Okay, let's head back," I conceded before we'd even made it under the columns.

Without protest, they immediately turned and started down. As Dad marched ahead, Mom slipped her arm through Erica's and mine and I could smell her perfume—a department store scent she'd worn forever. "Maybe tomorrow we can off-load your dad at a movie and go shopping." I couldn't ever remember shopping with both of them as adults, having been scarred by the checkout counter screaming matches of Erica's adolescence. Erica would ask for something we couldn't afford—Dad would say he hated it to the point where he was insulting her. Mom would get stuck in the middle, wanting to mollify Erica, but still truly unable to afford whatever it was. By the time I became a teenager, Mom was so worn down, I probably could have come out of my room wrapped in a tatami mat and she wouldn't have noticed.

"Oh, actually, I'll be in Georgetown," Erica said, continuing to flap her shirt away from her stomach, revealing bands of hard muscle.

I could feel Mom tense. "You will?"

Up ahead we saw Dad answer his phone.

"Oh, yeah, Stacey—you remember Stacey, from high school?"

She thought for a moment. "Not the girl with the lip ring?"

Erica blew out through her nose. "Oh my God, Ma, that was, like, a hundred years ago. She works for a lobbyist now. I told her I'd meet her for lunch."

"Okay." I could feel the Outlook calendar pop up in Mom's field of vision like *Minority Report* as she shifted the day—and her expectations. "Well, we'll hit the museums when they open and then meet up with you after lunch."

"I'm going for a run in the morning." Mom didn't even bother to ask if Erica could skip it. "And then I'm going to a meeting. But I'll catch up with you guys later—" She stopped short as all three of us saw Dad lob his phone into the gutter. Mom immediately ran over, scrambling to her knees to retrieve it.

"Dad!"

"Fucking assholes."

"Dad, what happened?" I tried again.

He stormed away from us, then whipped back. "Fucking assholes!"

"We got that part," Erica said flatly. The kind of line that would have gotten her a smack when we were kids.

"It was Cullen." He turned to Mom as she pushed herself to her feet, cell phone in hand.

"Who's Cullen?" I asked.

"Fucking asshole, that's who."

"Dad!" we said in chorus.

"He runs the citywide athletic program—decides which programs get funding."

"He's cutting your funding?" I was stunned. They still hoped to sell the house one day and retire someplace hot and cheap. They'd never make it if Dad lost his job.

"Not yet, but he can if he wants to—what did I do with the keys?" He patted his pockets. "They met tonight. They've decided to make a special presentation to Baker at the Thanksgiving game. Get all the boys—get *my* boys"—he thumped his chest—"on the field to present that piece of shit with some trophy."

"Dad, I'm sure you can—"

"One hundred percent participation, that's what Cullen kept saying," he continued as Mom pulled the keys out of her purse. "One hundred percent."

Erica swiped them from Mom's hand and shut herself in the backseat. The three of us were left looking at each other.

"Well, we've got tomorrow night," Mom comforted herself as she got in next to Erica. "That'll be fun."

When Bushy Eyebrows finally nodded that I could leave the office, it was already sometime after midnight. I quietly let myself in and immediately saw that Gail's couch was empty. I put my keys down on the side table in front of Lena's high school graduation portrait in its heavy sterling frame. The straps of her Vera Wang dress were strategically placed to hide the tattoo intended to rile Gail. What I wouldn't have given to be coming home to her that night.

Getting some ice water, I went out onto the balcony where Erica was leaning against the metal railing. "I didn't know you still smoked," I said as I slid the door shut.

"I don't," she answered without even turning around, a strong plume blowing over her head. "It's better up here—there's a breeze."

I stared into the distance, the hovering moon and the languid heat making the city, which usually feels like the world's largest open-air library, unexpectedly romantic. I wondered what Greg was doing at that exact moment and if it included picturing me sleeping peacefully.

"How's work?" I asked.

"Oh God, don't do that."

"What?"

"Ask me like you're Dad."

"I wasn't," I said, not even sure what she meant.

"I'm in line for a good promotion this fall. No one seems to mind that I finished college at night school, Miss Summa Cum Laude, as long as I'm there twice the hours as everybody else."

"He knows you work hard."

"Does he? Because I think the expression he uses is 'failing upward.'"

I studied her profile. "Is it fun? I mean, do you enjoy it?"

"I did fun." She looked out, her slim freckle-free wrists resting on the bars, the wind ruffling her cotton slip, and I marveled at this incongruity that's always been there between the delicacy of her features and the intensity of her energy. She's like an orphan in a Japanime cartoon wielding a samurai sword. "Dad has to deal with his shit," she said forcefully. "If he did the program, went to meetings, he could accept responsibility for his life, for his disease, instead of continuing to blame Baker for all his problems."

"Well, he's sober now," I offered lamely.

"He's a fluke. No, he's worse than a fluke, he's a fucking time bomb, and it's not fair to Mom." She stubbed out her cigarette and lit another.

"How's Peter?" I asked something Dad would never ask.

"He wants to have sex a lot."

I raised my eyebrows.

She shrugged. "It's common for guys in AA. They can't use, so they eat too much—or exercise too much—or both. And sex becomes this calorie-free permissible thing. We're working through it. I need to feel needed for me." The last sentence was one of her pronouncements.

"I'm seeing someone." I blurted out this exaggerated truth realizing I'd been dying to tell her—get her opinion, her advice.

"An intern?" she asked, flicking her butt off the balcony.

"No, actually, he's, um, on salary. He's super cute, in this kind of unexpected way. He smells like mulling spices, and he's really funny—"

"Is it a sex thing?" I loved this side of Erica. The side that would come home smelling like Boone's, get under my Barbie sheets, and give an unsolicited explanation of finger-banging. "A sleepaway-camp kind of thing?"

"You had sex at sleepaway camp?" I asked.

"Of course."

"I never went." By the time I was in fourth grade, her tutors and learning specialists and behavioral therapists were already eating through our parents' income. I spent summers at the Y or riding my bike to the town pool with friends. "I don't know—I guess so—he knows I'm just passing through and he's—he's permanent. Well"—I shrugged—"as permanent as anyone in the administration is."

"That's hot."

"Yeah, it is."

"Nothing hotter than temporary."

"Right." I let that assessment sink in. "Right."

"You want it to be more?" she asked.

"No, no—that's not really . . . on the menu." I chewed my lip, enticed by the smell of her freshly lit match as she fired up another cigarette. "Can I have one?"

"I'm low." She blew out through her nostrils. "I've moved in with Peter."

"Wow, okay," I answered, because we'd somehow shifted back to her.

"What?" She tensed.

"No, nothing."

"It's not a big deal," she said in a way that meant it was.

"No, of course it isn't," I reassured her. "I mean, it *is*. But not like that."

"Don't tell them—I can't deal with their shit right now. Jamie, you have to promise. Not until they've met him, and I don't know when I'll be ready to let that happen."

"No, no, of course." Even though I'd never had a relationship with them that entailed getting their shit—they didn't yell at me. I didn't snipe at them. Or disappoint. And I never sounded over them—she always sounded so completely over them, as though they were just this problem she had to manage until they died. Then I wondered if that was how she talked about me to her friends—so over me.

She returned her full focus to the view and I knew she was finished with the conversation—whatever she needed, she had gotten.

"Um, I guess I'm going to try to sleep." I needlessly pointed to the glass door.

She didn't answer, and as I sealed myself back in the recirculating air I shivered, wondering if she was right, if the hottest thing about me was that I was leaving.

I spent Saturday morning confirming that all the union leaders being flown in for the fireworks were getting face time with POTUS. And that their wives were being entertained by the First Lady. Who had planned, according to Abigail, to "get through the day" by showing them how to prepare Oreo banana pudding. Rutland had made an off-the-cuff remark on the campaign trail about loving it and it will dog the man till he's dead.

I found Mom waiting for Dad at the museum café, flipping through *Real Simple*, and watched her for a moment before crossing the concourse. She was wearing her best clothes for this trip; I knew that. Her favorite twin set and her good linen pants. At graduation I'd noticed that she looked older than the other mothers. It had been hard for her, commuting back and forth every day, being the only link to stability and health insurance, needing to be sure she didn't lose her job as Dad moved in and out of various junior athletic programs, his confidence tattered after Baker fired him from his dream job. She couldn't leave work for the school plays or doctor appointments, and he didn't know how to navigate us through that stuff.

One Halloween we almost missed trick-or-treating because the strap broke on Erica's tutu, then one of my cat ears ripped off and Dad had to sew our costumes back together, cursing the whole time and making us promise, on pain of death, not to tell her. Now it sounds kind of funny. It wasn't.

"I gave up somewhere between air and space. Any word from Erica?" she asked as I set down my tray at her table.

I needlessly checked my phone, knowing I hadn't felt it buzz. "Nope."

She reached over to break the edge off my cookie. "Has she said anything to you about Peter?"

"No, why?"

"Oh, nothing." She swirled the straw through her iced tea. "It's just that she doesn't have the greatest track record and she won't even let us meet him."

"You can't really judge her life now based on before." I took a bite of salad. "She seems fine."

She nodded down at the plastic cup. "No, you're right." Looking up, she reached across the Formica to squeeze my hand. "Thank God for you. If I'd had two girls like your dad. . . ."

"You think she's like him?" I asked, a little taken aback. "I mean aside from the obvious."

"Are you kidding? That's why they rile each other up." She took more of the cookie. "I'm just grateful you focused on the scholarship, waited until college to date—you're on the pill, right?"

"Mom!"

"Look, I'd rather you were a bad Catholic than a good mother right now." I smiled as she glanced at her watch. "Your dad'll be here any second."

"How's he doing with this Baker thing?"

She didn't answer.

"Erica thinks he needs to accept responsibility," I paraphrased her.

Mom's eyes flashed. "Does she now? He has been sober for eight years. Enough said."

"Okay." I put down my fork, thinking of those nights he wove into the house, the time he fell asleep in the flower bed, not sure how she was calculating that. "I'll need to get going soon."

She dropped her hands on the table. "Really? They're not paying you."

"No one at my office sees their families. And they *are* paid. I'm sorry," I said, even as I saw a slide show of school auditoriums full of parent audiences that didn't contain her. "It's just that there are no jobs out there right now—"

"You're smart. You'll find something—" She stopped herself, spotting Dad making his way across the grand hall. "Don't talk about the job stuff, okay? I don't want him to have to worry about you."

That night we waited with what felt like all of humanity for clearance to the White House lawn. "Oh my God, am I late? I'm totally late," Rachelle answered her own question as she squeezed in where we were shuffling toward the metal detectors. "They've closed off *everything,* but I mean *everything.*" As she spoke, she kissed my parents' cheeks, and even Erica's, blowing right past Erica's recoil. "How long have you been standing here?" I admired how at ease she was.

"Not long," Mom lied.

"We really hoofed it today," Dad said with crossed arms and a set brow.

"And I never properly rehydrated after my run," Erica added.

I pulled my ID and ticket out and they followed suit. "This—this—" Rachelle looked through the fence, where we could see the stage draped in bunting, the building majestically lit.

"Is the single greatest place to celebrate July Fourth, unless you own Macy's," I finished, and she grinned and squeezed my hand.

"Miss, your face." A security guard instructed Erica to remove her sunglasses.

She looked up for him, squinting against the sunset. As soon as he cleared her, she put them back on.

"Oh for fuck's sake, Erica," Dad scoffed.

"I'm taking care of myself—"

"So, here we are," I cut in, tipping up onto my toes to try to see what—if anything—was happening on the stage. "Where I work," I couldn't help adding, because the tickets I could have traded for a kidney were being treated like something they showed up for as a favor.

"Stop being such a—"

"A what, Dad?" she baited him, all of us shuffling forward on the crowd's heels.

"Erica, let it go," I implored.

"No."

"Fucking princess." Just as he said it, he was pushed so hard by someone trying to get through that he teetered off balance.

"Jim." Mom grabbed his arm before turning to me. "Can he sit down?" she asked.

I pointlessly looked in the free inches to my left and right for a chair.

"I bet there might be something at the comfort station," Rachelle suggested, pretending she wasn't standing in the middle of whatever this was with my family. I shot her a look of gratitude as it occurred to me that in the same situation Lena would have just clammed up, adding an extra frosting of awkwardness. "I'll go check. Be right back!"

"I'm fine," Dad said as she elbowed away. "My knee is fine."

"What's wrong with your knee?" I asked.

"Nothing."

"It's been acting up," Mom explained.

"Getting help isn't being a princess," Erica, stewing, shot back at him. "Knowing your boundaries isn't being a princess. We can't all be tough Irish fuckers, or whatever you call yourself." Mom tried to take her hand. It was Freshman Weekend all over again. Except this time Erica was ruining it in person.

Suddenly the crowd rippled as the Secret Service cut a path for the President, clipping ropes up with the speed of FoxConn employees. We stepped back off the red carpet I didn't even realize we'd been standing on, our toes on the edge as Greg made his way toward us in his khakis, shaking hands, slapping backs, Susan right behind him, her hair twisted up smartly against the heat. I was stunned—I'd had no idea he'd be walking the lawn, and I instinctively shrank a little behind Erica, my face turned to the ground.

"Jamie!" I looked up, taking in his delight. Susan moved on to greet the Majority Leader's wife. "Are these your parents?" the President asked of the gobsmacked people on either side of me.

"Y-yes. Mom—Betsy McAlister, James McAlister, this is—"

"Gregory Rutland, great to meet you." He pumped their hands while they stared at him, speechless.

"And this is my sister, Erica," I added as she whipped off her shades.

"Lights give you a headache?" he asked.

"Yes," she almost whispered as if she were hearing from a psychic.

"Susan, too. She wears tinted contacts to get through these things." He turned his attention back on my parents. "Your daughter was a real trouper during the furlough. Couldn't have pulled through without her."

My parents didn't seem to understand his language.

"All the interns," he added. "They were our cannon fodder. Heroic."

"You having fun, sir?" someone to my left asked, thrusting out a photograph for Greg to sign.

"Nothing better than celebrating our nation's independence. On nights like tonight it's always good to see friendly faces"—he glanced at me as he handed back the autograph—"amid not-so-friendly faces." He tossed his head in the direction of the Majority Leader, who was making his way up the line with Ronald, but I will always think he privately meant Susan. Everyone laughed. "Well, enjoy the fireworks."

He moved on.

My parents turned to me. *"The President knows your name?"* Mom asked when he was out of earshot.

I watched his broad back as he worked the crowd. I could feel the electric jolt of his hand slipping between my legs, and my name felt like the least of what he knew. "Well, there weren't very many of us here during the furlough and—you know—politicians are good with names." With remembering what's important to people.

"Jamie," Mom marveled, looking younger from the thrill. Basking in her full attention, I beamed.

"I don't like him." I heard the words, but still had to turn to confirm it was Dad's voice and not one of the "unfriendly faces."

"What?" I asked.

"I don't like him. In person. He was . . ." He struggled, his face darkening. "Glib. Politician-y. I—"

"Okay, this is a migraine," Erica announced, cutting him off. "I'm going back to the apartment."

"I'm with you," Dad agreed. He turned to follow her toward the exit. And I realized Mom was right: ultimately they *were* the same, leaving me and Mom to be the other pair, but we were just—not. With an apologetic look over her shoulder, Mom, confused, followed them, quickly swallowed into the crush.

No one suggested one of them stay with me. No one asked if I was coming.

I remember feeling momentarily suspended as the sky bruised black, my inhale trapped, ribs flared, lips parted.

Then I was moving before I realized I was moving. Aggressively elbowing my way in an arc to wriggle into a spot down the line. "Excuse me, pardon me, forgive me." I made a few inches where there were none, anger abutting me, the velvet pressed against my hips. But I didn't care. He spotted me, his face shrinking as he saw my watering eyes, and he hugged me.

He hugged me.

Chapter Five

July 12

Over the next week I had to bully myself to leave the vicinity of Gail's landline for anywhere other than the office, living to get back inside those seconds in which I sought rescue and for once in my life found it waiting. For Rachelle, I framed my hermit status—not untruthfully—as a budget issue. But there was no arguing when she showed up Sunday morning, sucking her third iced espresso, her Groupon app loaded with Chinatown mani/pedis. Dressed in a vintage Vivienne Tam Mao-in-pigtails minidress, she followed me around the apartment as I reluctantly collected myself, making little "let'sgo-let'sgo-let'sgo" claps.

Matt McGeehan had swung through town. The previous night she'd been stunned to run into him at a cocktail party she'd expected to be tedious. Instead, they talked for *hours* before he'd had to leave with friends. But he'd suggested they meet for coffee before he went to the airport, and the possibility that he really meant "coffee" necessitated emergency full-body grooming—"So find your other fucking flip-flop and let's GO already."

It was one of those thickly wet days where you felt trapped in a water balloon simmering in the sun. Plus, we weren't the only ones trying to cash in, so the tiny unair-conditioned salon was packed with girls dissecting their big weekend dates—those accomplished and those they still hoped to make happen. It was torturous to sit silent among all that strategizing chatter and not stand in my bucket and beseech, "Help! The President of the United States grabbed me—I know, *me!*—now what?!"

"I'm going to wear my eyelet sundress with a great bra peeking through. Nude lips, bronzer . . ." Rachelle planned her Look, as she would call it. I used to tease her that I was going to pull her building's alarm one night just to see what she'd wear to the street. But I loved her for her costumes, and more so for what they revealed about her sense of the ever-present opportunities awaiting. Her favorite story was about Jerry Hall, from Nowhere, Texas, who used her pageant money to get to the coast of France. Once there, Jerry put on her bikini, curled her hair, threw on platform heels, and went to the beach proclaiming, "I am getting discovered today!" And she promptly was. Rachelle was perpetually straightening her hair and proclaiming her intention to succeed.

"But *where* is this sex actually going to happen?" Rachelle, test-running her pending date, had arrived at The Deed. "My room-mate's random-ass acquaintance from Semester at Sea is crashing. Plus this girl's—and I use the term loosely—boyfriend is lying in the middle of my living room like a downed elephant. She said depres-sion, but he's so obviously sleeping something off. He has this smell—just stale—like socks on a road trip with the windows rolled up. Maybe if I smoke on the walk back? It would at least fill Matt's nostrils while we get to my room. I was going to leave a candle burning, but that seemed, like, trying. And dangerous. Oh my God, you are so lucky to live alone. You can do *anything* at your place. I can't even imagine."

My anything consisted of a singular activity: phone-staring. At the nail parlor, surrounded by estrogen being channeled into finding/ getting/keeping The Guy, I panicked that I should be doing *so much more.*

"The way he hugged me last night was just so . . . it went on that second too long, you know?"

I felt a wave of déjà vu—junior high school, sitting on the dog-haired carpet of someone's den, the same smell of polish remover making me light-headed as I forced myself to refrain from talking about Mike. "Um-hmm." I focused on flipping through the week's *People*, slick from drying oil.

"I can't just ask Matt to come back to my place. Unless he *wants* me to ask him because he's too afraid to put it out there." She snapped her fingers. "Maybe I'll offer him a cigarette, steer him in the direction of my apartment . . ."

And suddenly I was facing the photo I'd been turning away from all week, the White House silhouetted, fireworks illuminating their faces. Greg, one arm around Susan, the other around their sixteen-year-old daughter, Alison. Their seventeen-year-old son, Adam, laughing, the little lines around his eyes just like Greg's—

"Matt's ex was a total bitch. She wore this perfume handmade on a farm in Italy—*that* girl."

I looked around for somewhere, anywhere, to toss the magazine. Instead I flipped it over on my lap and put my bag on top as if to smother the intruding reality. I turned to Rachelle, mouth open to tell her. "I . . ."

Deeply immersed in her possibilities, her brown eyes returned my intense gaze. "Sky."

"What?"

"Sky Hoppey. She and Matt were together for junior and senior year. Forever. But every time we talked, there was always such a *thing* there. Matt looked content with her, I'm not an idiot, but with me he looks . . . intrigued. Don't you think that means something?" God, I wanted it to.

But then I felt the pages adhere to my sweaty thighs, afraid the image would be transferred onto my skin like a Cracker Jack tattoo. "Don't you?" Rachelle repeated urgently, lifting her freshly depilitated brows as the balloon popped outside and heavy drops spattered the street.

I honestly didn't know what I thought—for either of us. "Of course."

Half an hour later, I made a sloshy beeline to my bathroom, the remnants of sodden tissue still between my toes. Shivering, I twisted on the hot water and was just peeling off my shorts when I heard the ringing. I flat-out ran.

"Hello?"

"It's raining," he said as though he'd just looked up.

"I'm aware." I beamed at the ceiling. "I am, in fact, soaked."

"Are you, now."

"I was out in flip-flops."

He laughed. "I want to be out in flip-flops."

"Pink ones? Do it. Your public awaits."

"So . . ."

"Yes?"

"Do you want to hang out?"

I jogged in place, my fists jabbing the air as I strained for a casual response. "Sure. Meet you at the Crystal Mall Smoothie Barn in, say, thirty?"

"How about a yogurt beneath the ficus in my office. It's relatively quiet around here this afternoon."

"I don't know . . ." I pretended to hedge.

"I could hum some Muzak."

I laughed. "You're dating yourself."

"Come over, Jamie."

"Okay."

As the founding architect had so aspired, it was impossible to imagine I could ever feel unintimidated approaching the Oval. If the jewel-toned brocades behind his secretary's Chippendale desk were intended to check the demands of those at the height of their power, the effect on my twenty-one-year-old self was such that my legs literally trembled.

Jean looked up from her novel to welcome me. "He just stepped out, but you can go ahead in, dear."

"Thank you." I tugged at the blazer I'd thrown on over my sundress in a last-minute insecurity fit. The lamps were on, casting a warm glow against the dark sky. Behind his desk there was a new addition to his sterling framed photos: Alison's ponytail flipped over her shoulder as she gazed at those fireworks. Looking away, I cauterized my shame while hastily reaching up to tug out the one I'd spent ten minutes brushing into place.

"Jamie," Greg called as he arrived behind me from the reception area, looking relaxed in a loden polo that matched his eyes. "Thanks for coming in."

"Hi." I waved.

"This'll be good." He rubbed his palms as he passed Jean's desk. "We can go over those details and you can get them in to Margaret tomorrow morning. Save us all a meeting." Jean continued reading. It's true what they say. Greg has the ability to reset your perceptions through sheer force of presence. He's notoriously rerouted more than one foreign leader between their arrival and departure. And that afternoon he radiated a decorum that made me immediately ashamed of the erotic curiosity that had brought me there.

"Yes, well." I buttoned my blazer as I walked over to meet him. "I'm glad I could help."

"Hell of a day out there." He dropped his broadcasting tone as he crossed the threshold, leaving the door purposefully open.

"Yes."

"Have a seat." He sat on the blue couch and I cut across the oval, avoiding treading on an eagle wing to sit opposite, unsure of the script we were reading from for Jean.

"So you wanted to go over some scheduling?" I glanced at the doorway.

He stared at me. "You look like summer," he said, his voice much quieter so that only I could hear. "Cheesy?"

I nodded. But truthfully it was the most romantic thing anyone had ever said to me. To this day it probably still is.

"You just . . ." He shrugged. "Do."

"Thanks." I smiled and he blushed. He was blushing. "So how was your thing yesterday with N.A.S.A.? There was a lot of discussion about whether the fans in the tent would be too noisy—were they?"

"Didn't even notice, so there's your answer. It was sad, honestly. Strange. I hate that that era is coming to a close under me. No more final frontier." He sighed. "What did you do last night?"

"I, um." I stared at the phone. "Went out—with friends."

"To a bar?" He picked up his glasses from the coffee table between us.

"Yes. Yup. Just a few drinks out."

"Fun." He fingered the frames.

"It was no state dinner, but it was good."

He blew a huff of steamed air on the lenses and cleaned them with the hem of his shirt. "Only someone who has not suffered through a state dinner would say that. I bet you were fending them off with a stick."

"Well, you know," I demurred. Contrived demurring. His brow dropped and he folded his glasses back on top of his papers. Was that why he called? To make sure I hadn't spent the night out? It's strange looking back to think I was so flattered, taking his signs of possessiveness as some sort of currency. As if it could be cashed in for having a real relationship.

"Sir, your lunch is here," Jean called.

"Great, thanks." He hopped up to greet the server and take the tray. "Hope you don't mind. I'm starving."

"No, please eat."

"It may not be the Crystal Mall." He set it on the coffee table between us, the muscles of his forearms momentarily defining. "But!" He gestured to three tall glasses. "Mango, strawberry, and pineapple—no, not pineapple—peach. Tell me you're not a blueberry. Or tell me you're a blueberry and I'll have one sent up." He looked hopeful. "Christ, say something."

I was stunned. "You made me a smoothie." My hands crossed below my collarbones. "*Three* smoothies."

"By proxy."

"I love it. Any of them. Peach, I guess."

Beaming, he handed it off to me and removed the silver lid to reveal a cheeseburger. "You want to split it?" I shook my head and he disarmingly slid down to the floor at the coffee table to hunker in. "So did your folks have a good time at the party?"

I took the straw from my mouth, unsure if we were going to acknowledge how I sought him out after they bolted. "Thank you for that."

"I was just giving thanks where thanks were due," he tossed off, studying me for a moment.

I held his gaze with an appreciative smile before daring, "I mean it."

"You didn't answer the question."

"That's funny coming from you, Mr. Evasive." I took a sip, smiling to myself as I realized we had an in-joke. "It was great."

He grinned, wiping at his mouth.

"What?" I asked.

"I'm starting to be able to interpret your positive summations."

"Oh? Care to translate?"

"That one was something closer to 'not so great.'"

"They're just . . ." I shrugged. "My sister's kind of the main attraction. As she should be," I hastened to add, out of habit. "She's overcome a lot. A learning disability—which my dad treated as a discipline issue. By the time she was formally diagnosed she'd kind of come up with her own way to cope, which took so much to kick. You're probably picturing some mess, but she's, like, the total opposite."

"So you two are close."

"Yes." I put down the glass, unprepared for his interest.

"Did you tell her?" he asked without pause.

"I told her that I was having a . . ." I didn't know how to name what was happening between us. "But not that it was you." I watched for his response, but he continued chewing. I pushed the fact that Lena knew from my mind. It wasn't as though I'd told her everything. "I know not to just spout off about this."

He set down the burger. "Let's be clear, Jamie. I'm not now, nor have I ever, telling you what to do."

"I know." Stung by the indirect directive, I leapt to change the subject. "So you're an only child, right?"

"Wrong. But it's nice to know you haven't Googled me."

"Brother or sister?"

"Brother."

"And did you tell him?" I dropped my voice in imitation.

"That would be difficult." He balled his napkin. "He's dead."

"Oh my God, I'm so—"

"No." He reached across to me. "I didn't mean it like that. He died in Nam. One of the last casualties. I was ten. Then it was just me and my mother. But Sam was that same thing for us, the—how did you say it?"

"Main attraction?"

Greg wiped a stray dot of ketchup marring the E Pluribus Unum on the plate's rim before pushing the tray to the side. "I used to watch Sam shave before he'd go out. He had this antique kit with the brush and everything. He'd wink at me in the mirror. Bright, smart, smooth."

"And now you're the President."

His eyes were focused somewhere in the middle distance. "I was certain I'd get that kit when I left for college, but my mother couldn't part with it. She was . . ." He screwed his face up and then exhaled. "Out in the woods I had this makeshift zip line, all of four feet off the ground. I'd pull myself up to the jerry-rigged platform he built for me and, you know, zoom." He shot his palm into the air like a plane. "Sam'd hide things under the base—liquor, condoms. I'd leave him messages sometimes. That's where I found the note he left me."

"Note?"

"Rolled up in an old Coke bottle." He looked down, noticing a small rip in the seam of his worn khakis. "I reread it whenever I visit."

"What did it say?"

"Sir?"

"Jean!" We looked over as she stood from her desk. "What can I do for you?"

"I'm going to go out now for some lunch." She came to the doorway, tying a rain bonnet under her chin. "Will you need anything?"

"We'll be fine, thanks."

We heard the outer office door click closed. We were alone. As alone as the President ever was.

"It's weird to be higher than you," I said, referring to my position on the couch. The rain started to pelt the glass.

"I like it. Go ahead. Decide something, anything."

"Ummm, college tuition shall now be subsidized by the tobacco industry," I decreed.

"Done." He threw his fist up.

"That's all it takes?"

"Yup." Lightning flashed. "I've never told anyone about that shaving kit," he said, unaware—or perhaps not—of the potency of having earned his secret.

"If Erica died, I think my family would spin off into space or something. She's the thing we've, I don't know, figured out how to do," I admitted—sharing it to forge something with Greg. He nodded, and that potent combination of past pain and present recognition, which informs my desire even now, pulsed beneath my ribs. The thick air from outside seemed to be seeping in. "Let's open a window. Can we?" I stood to break the intensity of his gaze.

I heard him follow me over to the heavy gold drapes bordering the French doors. "My men are just outside, Jamie."

"Right. Sorry. I know it's raining, but it looks like there's a breeze. It would be nice to get some air . . ." I turned and he was inches from me.

"If I were twenty years younger . . ."

"You'd what?" I asked, meeting his eyes.

He cupped the back of his neck with his hand. I dared to lift my finger to his hip, to the rip he'd been worrying into a hole, feeling the warmth of his skin as I darted it inside. He pulled my hand away. "I hoped we could just . . . I'm trying to be good."

"Okay," I breathed, his hand hot around my wrist. We stood like this, me looking into his chest, him peering down. *Don't you think that means something?* Beyond the glass and the ever-present guards, the wind tossed the branches. Suddenly he bent my arm behind my back, stepping me to the wall between the windows. He dropped to his knees, gripping me to rove under my hem before pulling me onto the floor. His mouth warm, his tongue darted into the side of my panties, the lace edge cutting into my skin. There, beside his desk, the sky flashing, the rain beating, he took me in until I was gripping at his hair and turning my mouth into the rug to muffle my cry.

Then I was limp, the seismic undercurrent rendering my surface still. "Was that okay, baby?" He lifted his head to implore so tenderly, I was reminded instantly and acutely that this man was in a relationship. Only guys who've loved touch like that, care like that. He was trained to ask . . . from kindness. It was habit and I was the beneficiary. I reached down to lift him up, to reciprocate, to sear anyone else out of both our minds, but he rolled onto his back to hold me against him until his body was able to relax. We lay like that, my ear pressed against his heart, his thumb stroking my cheek, until the rain slowed and our breathing quieted. We talked about books that had changed us, camping in backyards, bad teachers we'd had, why the French refuse to put a satisfying ending on a movie. When we finally returned upright sometime later, we hugged each other fiercely. "God, Jamie, it's never enough time with you," he said into my hair. Passing Jean as she returned with a dripping umbrella and pleasant smile, I was dizzy from the attention.

I walked home slowly, flooded by impulses to open a bottle of wine, eat a box of chocolates, dance atop a table to Beyoncé—anything to keep my endorphins skywriting and stave off the doubt I knew would creep in by morning. *"OMG HE KISSED ME!!!!"* Rachelle's text came as I stepped into my elevator.

At that moment, I just wanted to be lounging in the unforgiving plastic chairs of the cafeteria *so badly*. Sunday morning. French toast sticks. Nothing more pressing than comparing the triumph of last night's touches and glances. *"Me, too!"* I texted back, since getting Lena to celebrate with me threatened to be more complicated than I had the space for, and no longer just because of the logistics.

My phone rang a second later. "What?!"

"I hooked up," I blurted, hastily adding, "with this guy in my office."

"Oh my God! Who? This just happened now?"

"You don't know him. He called me in to work, I thought, but he really wanted to see me." I told myself to *shut up*. "Want to take a victory lap?"

"Matt Mc-Gee-han kissed me!" she shouted the way Oprah used to announce her guests as she walked in. We ordered dumplings, shared our successful one-liners, and inhaled the lingering cologne on our skin. While Rachelle's hook-up consisted of what could reasonably take place under a restaurant awning before Matt got in a cab, it was

still seriously gratifying. Given that there were over three hundred men it could have been, I was careful not to specify the office where mine had occurred, referring to Greg only as "he," and Rachelle, delighted just to have a partner to burst through the finish line with, didn't press it just yet. So, having given in fully to one temptation for the day, I managed to partially stave off the other.

Slightly hung over but still skywriting, the next morning I eagerly stepped in when Margaret asked for me. "Do you have a delivery?" She didn't, but informed me that one of her staff was sick, so Dana was taking over his work and I was going to assist her.

A harried Dana handed me a binder without even looking up. "Get the proposal hammered out and then get a copy to Security for vetting. And then get a meeting scheduled with FLOTUS—"

"Sorry?"

"A meeting with the First Lady and the kids—"

"Kids?"

"To make final itinerary tweaks." My feet struck the ground— below ground. Feet lapped by hell flames. "Don't tell me you're going to be all star-struck and tongue-tied. I asked for you because you seemed the least maintenance."

"You asked for me?"

She dropped her head. This conversation was taking so much longer than she'd anticipated.

"Yes, no maintenance." I saluted, and returned to my desk with the binder, which contained the plans for a weeklong trip for Adam to check out colleges before they were back in session. Meetings with professors, private campus tours. Most important, trying to simultaneously stay off TMZ and under the radar of "elitism" accusations. (From Partridge. Who went to Yale.) I stared at one of the notes scrawled in the margin of a spreadsheet. *"POTUS to join?"*

For two weeks I plotted every mile of the pending tour, while trying to resist absorbing any information that colored the President's family into the people they were from the silhouettes I needed them to be. Alison was a vegetarian. Adam wanted to meet with the biology and chemistry professors. Susan traveled with her own pillow. That was the one I couldn't deflect. Did she have only the one? Did Greg lie in bed and stare at the empty space? Did he miss her?

So those were my days.

My nights were spent sitting in the tub for too long, the phone stretched to the bath mat—even though it was always much later when it rang, two, three in the morning. He called—the records show he called—at least every other night, keeping me on the phone for hours sometimes. To tell me jokes, ask about my life and my day, and yes, believe it or not, seek my advice.

I want to make that point about the calls, because I know that's not what people remember.

When the scheduled day arrived and everyone but those the trip was for had vetted the itinerary, I contemplated feigning food poisoning. But I couldn't allow myself to wuss out, couldn't live with the idea that I couldn't even face her—them. Which made zero sense compared with what I apparently could live with, but that's what it was.

I'd been informed POTUS would join "if able," but I didn't imagine he'd see my name on the agenda and come. But then, I had no idea what mental box he'd put me—or them—into. I wanted him to join us so I could finally know. And I deeply didn't.

Utterly unaware of all this, Dana had taken the time to blow-dry her hair and appeared to have gone all out with the tinted ChapStick. She repeatedly cleared her throat on the way up to the First Lady's office, then, as we were about to walk in, lost color when she realized she'd forgotten her binder. "Make small talk," she instructed as she flapped off in her Bally slingbacks.

I was ushered through the waiting area into a butter-yellow room, the same color as the swimsuit Susan wore in that photo, and I wondered if it was her favorite. The linen shades were drawn against the morning light, preventing the subdued floral on the settee from fading.

"Hi, I'm Alison." The President's daughter put down her phone to come over and shake my hand, the mature gesture incongruous with her shorts and tank top. She wore a dirty string anklet—the kind we made for each other in middle school—that many swims and showers ago was pink and purple. I wondered if there was another girl out there wearing its match. If its dogged permanence had been a point of contention for the campaign stylist; if her parents cared.

I found my voice. "Hi, I'm Jamie. Dana will be here in a minute."

"I think it's just going to be us, anyway."

"Oh?"

"I mean, my mom's secretary and Adam and mine's. Adam's working and my mom's got another thing."

"But isn't this trip for Adam?" I asked.

Her eyebrows lifted as she shrugged, to telegraph that she was accustomed to the absurdity. "Ten meetings per half-step taken, right?" she quoted her father.

Small talk, small talk. "Adam has a job?" I asked what I already knew.

"Yeah, some research study at American U. A premed thing." She stayed standing, and I'm uncertain which of us sat first.

"I'm so sorry to keep you waiting, Alison." Dana sailed back in, perspiration beading her nose while Abigail and another woman trailed her. "We're eager to get your feedback. We want to be sure you have an *awesome* time!"

Alison's eyes flickered to mine. "Yes, me too, thanks," she offered, waiting for them to continue. I was mostly aware of her poise, her manners. Of how many rooms she'd sat in listening to places she would go and things she would do that were not remotely of her own choosing. As they briefed, she occasionally eyed her phone buzzing with texts she didn't read. "What about Vassar?" she interjected, sending me into a small coughing fit.

"Oh, we didn't know he wanted to—did Adam want to visit Vassar?" Dana asked, scrambling through her notes as if Diane Keaton were playing her.

"My dad's suddenly all into it. For me. He says he thinks if I went there, I'd turn out well." She shrugged as a hot flush blasted up my neck. "I mean, I just thought if there's time—"

"Oh, no, of course, we can make that happen!"

"There isn't." Abigail cut Dana off. "We have to bang this out before the convention. Next year."

Alison's eyes glazed. "Wow, if Dad gets reelected *and* Adam goes off to college—Adam's what makes this bearable." An embarrassed smile immediately broke and she hastily stood. We followed to our feet and she shook our hands again. This very real, lovely girl with her father's eyes and mother's mouth. "I mean, it's all awesome," she said, blushing from her admission. "Whatever. Thank you."

And it was laid excruciatingly bare. My recent fantasies of First Ladydom, my debates over American designers versus foreign, were laughable, embarrassing. Wrong.

The next morning was a Saturday and I, marinating in self-loathing, with my twenty-second birthday just hours away, called Rachelle, herself marinating because Matt had posted pictures on Facebook with a girl hanging on him at what we couldn't decide was a bar or a house party, which was akin to trying to decipher the caliber of bullet speeding toward you.

"And Geoffrey was extra wet sand in my bikini this week. We need out of Dodge," she said. "Meet me in Chinatown."

We arrived in Manhattan on the Fung Wah bus by lunch, without a destination or host. We had Facebooked our arrival, expecting immediate invitations, but instead walked for hours, wending north up Broadway. Rachelle shopped, I consulted. Dusk fell. I'd have thought Lena would have at least suggested a restaurant, but all she posted was, "Too hot for NY—yuck! Love from the beach!" I know she meant it to be funny, but it rankled.

"I could call Mathew," Rachelle offered—any opportunity to reengage.

"To ask if we can crash on his couch? I'm not letting you do that.

I've been there." I thought of all the times after Mike left that I reached out, the pretenses, the questions only he (and Wikipedia) could have answered, each one met with a silence that etched my humiliation deeper. "It does not lead to the sex."

She narrowed her eyes. "If I just fucking lived here, we'd have sealed the deal this week and I'd be his girlfriend right now."

"I'm so sorry. We can solve this," I insisted. "We're two adult women! With cell phones! Your other friend hasn't called back yet?"

"She's in the Hamptons—wait, we'll surprise your sister!"

"My *sister*," I repeated skeptically.

"She'll love it."

"She won't."

"Inside she'll be doing a Snoopy dance. Don't overthink it."

If she was remotely close to dancing, Erica didn't let on. Three women she was entertaining snacked around a white marble kitchen island while something with rosemary was cooking. "This is Sara, Megan, and Blair. Guys, this is Jamie and . . ."

"Rachelle," she reminded her, stepping in around me. "So great to see you again! This place is in-*sane*. Do you rent or own?"

"Sorry to interrupt," I said quickly as I joined Rachelle, who was taking in Peter's Chelsea condo, the high-end everything, the floor-to-ceiling windows looking down Sixth Avenue. "We were just meeting some people and I thought we'd say hi before heading home."

"But, oh my God," Rachelle talked over me, "if we didn't have to take the late-night Chinatown bus back that would be *amazing*. The drivers are so sketch."

"Well then you should stay," Erica said on an inhale, ribs visibly splaying.

"Carrot?" Megan offered. "Your sister forgot there are only four of us."

"I'll eat it all," Blair said through a full mouth. "I was at the office all day, which kicked off with one optimistic wheatgrass shot and bottomed out with one four p.m. hot dog."

"Whose Goldman bag is that?" Rachelle flung a finger at the tote by the door as if it were the face of Jesus in a bowl of Jell-O.

"Guilty." Blair raised her hand.

"That's so random." Rachelle turned to her, full wattage. "Do you know Mathew McGeehan, in the associate program? Just started in June—"

"Blair isn't working with associates at this point," Erica said, putting a period on the inquiry.

"Of course." Rachelle grabbed a Parmesan twist and cracked it in half. "He's just a friend of mine. From boarding school. Had to ask. God, I can't *wait* to get to my 'at this point.' My boss is a round hairbrush in my asshole."

I pivoted to Erica. "It smells delicious—what did you cook?"

"Fresh Direct," she corrected me.

"I'm shocked that guys are always asking me on dates if I can cook," Blair said. "Apparently my distaste for it reveals a deep character flaw about me—worse than being an addict."

"They really want a mommy," Sara answered.

"Well, *I* cook," Megan said proudly.

"I swallow." Erica refilled her Perrier. "Ovens are for shoes. Ten-minute countdown. Plate up." She handed me one, our eyes meeting for a second. "*Mad Men* season finale," she explained.

"It gave me *chills*." Rachelle was emphatic.

"Don't say anything!" Megan plopped down on the cowhide rug.

"I've been chained to my desk, so no spoilers here," I reassured them. I had no context for the world of AA, had to get subway directions to her apartment from a stranger, but I knew how to watch TV in a group.

"Best show about alcoholics ever made," Erica said, making a spot for me next to her on the low couch.

Blair spun around from the floor. "Oh my God, how fucking sick is it they're opening a Magnolia on the same block as our meetings? There's going to be, like, a worn groove in the sidewalk."

"We should just meet there," Erica agreed. "Occupational therapy. Talk while we frost. So much better than church."

"You go to church?" I couldn't help asking.

"The basement," she clarified, eliciting a laugh from her friends.

I considered this for a second. "Churches give me the willies."

Suddenly she leaned over and kissed my forehead just like Mom. It was so unexpected I didn't dare breathe.

So I thought Erica was happy we came, in her Erica way. And while Rachelle was already planning her Tumblr feed of the adventure, I quietly studied a sister I'd overheard on the phone and seen piling into cars, but never been invited to join.

A few hours later, having seen everyone off, Erica shuffled back to the kitchen where we were attempting to tidy up. "Blair's a trader?" I asked. "Have you known each other a long time? I always wondered if the meetings put the friendship track on warp speed."

"Yes." She piled her hair into a makeshift bun as she took in the mess, dropping her head to the side. "What are you looking for?"

"Saran wrap. You want to save this stuff, right?" I continued searching drawers.

Erica reached into the back of a cabinet, placing the yellow box on the counter. "You don't need to clean up."

"Oh, we don't mind. It's only eleven, we were thinking we could—"

"I have a race tomorrow," she informed us. "Check-in is at seven a.m."

"Oh."

"So you guys are welcome to stay, but you need to sleep now. Leave the door unchained for Peter."

"Can I take a quick shower?" Rachelle asked.

Erica pointed her to the guest bath. "The fresh towels are rolled under the sink."

We cleaned in silence, the only sound the running water until Erica's cell rang. I was surprised to see my mother's number at this hour. Since she wasn't moving toward it, I answered. Erica crossed her arms, her jaw jutting abruptly to the side. I looked away. "Everything okay?"

"Jamie? Oh, I'm sorry, I meant to call Erica."

"You did."

"I'm confused."

"I came up to see her."

"You did?" Her voice brightened. "Oh, that's great. Her roommate isn't there, is she? She's a pill."

"Maureen's away this weekend." Erica watched me lie for her, expressionless. "That's why she invited me up."

"Well, I'm happy to hear it. That makes me feel better, actually."

"Is everything okay?" I asked again.

"Yes," Mom said too forcefully. "You guys have fun, just—have her call me, okay?"

"Sure." I hung up and felt the vague downward pull of insecurity. "She wants you to call her."

"Okay."

"Why's Mom calling you at eleven at night?"

"To talk," Erica said with annoyance, picking up the sponge and rubbing at the counter.

"How often is she calling you to talk?"

"More often than I have time for."

"About what?"

"I don't know, Jamie. Dad, life, work. What difference does it make?" She threw the sponge in the sink.

"Are you mad that I came?"

"No! It's fine, just . . . for starters your friend is—she takes up a lot of space. And it's weird! It's *weird* that you just showed up. A call would have been—whatever, it doesn't matter."

"Well, I had to get out of D.C.," I said defensively, not bothering to remind her about my birthday. "Rachelle is fun, Erica, she's not—"

She slapped her palm on the counter. "What do you want, Jamie?"

"The guy I'm seeing. He has a girlfriend."

Her expression shifted, her surprise satisfying.

"And it's all—it's—I feel pretty gross about the whole thing." I was prodding for the kind of pronouncement that was her forte and, on some level, aching for the judgment marbleized through it. "I mean, do you think it is?"

"Gross?" she said in a way that made me embarrassed for the word choice.

"Actually, he's married." She pivoted and walked away down the hall. "Please tell me what to do." She returned with a set of bedding and snapped out a flat sheet, her expression impassive. "Please?"

"Fuck, Jamie, no." She said it as if I'd tried to throw her a scorpion.

"Erica, I'm asking—I need help with this. It's really big. I don't know if I can handle—"

"No. Jamie, you can't just push your way in here and—no." She lifted her hands. "I can't. I'm already dealing with Mom, and no. No."

"You can't," I asked her, my voice thickening, "or won't?"

"You don't get to put this on me—"

We heard a sneeze and turned to see Rachelle dripping in her towel. She smiled as if this were all totally normal. "Did you say you had a hair dryer?"

Rachelle saved me. She got me out of there and into a speakeasy beneath a barber shop, or maybe it was a store with a barber's pole in the window—either way, I remember it was on the Lower East Side. She deposited me on a banquette, worked the room to procure drinks, and then, once I had something muddled in each hand, ran out for snacks.

"The next time you say your sister won't like something, let's go with that." She plopped back down to unwrap a cellophaned bagel and place it ceremoniously before me.

"What's this?" I asked, whiskey and sugar defrosting the block of hurt in my stomach.

"In about . . ." She checked her phone, the glow momentarily illuminating her smoky eyes. "Two minutes, it'll be your birthday." She tore open a box of Shabbat candles and stuck one in the hole, lighting it with her Bic. I made my wish as instructed, exactly what you'd expect. The music got louder and we sipped yet another cocktail as she lolled her head to me on the worn velvet. "So . . . married?"

I nodded.

"Kids?" she asked.

"Two."

"Holy wow."

"Yeah." I peered at her in the lantern shadows that shifted with the crowd. "I know, I feel like shit about it."

"So that's why the office hook-up. Does he come over? Is he going to leave her?"

"No. I don't know. No."

"Aw." She squeezed my knee affectionately. "My very own other woman."

"Uck." I took another long draw. "There are two versions in my head: one where I'm meeting my soul mate under less-than-optimal circumstances that we will somehow rise above. And one where I'm evil." I hoped that hearing it out loud would make it feel less corrosive, but it was the opposite. I hated myself.

"The whole soul mate thing is *supposed* to be messy. There're a thousand stories where someone leaves the wrong person—Sky Hoppey—to meet the right one. Oh God, it's not the guy with the 'Don't Frack with Me' cuff links and the wedding picture on his desk where his wife is wearing a cape? At least tell me it's not him."

"Definitely not him." Which kicked off an inquisition that I was determined, despite my prior lapses, would lead nowhere, except eventually (though the memory's fuzzy), to dancing with a group of Polish—Scottish—tourists—construction workers? I quickly realized that my seeing a "married guy at work" was infinitely sexier in Rachelle's world than the mundane detail of the guy's actual identity. Given the less-than-virile workforce of my office, a name would have taken my story from fabulous to pedestrian and perhaps even tawdry, so she happily left him a mystery and called him my Mister Man.

Later, as we fought passing out on the dawn bus back to D.C., our arms looped precautionarily through our bag handles, Rachelle smiled at me with closing eyes. "You're amazing."

"I am?" I asked, the black thickness taking hold. "You mean disgusting?"

"I mean . . ." I heard her murmur with the brightening skyline looming above. "I have to get to New York. My life has to start here already. It just . . . does." Her hand still holding mine, her grated breathing mixed with the traffic funneling us into the tunnel.

≡

Squinting against the whiskey clamor in my skull and the maw of guilt in my stomach, I managed to find my way back to Gail's and a ringing phone. Greg greeted me by very quietly singing in my new year. "I had to call," he said softly.

Gripping the receiver to my shoulder, I clutched Gail's keys. "I leave in nine days," I leveled at him.

"You can't go." His anguish took me by surprise.

"I have to."

"I don't want you to."

"You don't?"

"Fuck, Jamie, I'm risking the world to sing you 'Happy Birthday.'"

The thoughts I'd been locked in with came bursting from their dehydrated compartments. "But I can't—how can I—*keep* doing this? I'm not allowed to want it to go where it can't. And I can't make sense of—I need you to make sense of—more sense—"

"You can handle this, right? Jamie?" He shut me down.

Looking back, I realize that he was revealing what he believed: we didn't deserve to ask for a solution to our situation, only for the capacity to withstand it. "Of course."

"In three years, I won't be running for anything ever again and no one can tell me what to do. I love you, Jamie."

"You do?"

"Only when I'm with you does any of this feel like I thought it would. I've made so many mistakes. Mistakes that should have been undone a long time ago." Did he mean Susan? "But then I chose a public life and those doors closed to me. I know I have a lot—everything—I know that." There was a pause. I sensed him struggling for the words. "But somehow along the way, happiness became something I had to . . . trade in—until you." We stayed on the line in silence. "Let me make a wish for us on your candle, too?" he asked tenderly.

"Yes."

≡

In an unprecedented turn of events, the essence of that birthday wish—however conflicted—was granted. I was so unaccustomed to getting what I asked for that Margaret had to repeat herself. "A full-time junior position."

"Really?"

"You did a solid job prepping the college trip. Dana says you were like a robot. So you accept?"

I swiped my pass and jumped over Brooke's foot, which I swore was extended to trip me. Texting Rachelle and then Lena, I took the stairs two at a time.

"Jamie, he's—"

"Jean, I got a job!"

"Congratulations—"

"Junior staffer. I'm so excited! Is he in?"

"The President is in meetings all morning," she said stiffly. I looked over my shoulder to find Amar Singh sitting by the door in his bow tie. He looked at me strangely. *Fuck.*

"Right. Margaret sent me up to ask—because she needed to schedule some time to review—to update the President—on the college trip. And of course I wanted to tell you the good news, so I offered to come up instead of calling because you've been so encouraging to me. So—thank you."

"Well, you're very welcome, dear. I'll call down to schedule that review once we get an opening."

"Which I'll tell Margaret. Okay, then. Thank you!" I punched the air goofily, nodded at Singh, and left with a dry mouth.

The news of my promotion rapidly circulated throughout the department. But no congratulations were forthcoming. While she admitted it wasn't fair, Lena still felt rejected. I kept reminding her that *technically* L.A. had rejected *me,* until I felt like I shouldn't have had to keep saying that and she should have just been happy for me. Coupled with the poisonous nausea as I waited for Greg's admonishment for rushing to his office unbidden, it was not at all how I'd imagined finally getting a job would feel.

Then, on nearly the last day of my internship, my desk phone rang. "Department of Scheduling and Advance, Jamie speaking."

"Meet me in the south hall on the way out to the chopper," he instructed. "About ten after four." And he hung up, leaving me suspended in adrenaline.

I used my lunch hour to case Wm. Fox & Co., looking at pocket squares and cuff links I couldn't possibly afford. In addition to my note of apology, I hunted for something that might delight him enough to overlook my misstep. I passed my hand over the tie tables like I was spreading a freshly shuffled deck. And then I found it— royal blue with a quiet white pattern suggestive of the tiniest lightning bolts. And at 4:07, palms sweating, I walked the administrative carpet with it tucked discreetly into a manila envelope.

His security rounded the corner. And then it was him, in his black pinstripe suit. We both continued looking straight ahead as people chattered in their offices abutting the corridor. Phones rang and were answered.

"Oh, great." He slowed, and his detail stopped. "Could you, uh, bring this to Margaret?" He tugged an Oval Office envelope from his bag.

"Yes, sir. She just asked for me to bring this up to you, actually, but I'm happy to bring it to Jean—"

"That's fine." He grabbed my envelope in return as he walked on. I held mine casually until I crossed the threshold of the ladies' room, where I locked myself in a stall. I broke the seal and breathlessly tugged out a small orange box that looked like the ones Gail kept stacked in her closet. Hermès. I slipped off the ribbon to discover the most beautiful silver—ring? It was too big to be a ring. A thumb ring? I opened the diminutive brochure. A scarf ring. Fingering the equestrian links, I opened the card. *To your future. Congratulations, G."*

And there was a book. J. D. Salinger. Leather bound, inscribed with, *"Many Happy Returns."* I flipped to the page where he'd stuck a Post-it:

> . . . *walking toward her quickly but with a slow face, reasoned to himself, with suppressed excitement, that he was the only one on*

*the platform who really knew Franny's coat. He remembered that
once, in a borrowed car, after kissing Franny for a half hour or so,
he had kissed her coat lapel, as though it were a perfectly desirable,
organic extension of the person herself.*

Wow. WowwowWOW. A future. Of happy returns. I hugged the
presents as if I were pulling him against me and floated out of the
stall—into Brooke. She looked at the orange box at my chest and
the Oval Office envelope, her eyes narrowing. I washed my hands,
staring her down in the mirror. I grabbed a towel, collected my
treasure from the counter, and walked out. Her last day could not
come fast enough.

And neither could my first.

Part II

Part II

Chapter Six

August 15

I don't remember how I got across town to the address where I'd been directed, numbly clutching that stupid cardboard box with the few possessions I'd accumulated at the White House rattling around. I kept thinking I should fucking stop at a deli and grab a plastic bag and dump this clichéd thing that made me look so—rejected. Instead I carried it in a fugue state until I found myself following a guy I'd been assigned to down several flights toward some sub-basement's subbasement, my body, stomach, and will to live all sinking in tandem.

"The stairwell's a little Gringotts," he said, briefly touching his tented fingers to the raw concrete walls, and it took me a second to realize he meant Harry Potter's underground bank. "But the bullpens are bright." I trailed his narrow back down yet another flight. "And I've found a small vitamin D supplement keeps the suicidal tendencies at bay."

Still reeling, I couldn't compute what he was saying. I also wondered how he got away with just a V-neck over his oxford. Maybe this place was more casual than one would think?

"Here we are." He held up the ID dangling from his red lanyard to the security panel and the door clicked. "See? Bright." He had a bemused sardonic energy, implying he didn't want to be there, didn't want to have to say what he was about to say, and wished he could just narrate his life with thought bubbles.

"Yes. Yes, it is." The fluorescents banked off the unbroken field of polished white linoleum, making it feel as though I'd be processing the recently deceased in an Albert Brooks film.

"You have Tabby's old desk." He led me across other people's paths, everyone moving in focused silence as if weaving a tartan in a Vassar dance recital. "And voilà," he said flatly, gesturing toward a battered metal desk surrounded by a field of the same. "Hot tip: make sure you clean your phone. After Nicaragua, Tabby didn't like anyone meddling with her things, including janitors. Alrighty." He bit the inside of his mouth as I set the box down. "I'm over there once you get yourself settled, and welcome to the Department of Homeland Security."

There'd been a mistake. There had to have been a mistake.

"Just remind me to help you get your cafeteria pass."

"Um, you know—sorry," I prompted him.

"Paul," he reintroduced himself. With his unlined face, blue eyes, thick black hair, and a cleft in his chin like a cartoon hero, I guessed he was only in his early thirties.

"Yes, Paul, I don't think I'm going to be here that long."

"Planning to get fired?" he asked dryly.

"No." I blushed. "Help with the pass would be great, actually—yes, thank you."

"I'll come get you at one."

Not if I've chained myself to the White House fence first. "Perfect."

"And I'll give you your assignment as soon as your security clearance finishes processing." He started to leave, but then pivoted back. "They usually have that done in advance—when you interview."

"Right. I was—um—sent here."

He graciously nodded, but it seemed to make as little sense to him as it did to me. "Okay, then." He returned to his desk and I looked down at the coffee-stained blotter Tabby left behind—still torn down to December 2008. I couldn't let myself sit, because then I'd be there. Really there. I picked up the phone, wiped the receiver across my thigh, and dialed.

"Office of the President, Jean speaking."

"Jean, hi," I said quietly, "it's Jamie McAlister."

"Does Margaret need something?"

"Um, no—actually—that's why I'm calling. I was supposed to start officially working for her today, but when I arrived this morning I was told I'd been reassigned to an *unpaid* internship at the DOHS." I felt the clammy rumbling of a panic attack threatening. My loans would come due at Christmas. A thousand dollars a month.

"I'll put you straight through to personnel."

"Right, of course." Not the President of the United States. "Thank you—um, Jean?" I halted her.

"Yes?"

"Can you tell him I called?"

"Of course, dear," she said warmly. I hung up as soon as I heard the musical hold. Dropping into the chair, my eyes on the phone, I irrationally expected it to ring immediately. *I've fucked it up*, I thought. Were those goodbye gifts? Was that his way of telling me this was over? *Please*, I bargained, *just let him forgive me for rushing to his office*, and I vowed I'd never be impulsive again. After a few long minutes, I picked it back up and dialed the one person I could consult without having to redact this story.

"I just realized I put my underwear on backwards," Lena greeted me.

"How did you know it was me?"

"Area code."

"It's so good to hear your voice."

"Sorry, I've been so busy here. Miserably busy. But I just found out I'm bonus eligible this year, so that's cool. I feel like my boss can totally tell about my underwear and it's—"

"I've been banished." I tucked my head and put my hand over my mouth.

"Banished?"

"Lena, he punted me to the Department of Homeland Security. To another *internship*—"

"Whoa."

"I know, right?"

"No, I mean, that's the government government."

"Huh?"

"Like, not the white building with the fancy china and not Congress, passing bills on dog food—these are the people who can drop you down a well. Jamie, stop. Seriously, get out, go home," she said bluntly.

"Have you had your coffee yet this morning?" I tried cajoling her.

"My opinion can't be turned on a latte. There's no solution here. I'm sorry, there just isn't."

"Lena, I'm getting a cafeteria pass, it's not Guantánamo. I just need to talk this through. We used to talk about things *because* there was no solution—that was the core criterion. Hour ten dissecting Malik was not going to make him love you."

There was a silence.

"Lena? You still there?" I was about to call back when she finally responded.

"I'm uncomfortable, Jamie. Like, in the pit of my stomach. I asked my mom—"

"What?"

"As a hypothetical friend of a friend—"

"What other friend of a friend lives in D.C. and works—fuck—*worked* at the White House?"

"Exactly. I can't talk to you about this anymore."

"Are you kidding? You were mad at me because I didn't share enough. I finally—look, there's no 'this'—I just—I don't know what to do."

"I told you what to do. You don't want to hear it. Jamie, get on a plane or get on my mother's couch—what does it matter which coast it's on—and learn how to bartend."

"While you earn real money and start your career?" I was stunned. "You sure you don't just need a maid?" Her arrogance, my jealousy, the years she'd spent spotting me cash so we could do things at her level, all bubbled over.

"Jamie, that's not—I gotta jump," she added hastily, hanging up.

Heart audibly pounding, jaw set, my brain spun around one word like a weather vane: I *can't* talk to my best friend about the one thing I really need to talk about. I *can't* talk to Greg and find out what the fuck just happened here. I *can't* quit the only opportunity I have right now. And I *can't* be the sad broke girl on her rich friend's couch.

When Paul came to collect me for lunch, I'd tracked down a bottle of Fantastik from the closet. That phone sparkled.

As we sat across from each other, the rushed movement of those around us getting food, getting it down, and getting out of there as fast as possible created an audible rustle like wind through a cornfield. He picked at his roast beef sandwich. "So you have no personnel file."

I startled, pulled out of my imaginary pleadings. "Well, *technically*, I'm not personnel yet."

"But we don't really do interns. We've had, like, three since I've been here and they were all kids of senators and generals. On their way to West Point—mayonnaise." He snapped his fingers, twisting around like some packets might be sneaking up on him. "That's what I always forget. So, are you somebody's kid?"

"Um, my dad runs an intramural program on the South Side of Chicago, so no."

He took that in. "It's just that everyone else *wants* to be here," he said, opening a lemon yogurt, and I couldn't tell if he was including himself.

"Of course," I agreed, unprepared for the job interview this was turning into.

"No, I mean, they *want* to be here. Since 9/11. It's like patrolling the Arizona border to them—even if they're just braiding paper clips. I'm only telling you this because you got popped over here from the White House, which means you did an exemplary job. But you showed up this morning looking like you were trying to find the nearest Red Cross gymnasium."

I was mortified. "I—I am very excited to be here. It's an honor. I just had a rough morning—family stuff."

He nodded. "No, my first day was rough, too. But we promote internally, so if you prove yourself like you did there, you could land a position."

"Thank you for sharing that. I appreciate it."

He peered into his yogurt. "I came from the White House."

"You did?" I asked through a full mouth.

"Originally I started in Rutland's office back in Harrisburg."

"What was he like?" It came out before I could stop myself.

He considered for a second while I tried to temper the signs of my curiosity. "Even then, him being the President just felt inevitable. Like we all heard 'Hail to the Chief' when he walked in the room. Anyway, from there to the campaign—and . . ."

"They placed you here—why?" Everyone knew Rutland had taken only a handful of people from Pennsylvania.

"Eventually. It was a huge promotion," he said in a way that connoted the exact opposite. "Keep your friends close," he added airily. His cell vibrated and he glanced at it, blowing out "fffff" like he was about to say fuck.

I asked if he was okay and he abruptly stood, still staring at the phone.

"Paul?"

"My ex wants to stop by tonight to get his steak knives," he said as if he had just bitten into something acidic. "Only they're *my* steak knives and I will happily furnish him with my credit card statement from our ski trip to prove it."

"That sucks," I said.

"It does."

"Thank you for lunch," I said as he raised his tray. "And I'm really sorry."

"Well, just try to look like you want to be here and you'll do fine."

That night, with razor wire in my chest and nothing else to go on, I priced out flights to L.A. I was determined to be a grown-up and look at this pragmatically, stay focused on what had happened to my fledgling career. Even if the DOHS position transitioned into a paying job, I could spend years waiting on promotions to gradually move up out of the earth like a seed in Siberia. Advancement at the White House had felt like it could lead somewhere, open doors to unforeseen possibilities. That DOHS basement felt like it would lead to scurvy.

"I don't get it," Rachelle said on the phone from a VP campaign stop in Des Moines, where Geoffrey had forced her to lug the equipment through the muddy state fair. "How does your guy have the power to pull off something this big?"

"He doesn't," I rushed, stubbing out my third cigarette. "Not power—exactly. Just . . . influence."

"Ooh, influence, I *like* it. Jamie, reframe: how many girls can say they've been banished? He wants you so much he can't even handle having you in the same building."

Despite doing her best to find me a silver lining, I was desperate to regain some control, and pressing "purchase" on Expedia seemed the only way to achieve it. I told Rachelle we could talk more when she came back, but for sanity's sake I had to reserve a flight in two weeks to L.A. It was enough time to give my notice, nut up to grovel to Lena, and pack. I drank till I could pass out. But the ringing phone soon invaded my dream.

"I woke you," he said, sounding unapologetic.

I bolted up, the slap hitting me afresh.

"Jamie?" he asked uncertainly.

"I use some of my free time to sleep, yes." I sounded cold, which only made me sadder.

"You called Jean."

"To tell you I'm leaving." It felt so good to say, I queasily realized that I may have booked the flight for only that reason.

"But I got you the post."

"Um, actually, Greg," I corrected him, anger flaring, "*I* got myself a job at the White House by rocking my internship and not being all Children of the Corn. *You* banished me."

"I'm *keeping* you." He was shocked.

"Keeping me? Like a pet?" I was completely put off.

He took one of his characteristic pauses. "Singh made some strong suggestions after he saw you outside my office. That internship was our compromise."

"And I'm sick about that, but why didn't you tell me—"

"I'm in the middle of a campaign."

"I just don't understand how you need to follow anyone's anything."

"Jamie, I surround myself with smart people and I listen to them. That's how this works." He blew out hard and I pictured him looking at his desk, running his beautifully freckled hand through his thick hair. Would I get a chance to tell him that now—that I thought he had beautiful hands? It wasn't something you shared after being banished.

"I need to go—"

"Jamie." He snatched me back, the receiver already halfway to the cradle. "It's just until after the election."

Relief shot through me, contained by my skepticism, like a charge through a wire. I lifted the phone back to my ear. "Really?"

"Yes, of course! Why else would I have to listen to Singh?"

"Why didn't you tell me that? Call me before I had to carry a box across town like an idiot."

"Um, you know, Ms. McAlister, I've been busy," he imitated me as a blush drowned my own freckles.

"Uh, what could possibly be more important in, you know, the world, than my job assignment?" I joined in the joke to show him I got it, I was chastened.

"Listen, I just need to keep my head down until November," he said, his voice intimate again.

"No, of course."

"Then I'll bring you back."

"You will?" I threw my arm out in the dark—it was all I needed to hear.

"Yes!" He was almost laughing at me. "Margaret's pretty pissed at me as it is. Competent non—what did you call it?—Children of the Corn people are hard to find. You just need to trust me."

"I do," I said quickly, wanting to wrap his voice around me with the sheets. "I hope you trust me, too." He had given me what I'd prayed for, something I could finally count on—a plan for us. It was almost as though everything up to that point had to happen so I could have it. I wanted to return the favor of providing relief. I sensed how important this was, keeping him at ease, and reminded him, "I would never betray you—never. You know that, right?"

"You're special," he said softly.

"Like, needs extra help?" I demurred.

"No, really, you have a—a light around you that I can't get enough of. An energy like no one I've ever known. This between us—this is—" *What—what is this?* "Fun." Such a small, dumb word, but he said it as if it were cupped in his palms and he was trying not to spill it. And I felt protective of him all over again.

"When I hear those pundits tearing you apart on TV, I just want to reach in and break their noses."

He laughed deeply. "You're hired—oh, shit, there's the other line. It's daytime somewhere."

"Of course." I hated to let him go. "Greg?"

"Yes."

"You have my vote."

"Well, that's good. Illinois's a swing state. Night, Jamie."

I canceled my flight.

It was hard not to feel as if I were in a Greek myth, given the gift of hearing Zeus say I was special. Yet each time I replayed the memory, it faded, losing its potency, leaving me desperately needing a new memory to run thin. But there was none forthcoming.

Over the following weeks, on the sleep of someone with one ear open, I followed the campaign map and tried to immerse myself in my new internship, striving to prove myself as if word might get back to Greg that I'd collated three file archives in what Paul said was record time.

On line for an iced coffee to break up the monotony, I checked Facebook and saw that Kenny Richmond had announced he was gay. I immediately texted Lena. I hadn't even counted out my change before the phone rang.

"Why now?" she asked as a greeting. "Why not on any given day at one of the gayest schools in the Northeast?"

"And why September?" I countered, raising my cup to the barista in the sign for thanks, phone clamped to my shoulder. "Why not back during Pride month?"

"Where is he working?"

"Wells Fargo, Boston." I pushed outside into the tenacious heat.

"What does Wells Fargo have that Vassar didn't?"

"Or Boston, for that matter," I added, pulling down my sunglasses.

"It's like going to France and waiting until you get back to Trader Joe's to try Brie."

"I miss you." It popped out. She didn't respond. "Lena?"

"I've been busy," she answered tightly.

"Me, too. This new placement"—Paul's much-appreciated euphemism for internship—"is super time-consuming. But I love it," I added, because she'd made it clear that I couldn't be staying there for any other reason.

"That's . . . great."

"Yeah, though," I said, setting the groundwork for November, "I still think if something opened up at the White House, I'd go back, you know, maybe after the election."

"Oh. How's your family?" she asked politely.

I sat on a bench in the marginally cooler shade, unable to believe that this was us. That things could have gotten so strained. And I still wasn't entirely sure why. Was it me, what I did? Or was that just the excuse? Were we friends all those years because she'd had only a few hundred people to choose from and now she had all of Los Angeles? "My what?"

"You texted that your mom was calling Erica late at night—is she worried about her?" she flailed.

"Um, she idles there and you never ask about my family," I had to point out.

"That's not true."

"I meant it as a good thing." The ice in my drink was already transforming into a watery top layer.

"Jamie, I have to go."

"Lena—"

"Look, my mom says the RNC's just waiting for Rutland to sneeze wrong. You have to be beyond careful. They're searching for anything—*anything*—to hang him on. If the Supreme Court rules that Brianne Rice's case can move forward, the way my mother's friends are talking, they're going to mobilize behind Rice and it's just going to make them bolder."

"It's disgusting, the way she's gone after him with this trumped-up witch hunt."

"How can you say that now?" she asked too vehemently.

"*This* is not that. For you to even compare the two—"

"Fine. I'm sorry. But I know. *I* know I voted for a liar."

"No, you don't!" I was shrieking, but I couldn't reel myself back.

"You're doing that D.C. thing, Jamie, and you don't even see it."

"What?"

"Pretending the truth is flexible." She sounded pained, furious.

"And this has nothing to do with Greg and everything to do with your dad." Bringing up his infidelity was a low blow, and I didn't know why I'd dealt it.

"Okay." I could hear her breathe. "I see now why you don't tell anyone shit. Because then they can't throw it in your face." She hung up.

I wanted to call right back and tell her, *I'm sorry! I'm on the next plane!* And, *Greg who?* And, *Wasn't that crazy?*

But I didn't. I didn't. Someone thought I was special and I wasn't ready to let that go.

The Indian summer gave way to the first burst of an autumn that reflected my mood. The splashy reds and oranges arced overhead, forming a passionate canopy above my mind filled with equally passionate anticipation.

But as the chilling nights rolled on, one after the other, silent, the leaves drifted into the gutter, and my lust smoked like a damp fire in all that gray. The pumpkins were carved, the pumpkins were lit, and now they were starting to rot. And still he hadn't called.

Matt McGeehan had changed his Facebook status to "In a Relationship," and Rachelle and I were collectively spending too much money on crap wine and cigarettes. Halloween night she invited me to a DNC phone-banking party at the Marriott. It still amazes me that wherever I go, Halloween is the universal equalizer. Even there, in the nation's capital, we looked like a roomful of prostitutes working a pledge drive. I thought I was being pretty conservative in my navy yoga shorts and red tank top, my hair knotted up with a braid of rope I got at the hardware store; my red hair and blue brain had inspired me to go as a swing state. But I was surrounded by an astonishing amount of fishnets and cleavage, ass cheeks and high heels. The guys sported fake mustaches, crotch padding, and chest wigs, making it hard to tell what they were costumed to be, other than just generally repulsive.

"Hello?" the next person on my list answered.

"My name is Jamie and I'm calling from the DNC on behalf of President Rutland—"

"He can go fuck himself."

"Thank you for your time," I said, jumping down to the end of the approved script.

"Ew." Rachelle practically tossed her receiver on the table. She was dressed as a very sexy version of the Majority Leader's miniature Pomeranian. You have to take my word for it. "In hindsight, phone banking on Halloween was a horrible idea. Are we going to get through to a single sober person?"

"Doubtful." A man dressed as Callista Gingrich leaned in between us.

"Oh my gosh, Paul!" I leapt up. "What are you doing here?"

He sized up the room like he was expecting to run into someone. "I'll go anywhere for a free Oreo."

"I *love* your costume," Rachelle complimented.

"Ronald?" he appreciatively confirmed hers.

"Thank you. If one more guy calls me Toto," she said as we made the lady next to us move over so Paul could sit and filled three more Dixie cups with Hi-C. Suddenly, outside the double doors, the hallway air flashed white. "Is that him?" Rachelle pushed her chair back as I leapt up.

Paul nodded affirmatively, like this was all in a day. "Leaving the fundraiser downstairs."

We scrambled around our folding table and out to the grand staircase lined with Secret Service, skidding to a halt. "We just want to . . ." Rachelle pointed over their shoulders. I assume that since we obviously couldn't conceal a weapon in those outfits, they let us get close enough to peer between them. "Oh, this just made the story of tonight *so* much better," she said, sliding her phone out of the waistband of her faux-fur hot pants.

We watched him glad-hand his way across the lobby toward the exit, each person twirled inside his green-eyed charisma for a moment they wouldn't forget. Caught up in the excitement, Rachelle smiled and squealed at me as if we were at our first rock concert. I stared, allowing myself to drink him in, fully opening every memory until my skin ached and I was jealous of every patted shoulder, every pressed palm. "I'm so sick of feeling outside everything." Rachelle was suddenly deflated.

"I know."

"Like I'm on the other side of the glass from life and I can't seem to break through."

I nodded.

"When do we get our turn, Jamie?" I knew she was staring at me beseechingly for a pep talk, but I had no answer and just couldn't risk taking my eyes off him. I needed to memorize everything about how he moved and smiled and waved to get myself through the remaining days. In all the frenzy, I don't know what made him look up.

But he did.

After another hour, we gave up on polling and decamped to a bar Paul suggested. The place was packed with people who were Halloween drunk, half-naked, and ready to make a mistake. Rachelle was surreptitiously scoping, elbows clasped at her side, straw pursed between her glossed lips, while Paul lifted on his toes, actively scanning. "Shit."

"What?"

"My ex."

"What's the plan?" Rachelle asked like a Charlie's Angel, immediately fierce behind her whiskers and pink nose. "Dumping a drink, begging for more, making out with someone else—how you wanna play this?"

Paul just blinked his false lashes. "I'm such an asshole."

"No—why?" I touched his bare arm. "That wasn't on Rachelle's menu." I ducked my head and peered between the elbows and boas to see a group of guys getting bottle service in a booth. "Which one?"

"Dressed as a milk carton—I bet he's the one percent," he said, sounding gutted.

"He's really hot," Rachelle acknowledged, patting his back. "Even in that costume."

"He underplays it," Paul said wistfully like it was a phrase from his diary.

"How long has it been?"

"Two months. Let's get out of here." Paul grabbed his jacket. "I'd thought if we ran into each other—Halloween was kind of our holiday and we had an in-joke about Callista, but look at me—this is ridiculous."

"Want me to take you home—we could pick up ice cream?" I asked.

"No! No, that is *not* the story," Rachelle intervened, taking his jacket back. "Paul, a guy who I think is government cheese is checking you out. You're going to let him buy you a drink, swap stories and maybe saliva. Tonight's the night to feel *better* about ourselves," she said vehemently. "Jamie." She swung to me. "Donkey wants you."

"What?" And the moment it was out of my mouth, this guy wearing long ears swept me onto the makeshift dance floor. Beyoncé's "Ring the Alarm" was playing, and I remember he had incredibly strong legs.

I don't know who bought the drinks.

At one point I looked over and Paul was deep in conversation with the wedge of cheese and Rachelle was kissing someone wearing a white towel who was a Bill from *Schoolhouse Rock*. And then she left with him and Donkey programmed his number into my phone and the next thing I knew, I was helping Paul stumble into a cab. "How'd it go?"

"Awful." He clutched for the door handle. "He was boring and arrogant and I had to keep looking like I was having a blast, which just made it ten times worse."

"I'm so sorry."

"Fucking Rutland," he muttered as we swerved and he listed into me.

"What?" I pushed him upright.

"I'm just a little over him right now. Not that you'd understand. You ran out of that ballroom like Justin Bieber was downstairs."

I tensed. "So? Everyone reacts to him like that." I squinted against an oncoming car with its brights up.

"Spoken like a staffer." He stared out the window. "She denied it, too."

"Who denied what?" I asked.

"Brianne. That's why he left."

"Who left? Paul, what are you talking about?"

"Tom." Tears dripped out the corners of his heavily lined eyes, but his voice remained steady. "Him and his friends—*our* friends. They think I'll be a fucking embarrassment, a turncoat, toxic for Tom's career."

"Sorry." Drunk, adrenalized, confused, I scrambled to catch up. "What does Brianne Rice have to do with you?"

"*Nothing*," he said, wiping his hand under his nose. "That's what Tom refused to get. Just because I worked with her—witnessed one small thing. I'm one of hundreds of subpoenas they served in her case, which isn't even going to proceed. As if the Supreme Court is going to rule against the fucking President. It's a nonissue." His face contorted and he put his palm to his stomach.

"What's a nonissue?"

"My having to testify against Rutland."

That's when he puked.

I don't know how long Gail's phone had been ringing by the time I got Paul to his door and my key in the lock.

"What are you doing?" Greg was breathing heavily.

"What are *you* doing?" I unpeeled the vomit-crusted Lycra and flicked on the bedside lamp.

"Picturing you, leaning over the balcony like an angel—"

"I wasn't leaning."

"You have the most beautiful body. Your breasts, your thighs. I love touching your wet—"

I was sober. I stank of sour liquor and Oreos. Paul's words still clanged in my aching head. Greg was finally calling, but I was a million miles from wherever he was. "I'm taking my clothes off." It was true.

"You wearing a bra?"

"No."

"Panties?"

The smell was so bad I wanted to throw everything out the window, but it was across the room. Who doesn't own a cordless phone? "Yes."

"Are you touching yourself?"

. . . "Yes." If rubbing my arms against goose bumps counted.

"Where have you been?"

"I miss you so fucking much."

"You do?"

"Seeing your smile tonight—I live for that smile."

"My smile?" I sat on the bed, my feet throbbing from standing.

"I miss your voice, how it's just a little bit husky, your skin, your freckles, God, they're so fucking cute, the way you smell, like flowers and sex. I want you here with me right now. Always. I want to taste you. I want to hear you make that sound, how you groan when you come—" I heard him shudder.

The heat clicked on.

I rested back, mind reeling from all these new gifts, things I would always know. He thought I had a beautiful body. I would need to write it all down immediately before I jumbled what he missed and what he wanted with what he lived for. I let myself imagine him blissed out in my arms. I waited for him to speak.

A few minutes passed before I realized he'd hung up.

Paul came in late to work the next morning with a dry-cleaning reimbursement for me. I didn't push him more about Tom—or Brianne. I knew he was mortified. And I knew he was lonely. And I understood both.

Election night was only four days later, less then a week for me to run both potential takes on that phone call until my brain hemorrhaged. Was I the love of Greg's life—or a sex line? When the silence became unbearable, when I wanted to push myself to pull the trigger on leaving D.C. (if only so Gail's phone could ring on unanswered as he realized what he'd taken for granted), I would imagine every scathing thing Lena would say if I called her—which I didn't. The fact was

Lena's dad had married the woman he left her mom for. And he and his new wife had been together for years. They had kids. So which was the mistake? The "mistress" or the first marriage? I decided that's what I'd become the face of for her, pushing away the possibility that she was right—that truth had lost its moorings and I was submerged.

Paul had invited Rachelle and me to an election party near the office and as we walked from work, it felt like the city had reached such a frenzy of animosity, I half-expected the opposing parties to be coming down the street snapping their fingers like the Sharks and Jets. Rachelle was waiting on the corner, hunched in her red coat and jumping in her heels to keep warm.

"Ronald," Paul greeted her.

"Callista." She acknowledged him with a tilt of her head before abandoning any pretense of restraint and skipping up to us. "I'm sososo sorry if I made you barf from those shots."

"And I was worried no one would want to talk about it."

"We all do it."

"No, *we* don't." He dipped his chin into his herringbone scarf. "*You* do. Because you're twelve. I'm a hundred. Can we please go upstairs and eat shrimp now?"

"The Bill, whose name is Bill," she filled in for Paul's benefit, "is meeting us here and this is the one, I can feel it—how cute is that to meet on Halloween?" She slipped an arm through each of ours and led us to the entrance.

Upstairs it seemed to me the median age of the guests was definitely more on the side of a hundred than twelve. A few were pregnant, but most were starting to bald. Rachelle gamely asked everyone where they worked, what their core campaign issue was, and if they needed her to refresh their drinks. She was so perfect for PR.

The apartment was a duplex in the top two floors of a brownstone, hyper-modern and spare, with just one spiky aloe plant on the windowsill. The studied emptiness made it the perfect place to throw a party—that and the three TVs mounted beside each other. "Whose place is this?" I asked Paul.

"Carl Duggan. A friend of Tom's from K Street. Shmancy power circles. When he invited me tonight I thought he was making this grand gesture—turned out he just didn't know about our breakup yet. I'm pretty much here because I know Carl doesn't want me to be and I called his bluff." We pounded our second vodkas.

On the wall of screens the states turned color as they were called by the networks, waves of cheer or sick hush passing through the room each time. I felt crushed by conflicting desires. I wanted Greg to win because he wanted to win. And because the world would be a better place. I wanted Greg to lose so we could have a real chance. I believed we could have a real chance. I wanted him to choke on his burger and—if not die—then at least see his life flash and realize I wasn't porn. I wanted him to call and tell me he loved me. I wanted to get a grip.

If you're trying not to think about someone, standing in front of a bank of televisions repeating that person's name does not help. My phone buzzed with a text—from Mike. *"In the heart of it all, huh, James?"*

It was a volley from the wrong guy, but I'd been standing primed in Center Court for so many months that I reflexively lobbed it back. *"You voted, RIGHT?!"*

He texted back, *"For Partridge. Hahaha."*

"Not funny." I stared at the exchange with an agitated, uncomfortable twinge, then cleared the conversation. This made three times. Would it be the start of something? Would the texts grow more frequent, then get flirtatious? Would he want to see me? Would I want to see him?

I went to pour myself a third drink. I knew I should try to eat something, but the energy field across the nation seemed to warp around this room. Paul was letting himself be chatted up by a guy on the other side of the kitchen, but he didn't seem interested—he kept inching back to the brick.

I checked Facebook. Everyone had their virtual fingers crossed. Then a text from Rachelle. One word. *"Upstairs."*

I climbed the steps to the lofted home office. Over the TVs below I could hear soft sobbing. She was curled up in a nook between a bookcase and the wall. "I–I'm so p-pissed at myself," she said, and I knelt down. "He has a girlfriend."

"Bill?"

She nodded, rubbing her face, her mascara streaking across her cheek like rain in a painting. "We texted all week, he fucking asked about my childhood." She showed me the text that had just come in saying he hoped he hadn't given her the wrong impression. "Yeah, um, somewhere around when you put your penis in me I got the wrong impression."

"Rachelle, I'm so sorry."

"But he said he'd still be into 'meeting up' if I was ever interested."

"Are you?"

"*No.* How do you do it?" she asked aggressively.

"What?"

"Hang in being number two? I just want to be special enough that someone will *come* for me. Doesn't it kill you that he won't come for you? That he doesn't care enough to knock down your door, take a risk? Show that you're important to him? Don't you feel demeaned? Like you're a fucking nobody?"

"It's the President." Five syllables. Out of my mouth. The circle breaking open.

To her credit she didn't ask *what* was the President, or say *really* a million insulting times. She didn't get weird like Lena. She just held my hand, silently respecting the enormity of it as her tears dried.

"I'm never speechless," she finally said, and we laughed. "You have to get back down there. See if he wins."

"Not without you."

"I'm going to use the bathroom, sneak out, go home, and be disgustingly sorry for myself." She tugged me into her for a wet hug, whispering in my hair as I rested my chin on her shoulder, "You're so brave."

Downstairs, Paul appeared. "You *have* to see this view." He pulled me over to the windows that looked out at a sliver of what Gail's place faced. "They just called Pennsylania."

"Do you miss it?" I asked, making small talk as it queasily sunk in that, for the second time, I'd done what I'd promised Greg I would never do.

"Harrisburg? God, no." He considered for a second. "I thought there'd be more camaraderie. I thought join the government, join the campaign, share a common vision, a cause." He picked lint off his slim-cut cords. "But people suck everywhere, I guess."

A guy tried to squeeze past us to the sushi. "Hey," he said to me, smiling.

I stared at his face, the hazel eyes. "Donkey?" It came to me from Halloween.

"Guilty. Had it left over from going as Shrek with a group one year. Can I buy you a free drink?"

I looked to Paul.

"I'm good." He waved me off without a smile, but I followed my impromptu date anyway, being a bad friend because really I was anything but brave. Brave would have been having the strength to remain certain, to hold Greg's promise in my heart like a sea captain's wife. But it had been so long, I was depleted. And the despair had made me negligent.

We found a spot between the wall and a column and traded stories about college Halloweens, glancing periodically at the screens. Blitzer reported, "Our exit polling in Ohio is confirming that the Majority Leader's mishandling of the budget standoff created this thin margin for the Democrats. It's going to make a second term even more contentious than the first—if that's possible."

Possible. Inebriated, I got stuck on the word and how I couldn't access its lift anymore. I realized Donkey was leaning in to kiss me and I let him. His lips were sweet and curious. But they weren't Greg's.

The room screamed. Rooms all around us screamed. Boos echoed off the street below. Across the country, a chain of jubilation and dismay.

"And with Ohio's fifteen electoral votes going to Rutland we're ready to call it!" Rachel Maddow was elated.

Some minutes later, long enough for Partridge to concede, Donkey pulled back, his eyes warm. He slipped his hand into mine. We turned to the screens as Rutland bounded to the podium to address us.

Wearing my tie.

A jolt like wet skin in a socket.

"Victory!" he shouted, touching the blue silk.

We all know that now. How during his acceptance speech he touched the tie I gave him. How he never did that. How he had a carefully choreographed vocabulary of podium movements—and tie touching was not one of them.

"Victory!" he said again. The applause died down. He looked into the camera, staring into me, speaking slowly and deliberately. "This was a challenging campaign—and we made sacrifices. *You* made sacrifices." It was. I had. "But I promise you it was worth it. Because I stand here before you tonight pledging to serve you." I felt his roving lips devouring my thigh as he fell to his knees. "Pledging to rise to your challenges, to be worthy of the faith you have placed in me, to meet—and exceed—your expectations."

He touched it again, the tiny lightning bolts creasing beneath his fingertips.

I pulled my hand free.

Chapter Seven

November 22

It had been fifteen days since the election. Rachelle had parked herself on my couch every night, waiting vigil beside me for his summon, the job offer—the together part. The phone had not rung once, but she never wavered in her belief that I was telling the truth, and I couldn't even put my gratitude into words.

It was still early—she reassured me it was. And there were those back-to-back hurricanes on the Southern coast. But we didn't know when to decide it was late. How would I know? And what would I do?

I was lying awake, staring through the gap in the eyelet curtains at the snow-dusted branches of the elm in my parents' front yard. Which I once called the elm in my front yard, the one with the old tire swing long rotted and Erica's initials gouged in the trunk. For years, I thought F.U. was her boyfriend.

The Hello Kitty clock ticked on aggressively. 8:35 a.m. I should have been downstairs already, cutting, peeling, making jokes while Erica camped on the den couch watching the parade and griping. Hung over. Then, in the last few years, because she *wasn't* hung over. But I didn't want to go to the game. I didn't want to have dinner at three o'clock with Dad's drunk relatives, didn't want to listen to my uncles ribbing him, yet again, about his sobriety, about his wife and her education, her "shmancy desk job," our "snooty" neighborhood.

It was our little house that pissed them off. The front and back yards. That Erica and I each had a bedroom. When the fighting started I always wished we could do the meal at one of their apartments, but their wives were embarrassed, I think. My aunts always said, "Oh, no, Betsy, *you* have the space." And then Mom and I looked around at the square feet between the couch and the fireplace, the air between the hutch and the dining table, and *we* felt embarrassed. Not by what we had, but by the luxury of the emptiness around it.

My phone vibrated somewhere near my hip and I dug around in the bedspread to find it. *"Been up since 5. Family holiday=oxymoron."* Mike. Thinking of me. While I hid in the same bed in which I'd once conjured a future for us. *"PS. Coming to DC Jan 23."*

I stared at the sentence, feeling something. Like paper cuts.

"4 a conference," he added. *"Want to grab a drink? We can do that now, right?"*

I erased the questions and rolled over twice until I'd pinned myself in the blanket. In a cold flush of surprise, I realized I didn't want to see him. "Greg," I said into my pillow to drown out the unsettling feeling. Conjuring his fingertips touching the lightning bolts, I said it again and then again, focusing on the click of the second "g" at the top of my throat.

"Fuck!" I heard Dad shout from his room as he headed out. "Fuck, fuck, *fuck* it all to hell." And then the front door slammed. A minute later the Honda started, making that horrible grinding sound it always did, as he peeled out.

I waited.

"Jamie!" Mom called up the stairs brightly. "Let's get going! I've got to get the turkey in the oven!" Which was step one in a hundred of what had to happen next.

Three hours later, Mom, Erica, and I sat shivering in the bleachers of Stagg Field, a fleece blanket wrapped around the shoulders of our down coats. Mom had hustled us into the car, insisting we had to "be supportive," but now none of us were watching the game. I distracted myself by wondering who the White House entertains at Thanksgiving—heads of state, probably. I indulged in imagining myself at the other end of the table, my hair in a French twist that picked up the red of the dried maple leaves in the centerpiece—

Greg would smile at me before he said grace, before he asked God to bless us. And I know as I share this what it sounds like. It's hard to explain, but in retrospect my fantasies never existed in a world *after* Susan and the kids. Instead they ran childishly parallel, as if one reality could occur without disturbing the other. Like on *Sister Wives.*

"I'm really proud of Dad," I interrupted myself. "He obviously really doesn't want to be here, but he's getting through it." I thought I could relate.

Mom looked questioningly to Erica.

"What?" I asked.

"Nothing." Snow flurries started to kick up, the wind circulating in the stadium creating the illusion that the flakes were rising from the turf.

"Mom, what's going on?"

"She thinks he's drinking again," Erica answered, and I had a momentary sensation of the bleachers collapsing.

Mom studied my face, hers suddenly so sad and drawn, resigned, whether it was to his behavior or actually telling me I'm not sure. "He's been lying. Says he's stuck at work, but he's left. Gets home late, says he's with Joe, but Joe just called—dumb stuff, but it got me worried. I just—it's a horrible thing when you suddenly have to figure out if you can trust someone again."

The icy wind gathered speed off the lake as I flashed to the last time, how far away from each other it had felt like we all were, even under that small roof. Four people getting through the days and nights—passing bowls of peas, kitchen towels, the remote. It was too much to think about losing whatever ground of normalcy we'd gained in these intervening years. Her statement was unapproachable as a daughter—but not as a girl. Since Greg's first kiss I had been struggling with faith. Understood, I realized in that moment, with trust. I'd rewatched his acceptance speech almost a hundred times on YouTube. Were his reassurances all in my head? "I asked Erica to keep an eye on him this weekend."

On the field, the members of the Junior Athletic League sports teams were lining up to present Baker his honorary trophy that was practically as big as one of the players. As I tried to spot Dad, Erica put her arm around Mom, and I realized Mom hadn't been checking up on Erica, but consulting her, letting her inside something I hadn't even been aware of. How long had it been this way?

Each team's coach hung back as his kids marched forward in formation to pass by Baker and salute. It was a sweet tribute, nicely choreographed, nothing you would guess could literally drive a man to drink. But when it was his team's turn, Dad stayed abreast of the line, accompanying his boys right past Baker. It was a strange blunder that did not go unnoticed in the stands.

Back at the house, we didn't really talk as we waited for Dad to return. Erica moved in fits and starts. She'd set the table, then flip through a magazine or go outside for a cigarette, while Mom and I chopped and prepped to host fourteen people. Rachelle texted me from Tucson that her family had turned down the AC an extra 10 degrees so everyone could wear cashmere. I had nothing funny to reply.

The front door opened and Dad stomped in.

"Who wants coffee?" I asked, my voice going up as if I were singing a jingle.

"Hon," Mom said to calm him, her hands full of gizzards on the other side of the island. "Why don't you head upstairs and relax, lie down—we'll call you when everyone gets here. Jamie, the apples are in that bag—can you peel and core while I do the onions?"

"On it."

"Erica, you haven't said a proper hello to Dad yet—give him a hug," Mom added, brushing her bangs away with the back of her forearm. Erica had gotten in late last night after he'd already taken his Ambien.

Looking like a kid in a school play who's unsure of the directions, Erica walked over to hug him. They were both visibly stiff. Dad took in the preparations for a moment—"I don't know why we need to go to all this fuss—it's my fucking brothers, not the Queen"—before clomping upstairs.

Erica went to pull on her coat.

"Jamie," Mom continued, "after the apples, tackle the potatoes, and I'll start the pie crust as soon as I get the corn bread in the oven." I looked at the mountain of soil-crusted vegetables on the table and for the first time, I didn't understand why I was doing this by myself when I wanted out of there as much as anyone.

"Hey, Erica, grab a peeler," I said as she pulled her cigarettes from her leather bag.

"I don't want to."

"Well?" Mom asked her, glancing after Dad. "Could you smell his breath?"

"He was holding it." Erica wrapped her arms around her waist.

"I can't find my fucking cuff links!" he shouted from upstairs.

"They're on the dresser!" Mom opened the oven to baste, twisting as the heat hit her face.

"They are not on the fucking dresser!"

"Mom, you don't do him any favors," Erica said, searching her coat pockets.

"I'm giving him space." She wrestled with the enormous pan, sweating.

"Erica." I held out the peeler, all at once so angry that she wouldn't just help me.

"Betsy!" Dad called down.

"Jim, I am up to my elbows in bird carcass here! Erica—go find the cuff links."

"No, she's going to peel the potatoes."

"No, I'm not." Lighter in hand, Erica reached for the doorknob. "I set the table."

"Was that the deal you made with your sponsor?" I asked. "You'd make it through a whole weekend with your goddamn family without getting fucking loaded, but God forbid anyone asks you to do anything."

"I need some fucking air," she shot back.

"Erica, it's Thanksgiving, can we please just—" My phone interrupted Mom. I glanced over to the counter where I'd left it charging. The White House number.

"Hello?" I grabbed it, tugging the cord out.

"Hey." His voice was low and tender in that one syllable. *Oh my God*. This was it.

"Hi," my voice lifted. He'd found me.

"Are you eating?" he asked. "Is this a bad time? I shouldn't have called, but something about today made me miss you so fucking much."

I pulled open the back door and stepped two feet out into the building snow. "I miss you, too," I said because, despite the anxiety he'd put me through, I couldn't not.

"Who is it?" I heard Mom ask inside. "Who does she miss?"

I curled away over the ice-glazed trash bins.

"It's Jamie's boyfriend."

"Her *what*?" I heard the crash, the sound of the bird slipping across the floor. "Shit."

"I woke up thinking about you," he said. "I think it was a dream, actually."

"You dream about me?"

"Jamie, if you had any idea."

"Is it too much to get a little fucking help one day a year?!" Dad's voice stormed into the kitchen.

"Dad, stop fucking yelling!" Erica yelled. I stepped farther away, out of the buffer of the fence, the wind permeating my sweater.

"I've wanted to call every single minute since the election," he said fervently. "Did you notice my tie?"

I heard the back door swing open against the siding. "Jamie Stevenson McAlister, who are you talking to, the fucking President? You get your ass in here *now*."

"Wait, what did he say—"

"Happy Thanksgiving!" I chirped brightly down the line just like Mom, hanging up on Greg's question before he could hear one more second. *Fuck. Fuckfuckfuck.*

"Dad, are you drunk?" Erica asked as I scrambled inside, snow on my head and shoulders. That was it, the call. How would I—

"How dare you? This is *my* home." Dad, standing in the middle of the kitchen, slapped his chest.

"Jamie has a boyfriend?" Mom asked, maybe trying to distract us, scooping flour into a bowl.

"And he's married," Erica added.

"Erica's living with Peter," I retaliated.

Dad flash boiled. "You sicken me, *both* of you." He glared at us, spit flecking the corners of his mouth.

"*You're* sickened?" I demanded, furious at what he'd just cost me.

"*Enough.* You know what's wrong with you girls?" His eyes darkened flat. "You think the rules don't apply to you."

I don't remember the rest of the fight, some self-protective part of my brain knocked me out like a salamander, only that it escalated until I found myself, eyes sobbed swollen, on a half-empty flight back to D.C. I couldn't handle the possibility that Dad was drinking again, what it would do to Mom, our family finally splitting apart before I could build a new one for myself like Erica had done. Instead I focused with disproportionate intensity on the fact that Greg had called, had been about to offer me my job back, and that I'd have to wait until Monday to be sure Jean would be manning her desk.

"Oval Office, Jean Hargrove speaking," she answered as Rachelle rolled her wrist to prompt me, our bagels sitting between us on Gail's dining table.

"Good morning. This is Jamie McAlister. I'm returning the President's call." After much back and forth, we decided I should just say it.

"He's busy now, but I will make sure he gets the message."

And then that was played—the move we'd spent three days rehearsing. And I was back to waiting.

By hiring myself out for odd jobs on TaskRabbit and starting a dog-walking service I made almost a thousand dollars, plus what I saved because I didn't have to fly home during the most expensive week of the year. Erica refused to get on a plane until Dad admitted he was drinking again, so, confirming my fears, she ended up in St. Barts with Peter's family, where he proposed. And when I suggested spending Christmas with friends from Vassar in Virginia and waiting to come home until January when the flights were cheaper, Mom raised only the most perfunctory of objections.

The day of New Year's Eve, I'd been teetering between two sets of resolutions. In one, I went to the airport, slapped down my nearly maxed credit card, and boarded the next flight to anywhere; in the other, I dug in for the rest of Greg's administration—waving at motorcades, waiting on rope lines, reminding him of us in small ways until he was done, potentially free, and only then would I know unequivocally. I stepped off Gail's elevator, hearing music on the other side of the apartment door. He'd been full of surprises—maybe—my heart sped at the savory scents . . . and, was that jazz? Oh my God, he'd brought dinner and a tree and—

"Jamie?"

I froze in the entryway. "Gail?"

"Well, that explains the mess," she called out with a pointed pleasantness that always brought to mind a stewardess at the end of a hellacious flight. "I would've texted, but I assumed you'd be with your family through the New Year."

"Oh God, I'm so sorry." Heat rose in my frozen cheeks. "I left early this morning. I'll clean this all—" Rushing in, I lunged for a bra I'd hung to dry on the kitchen doorknob.

"Thank you." Her back to me, Gail opened the oven to three racks of foil containers.

"I had to work this week, so it didn't seem worth going all the way home just for the day."

"Yes, DOHS." She lowered her glasses to review the caterer's instructions.

"It's just an internship, actually. Still job searching—"

"You have plans tonight? Because I'd invite you, but the table only seats ten." She retied her lavender silk robe.

"Of course! No, I have a party, actually, so no worries."

Rachelle was skiing with her family in Tahoe, so we'd been planning to text at both midnights. Instead, I went to the movie with the longest running time that was reachable by Metro, part of a Terrence Malick retrospective. While Malick took me, and three other people, through every shaft of sunshine that could hit the earth against a sweeping symphonic accompaniment, I felt myself aging. I turned out the lights on the year, no clearer on which path to take, and with a gnawing feeling that I was wasting something, some part of myself that might slip away without ever being properly utilized.

"Jamie?"

"Yes?" I sat up out of a dead sleep.

"There's a call for you on my line." Standing in her nightgown, Gail pointed me to her room, where the stark winter light shone in. "Jean Hargrove."

"Oh, I'm sorry." I rushed to pick it up. She followed me. "Hello?"

"Hello, Jamie."

"Happy New Year," I said as Gail stood in the door, peering at me with her arms crossed.

"The President has requested that you come in this afternoon regarding a DOHS matter."

"Yes, of course."

"Very well then, dear, we'll see you at two p.m."

"Thank you." I hung up. "Sorry, it was my work. They prefer the security of a landline."

Gail returned to her bed, picking up her iPad.

"They must not have been able to reach me on my cell."

She plumped her pillow before nestling in.

"I, uh, have to go in."

"Jamie."

"Yes?"

"I've been delighted to have you stay here while you work." Her demeanor was disjointedly casual, given the severity of her tone.

"Thank you. I really appreciate it."

"However, I don't think it's a good idea for your work to come *here*. Do you agree?"

Mortified, and a little afraid, I emphatically nodded.

"I'll be needing your room soon."

The Currier & Ives journey to the White House did little to lull my panic about pending homelessness. I texted Rachelle, *"Lena told her a friend of a friend, but she MUST know who Jean is."*

"Evicting you has nothing to do with Greg and everything to do with your tampons on her counter. Put it out of your mind and GO ENJOY YOUR-SELF!!!! That's an order."

Determined to try, I crossed his threshold as Greg pushed back his desk chair to walk right over, beaming. *Oh,* I thought, almost letting myself slump like a marathoner being wrapped in one of those foil capes, *I've been right to believe in him, in this, in us.* "I love your no-poinsettia-left-behind policy."

He laughed.

"So, um, congratulations," I added, as Rachelle and I had planned.

"Thanks." He bowed, hands in the pockets of his khakis. "Can I take your coat?"

"Boy, they put you right to work, huh." He laughed as I unbuttoned it, my hand going to the scarf ring I was finally able to show off. (And making that work in a casual Sunday, hot reunion kind of way required a level of thinking that should have been a marketable skill.)

"Nice." He noticed.

"Sir?" Jean interrupted from the doorway. "I'm going to get some lunch. Would you like anything?"

"We're good. Thanks, Jean." He turned back to me as the door to the outer office clicked shut. "You have no idea how incredible it is to see you. I have something for you."

"You do?" My hands clasped beneath my chin.

He cocked his head, his blond bangs flopping. "Yes."

"Thank you!" I threw my arms around him. "I'm going to work really hard, I promise. It's going to be so awesome to be back—"

"Oh." He pulled away. "No, I meant a present."

"Oh."

"Come." I followed to his desk, where he tugged a folded shopping bag from his drawer and handed it to me.

"I have something for you, too," I admitted, trying to regroup. What was this? Had he not been calling on Thanksgiving about the job?

"Let's do it by the tree."

I raised my eyebrows suggestively, to his obvious delight.

"The exchange." He grinned.

"Of course," I said as he dropped to the red velvet skirt's edge.

"You first," he instructed, and I opened the bag to find a wrapped box. As I tore the paper, I saw the Lenox, Massachusetts, address printed under the shop's name. I'd read that they'd spent the holiday at a friend's estate in the Berkshires. Did he sneak away just to shop for me? I lifted the top to find a white plaster tile of a large bow. "Oh, it's beautiful . . ." I bought time.

"It's from Edith Wharton's house."

"The Mount?"

"A reproduction of one of the wall tiles. You had mentioned you were a Wharton fan—"

"No! No, I am. Thank you!"

"Someday you can put it in your home or use it as a doorstop or, I don't know. It seems silly now." He circled his arms around his raised knees.

"Well, while we're seeming silly—here." I withdrew the trove of gifts I'd been collecting since election night. A 1930s photo of the stud pup Leão, who was responsible for bringing the Portuguese water dog back from extinction. A copy of Richard Russo's *Straight Man,* a satire of institutional power struggles. A pair of cuff links in the shape of bicycle wheels that reminded me of his stories about the high school summer spent biking over the Rockies. And finally, another tie. Navy, with a tiny motif of raccoons—like Franny's fur coat.

I watched him take apart in seconds items I had made entire evenings out of wrapping, stopping only short of potato-stamping the paper. "Oh wow." It was the cuff links that seemed to most delight him. "Oh, Jamie, I love them. This. All of it."

"Really?"

His face was wistful as his thumb traced the little silver spokes. "I don't deserve you." After a moment, he slid his hand over where mine sat on the cool ridges of the plaster bow. He squeezed my fingers, then tugged me onto his lap, dropping his chin to my forehead. I pressed his arms to hold me even tighter, nestling against the softness of his sweater. "You're everything, Jamie. You know that, right?"

I inhaled, my face pushed into his chest, trying to memorize the feel of him—except that I didn't have to. "We made it," I said, lifting my face to his. I sensed the hesitancy that was the precursor to his kiss.

"You're not mad at me?" he asked, looking like a boy.

"I just missed you." Which is the answer he seemed to need to lay me down beneath the evergreen and sink his lips onto my skin. There was the familiar feel of my fingers slipping through his hair as he roved down my collarbone, working at the buttons of my blouse. He slid it open and nestled his warm cheek against my chest, pushing his hands under me to hold me tighter. Then he relaxed, resting his head, and I was struck by the weight of it. "God, Jamie. Everyone else needs so much, needs me to know—you're the only place I can—I should be able to just get you. You should be mine."

I stroked his hair off his forehead and smiled up at the elaborate molding. "I am." I reached down to his belt, pulling him up to kiss me as tenderness was replaced with frenzy.

Later, while buttoning my jeans, I tried to feel purely elated, instead of frustrated that he still wouldn't give over to me. I knew if he'd just let himself be inside me—come—that this would be over, the uncertainty, the longing; we'd be soldered together. I heard Jean clearing her throat as she returned to the outer office.

"So, my job." I combed my hair with my fingers.

"Yes." He finished tucking in his shirt.

"That's in process?"

"Yes."

"You've talked to Margaret?"

"It's being worked on. Everything is being worked on. We all just have to keep on it."

"By Margaret," I sought confirmation.

"It's an HR issue. So no, not Margaret."

"It's just that my student loans kick in this month. And I have to move out. So I need a paycheck ASAP."

"Jamie, if I could give you money I would."

"Oh, God, no," I said, mortified, "No, I don't want money. I'm not a—" I couldn't even finish the sentence. "Just a job."

He took my coat from me and draped it over my shoulders.

"Who in HR?" I asked as he kissed me.

"Jamie, there's so much I'm holding in my head—Iran and North Korea—and this damn harassment setup is dragging into a colossal waste of time—"

"No, I know! I know, that's why I was asking. Just if I knew who the person was I could, I don't know, will that to go well or something."

He sighed. "Chris."

"Chris. Great, I shall cross my fingers and toes and light my candles for Chris."

He winked.

"I can't wait to be back."

"It's amazing to see you."

"Hi, Chris?" I waited until after nine on the Wednesday following the inauguration. I had made it through a blitzkrieg of First Family pictures and Rutlandmania and now, huddled near the guard booth, I switched my umbrella to my other shoulder, my first loan bill dampening in my coat pocket.

"Yup."

"Hi, this is Jamie McAlister." I knew I shouldn't do it. But I literally couldn't afford to passively "keep on it."

"Hi."

"Hi, I know you're working on this, but I was wondering if maybe we could talk for a few minutes."

"Um—"

"I'm in the neighborhood now, actually. I thought it might be helpful if we touched base in person. I just want to be sure I'm doing all I can on my end to move this along."

"Move what along?"

"Sorry, is this Chris Doyle?"

"Yes."

"So you weren't, um, informed about my transfer?"

"I was not."

"Is there another Chris in Human Resources?"

"There's Christine Hooper . . ."

"Right! Hooper! Right. Could you, uh, transfer me to her? Thank you so much. So sorry."

The slush puddle rhythmically splashed the curb as cars passed.

"Christine Hooper."

"Christine! Hi, this is Jamie McAlister. I'm so sorry to bother you. I know you're doing everything you can—please know that I know that. But if you could just give me an overview of the situation I would so appreciate it."

"Is this for a medical or dental claim?"

"This is for my job. Didn't . . . he talk to you about me?"

"We don't speak directly with practitioners. If this is job-related, you need to speak to Maureen regarding disability. I don't cover that."

The wet flakes became harder. "This is Jamie McAlister. In the Department of Homeland Security. Nobody talked to you about my transfer?"

"You would need to talk to the DOHS about your benefits—"

"Are there any other people with the name Chris in HR?"

"Yes."

"Thank God."

"Chris Doyle."

Water seeping through my tights, I walked to my desk and sat in my sodden coat, my papers weighted under that porcelain bow.

I didn't know what to do next.

I dialed Rachelle, but the call went straight to voicemail.

Then Paul was over me, offering me the rest of his muffin. I stood up, steering him by the elbow right into the stairwell. "Jamie—"

"What do you know about Brianne?" I asked as the door clicked shut behind us.

"Brianne?" He coughed, spitting crumbs.

"*Was* he the reason she lost her job?"

"You're shaking. What happened to you?"

"Tell me." I stared him down.

"I can't. Jesus, Jamie."

"Tell me—I need to know. I need to."

"Why?"

"Paul, *tell me.*"

"Get back to work." He went to leave and I grabbed him.

"I *need* to know, Paul. I *need* to." I could feel my lips quivering, my cheeks wetting; I'm sure I seemed hysterical. "Please. *Please* help me."

He stared at me. A raisin fell on the floor.

Then his blinking eyes widened. He took an audible breath. "You . . . and *Rutland.*"

"Please."

His lids held open like an awning wound too far back. "It was late," he said without inflection. "I brought him something to sign about apples. A pesticide thing. Something from the EPA. She came in, passed something off; as she was leaving he said he wanted to bite that apple."

It was so gross, so tacky, stupid, like something one of my uncles would say, thinking it was suave. I couldn't imagine him saying it. And yet it was costing Paul so much, there was no reason to doubt him.

"I'm a tiny part of the case. There are hundreds of people on the witness list—"

"Promise you won't tell anyone," I begged him. "Nobody. Please."

He nodded.

=

I went back out in the downpour, forgetting my umbrella.

"Hello, dear," Jean answered.

"Is he there?"

"He's with someone just now."

"I need to see him." The rain cut against the back of my head.

"I'll try to schedule a call."

"No, not a call. A meeting. I can come in whenever."

There was the tiniest pause.

"I spoke to HR. Do you know if he spoke to someone about bringing me back? Because I called them and I don't think he did."

"I'm sure he'd like to talk to you directly. I'll have him call you, I promise," she added.

"Thank you." My phone hadn't even made it into my pocket before it rang.

"Jamie, the President would like you to come in right now."

I arrived soaked, my hair dripping down my coat. Jean stood, already in her trench, a look of alarm breaking through her disciplined face. He came to his door and they exchanged a nod.

"I'll be back in a few minutes," she told us, not bothering to invoke a coffee run as she departed.

He glowered. "Come in." I walked past him into the office, his curtains drawn against the storm. "I'm fucking busy, Jamie."

"I know that."

"If you're looking for attention, and I'm starting to wonder if you are, then stick with the boys on K Street. I don't have time for this bullshit. You're checking up on me? That is *exactly* why I didn't give you the real name of the person." He circled behind his desk.

"So there's a real person?" Drops fell to the carpet around me as if I were dissolving.

"How can I trust you?"

"Me?" A spring tightened in my chest.

"You're cold-calling people? Putting me in jeopardy? Did you tell your *father?*"

It sprang like shrapnel. "That was a joke," I rushed, "just his sense of humor—he's been saying that since I was—"

"The answer's obvious that I can't. I can't trust you, which is just, *uch*." He sat heavily in his chair and dropped his head into his hands, deflating. "I can't."

"Greg," I said, but he shifted his gaze to the wall, to some oil portrait of a mutton-chopped predecessor. He was pulling away from me; I could feel him making the decision right under my gaze and it was untenable.

I walked around the desk, right up to his bent head. I wanted him to seize me as he always had, but he didn't move. I didn't feel any sense of his will. I slipped my leg between his . . . he let me. I lowered to my knees. Still no response. I ran my forearm along his thigh, his legs opening as I brought my lips to his ear. "You can," I murmured as I arrived at the growing stiffness straining the wool of his trousers. My fingers deftly worked his belt. I watched myself do this, removed, wondering what I would do next. His eyes met mine. "You can," I said again. "Put your trust." I held his pained gaze. "In me." I lowered my head and his fingers wove into my hair.

Minutes later I sat in his lap, coat still on, my legs wrapped around him in the shadows. He brought his palms to my cheeks and kissed me deeply.

"Get this mystery person to hurry up," I said into his mouth as the patter of sleet softened. "I mean, solve world peace, and then, please bring me back."

"Thanks for setting me straight."

"Is that what I did?"

He laughed. And then pretended to faint back on his chair. His face clouded and he opened his eyes. "Someone's going to snatch you up."

"I'm snatched." I nuzzled him.

"Seriously, you're going to meet some virile kid without my baggage and you'll forget you even knew me."

"I prefer brooding intellects."

"Not football players?"

"No! My first boyfriend was a librarian."

"A librarian?"

"I mean, he wasn't, like, a dork. He revitalized one in the Lower Ninth Ward after the hurricane wiped it out. Then he took over in Naperville and started this literacy—"

"How old were you?"

"I don't know, it was, like, sixth grade."

"You were twelve."

I pushed back from his chest. "Well, at first. I mean, it wasn't— Mike was funny and sweet and it wasn't like—" But he was looking at me strangely. "I should probably place my soda order before Jean gets back." I climbed to my feet, wanting for the first time to get away from him.

He nodded, standing to buckle his belt, lost in thought.

"So, we're good, and you'll call me and I'll be back here soon," I said as if I were reviewing a grocery list with my grandma.

He gazed at me with unprecedented care.

"Jamie."

"Yes?"

"I'm sorry."

I nodded, trying to shrug. "Just get me a job, already." I found a smile and at some point realized I'd left.

Chapter Eight

January 23

It's such a flaw in our design that at the moment one's thinking is at its most scrambled and murky, emotions are staggeringly clear. Walking home from Greg's office that night, it was like my thoughts were boxing on steroids. I had to DO something, FIX something, STOP something from getting worse. A car honked and I froze in its headlights. Racing out of oncoming traffic, I silently screamed at myself that Greg trusted me—trusted me so much that he'd finally *let himself go.* WE WERE OKAY. We were okay! *I* was okay! He was finding me a job. *I'm okay I'm okay I'm okay . . .*

But my gut could give a fuck. I arrived at the dark apartment, too nauseous to even smoke, or call Rachelle. Falling back on a coping strategy from when my parents would be out searching parking lots for Erica, I paced the apartment's periphery. When that wasn't cutting it, I pulled off my socks and stepped out onto the snow-covered balcony, letting my feet burn into numbness. Ideas fragmented before I could follow them to conclusion, my insides shattering in concert.

I have no idea what time it was when I finally remembered Mike was here, in D.C., all of a cab ride away. Even though I had never responded to his overture, I picked up my phone.

"I need to see you." Seeing the text send made my chest loosen perceptibly. I stood in the dark hallway, sensation pricking back into my red feet.

A few seconds later the phone glowed with his response. *"Where are you?"*

"The Washingtonian off Virginia."

"Meet you in the morning. 7:30."

As if the key in my back had finally unwound, I crumpled atop my bed into a black sleep.

In the morning, I hurried to get my dog-walking done before Mike arrived. It was a blustery day, snowflakes blowing laterally in a way that reminded me of soup commercials. On the patch of shoveled grass across the street, there was a shivering man from the Nairobi Embassy in a quilted barn jacket that couldn't have been doing anything to insulate him. He inquired about my service as his Rhodesian ridgeback tried to play with—or devour, or play with, *then* devour—my charges.

Trying to imagine what it was going to be like to see Mike after so many years—he moved away when I was fourteen—I gave the diplomat the slip of paper serving as my business card (courtesy of the DOHS copy machine) that I'd been pushing on anyone with a stroller or leash.

Seeing a cab pull into Gail's circular drive, I quickly corralled the dogs, their noses magnetically pulled to every cryogenic yellow mark. What was I going to say? They tugged me into a gallop across the street. The cab pulled out and I saw a woman turn from the doorman.

"Jamie," Patty Harnet breathed, her voice thick with surprise.

I was so thrown by the sight of her, standing there on her own, that I irrationally thought he'd brought her with him. I knew Mike's wife from fundraisers at the library—car washes she helped organize, bake sales she'd helped man.

"Hi!" I became warm enough for palm trees to have cartoonishly sprouted between us. "Hi!"

"Is this who you were looking for?" the doorman asked her, pointing at me.

"Yes," I jumped in. "This is—we're great. Thank you." I nodded that he could return inside. "I didn't know you were in D.C.!" My pitch flew to a retrograde octave.

"For a conference," she managed. "For my job. So, yes."

"Oh, well, hi!" What was going on? How had this happened? Did she see my text? Did Mike tell her? "Are the kids here?" She'd been pregnant with their second when they left.

"No, four is a lot to transport—"

"Four. Wow."

"Well, I wanted three and then—twins—and, so, no, we didn't bring them—they're—no."

She shook her head, the flakes turning translucent as they melted on her short hair. When I knew them, it was long—almost waist-length. But she was still as pretty as she always was, as serious as she always was. "I want to take you for breakfast."

"Oh! That's so nice." I was frightened. "Sorry, these dogs are— ugh." Their leashes wrapped around us.

"Can I take you for a quick coffee?" she repeated, gripping the shoulder strap of her purse, her slim leather boots soaking in salt as I untangled us.

"Of course! I just have to drop them off. Come on in, and—"

Her face tightened. "Can't you just tie them up here? The heat lamps are on." She pointed to the awning.

"I guess if we're fast. There's a Starbucks around the corner."

"Fine."

We walked briskly, the blue crystals crunching beneath our feet. I held the door open. "I'll order for you," she said like a mother would.

"Um, just a coffee is great. Tall or whatever. Thank you."

She got on line. I found a table in the dark purple nook near the bathroom. With my hands clenched in my lap, it occurred to me that I was moments away from this finally being over—detonated— a white flash—everyone radiated into a cloud. I was stunned to realize I welcomed it.

She made her way back and set down a cup, taking the seat across from me, her coat left buttoned. "I'm glad we got a table—this place is always so packed," I prattled as I took off my parka, because that's what you do when someone is taking you to breakfast. She slid my coffee over. "Didn't you want anything?"

The corners of her eyes watered for a second at my question. Then her thoughts seemed to speed. "No, they have food at the conference. Tons, practically a cruise ship." She undid one button, a necklace with four initial charms there just below her pale clavicle. "All tastes the same. No small feat getting a roast salmon to taste like a fruit cup."

"That's too bad." I gripped the hot mug.

"No, I'll take anybody else doing the cooking. People always say I'm so lucky Mike works those library hours—must be such a help. But—" She caught herself, then squeaked out the rest of the sentence anyway. "He can't *do* anything." Her purse was still in her lap.

"So how are the kids?" I shifted to something she might want to talk about. "Do you have pictures?"

She rummaged for them and I took a sip of my coffee, sloshing it down in a scalding wave. "We just moved again this summer, which you probably know—"

"I didn't." I did. But I was reluctant to further cement the wrong impression. Because of my text she was assuming Mike and I were still in touch, assuming an intimacy that no longer existed. It was the opposite of how it had been years before, when she would make passing comments about him that seemed like she never got it—Mike—right. I knew that he hated pumpkin-flavored anything. That he didn't want to sell his guitar collection. That the smell of lavender made him sad. "From Missoula?"

"No," she said, nostrils flaring. "We went on to Akron from there. Anyway, Girl Scouts is the big thing at Julia's new school. There's no talking her out of it." She tapped her phone. "I don't know where we'll find the bandwidth. I keep trying to sell her on just getting a cool green dress. I told her she can pick out any one she wants and we can come up with badges for tasks that don't require driving for a half hour for a half-hour meeting." She handed it to me, and I saw that her hands were shaking.

"Maybe she can carpool with a friend?" I numbly swiped through shots of kids I had never met. *Just do it*, I willed her. *Just say it.*

"We may be moving again." She took her phone back. "Things at this library aren't really jelling."

"Patty, I'm—I want to tell you that—"

"One of the student aides—her parents have been making a stink." She talked over me, her gaze set on the center of the table.

"The mother doesn't work. She has *waaay* too much time on her hands and she's claiming—well. It's puppy love, right?—at that age. When I heard Mike get a text in the middle of the night, I thought she'd somehow followed us to D.C. Of course I erased it. I came here this morning to tell her to *get a grip*," she said severely. "But it was you."

I nodded, breath suspended.

"I can't ask to be relocated again." She raised her eyes to me. "But you could tell them."

"Them?" I asked.

"Her parents. The library. Girls fall in love with him all the time," she said, trying to laugh. "But obviously it's a one-way thing."

I stared at the top of her head, feeling as if I were watching this through a paper-towel tube. "I haven't seen Mike in seven years."

"You texted him at three in the morning."

It hung there between us.

"So you could still speak to it," she said evenly. "We can't move again. It's too hard on the family, on us."

It was a phrase Mike had invoked frequently for himself—how hard being married was on him, how trapped he felt. By being sympathetic to this burden he had to survive, I maintained his attention, which felt so deliriously fulfilling, given that my parents had none to spare. After years of being outside the whispered exchanges between Mom and Dad, between Mom and Erica, I was finally inside something. I had a secret of my own. But as I looked at Patty and absorbed her request, something came clear for the first time: by keeping me focused on being the other woman, he prevented me from thinking too hard about the fact that I wasn't a woman at all.

And some part of me, I realized, was stuck there.

"I should get the dogs inside."

In response to my unspoken refusal, she pushed her chair back angrily. "And I should get back to the hotel. I'm already missing the first session." We stared at each other. Years ago, Mike told me he was leaving for Missoula on a Tuesday afternoon. In the back of the science stacks, by the drinking fountain that never stopped running. There was no rebuttal; I did have my whole life ahead of me. And I had to agree that if I loved him, I'd want him to be happy and work where he was respected.

"You look different," she said, staring down at me.

"Older," I smiled faintly.

"No, just different," Patty said, and I realized it was meant to hurt. She turned, and quickly the clamor of those waiting to order obscured my view.

Minutes later, I was fumbling for my phone as I untied the leashes. "Jean?"

"Jamie?"

"I need to talk to the President." I wiped my nose with my sleeve. Patty had stripped me of something—the delusion of being special. Without it my mind suddenly seized on Brianne Rice. The fact of her and all that it implied. I had to hear it from him.

"I was going to call you, actually."

"Good. I can come in—" I tugged the dogs back from an abandoned bagel. "I can be there in twenty minutes."

"I don't think that will be possible. The President asked that I let you know—"

"Sorry?" I switched the phone to my other ear.

"—that he doesn't think it prudent to proceed with the study at this time."

"The study?" I gripped the phone, as the wind whipped so aggressively it sounded like a jet engine between us.

"The President will not be proceeding," she spoke very carefully. "And thinks it best that you put your attention elsewhere moving forward. There isn't a place for your study currently—or in the future." A woman tried to pass with two Boston terriers. The dogs yanked me. We were knotted, twisting around each other. I wanted to clamp my hands over Jean's lips. "Unfortunately," she added gently and with finality. Was he standing there? Was he on the line?

A snowblower barreled by, its metal blade scraping the pavement. *I can't—this can't be* . . . "Is he breaking—"

"I'm going to have to go now."

Half my brain was racing to say the perfect final thing and the other half just wanted to fight for this. "But—"

"Take care."

I saw the look on Greg's face as he said he was sorry. Sorry for me.

Freshman year, our dorm screened an animal rights documentary about puppy mills. There was this scene in the snow where a worker tossed a cowering cocker spaniel into a vat of flea dip that's supposed to be administered by the drop. When he hoisted it out by its scruff, the creature had gone rigid from the shock.

I was back by the library water fountain.

Rigid from the shock.

I don't know how long I sat on Gail's balcony, staring at my reflection in the glass doors. The late-morning sun was bouncing blindingly off the snow, making the living room inside appear black. The wind whipped my hair. The drift on the table peaked at the end, sparkling. My eyes stung, my skin tightened, everything constricted and shrank, deeper and closer, until all at once I was pierced. I pulled the door open and stood inside, the heat hurting just as much. There was nowhere to be. I became aware that the doorman was buzzing up, maybe had been for a while. I pressed the button with my knuckle.

"Ms. McAlister?"

"Yes?" But nothing came out. I cleared my throat, wet my mouth. "Yes?"

"There's a Paul Hoff here to see you."

"Paul?"

"Just a moment, Miss."

"Jamie? Are you okay? I've been calling—"

"He . . . dumped me." I would have said it to the doorman. I leaned against the wall, the flocked paper pushing into my cheek.

"Jesus."

I nodded.

"I'm coming up. Tell them to let me up."

"Miss McAlister?"

"Yes, please let him up." I unlocked the door.

A few moments later the elevator opened and I stepped into his arms, falling against his chest. "All right," I heard him murmur. "You'll be okay." He gripped my shoulders and bent to peer at me. "When did this happen?"

"This morning. I didn't want to—" The thought plunged my face downward with tears.

"What?"

"Start this part." I inhaled raggedly. "The after part."

Paul got me out of my wet clothes, drew a bath, and sat outside the door as I curled up in the steaming water, in no state to question his care. He talked to fill the agonized quiet, sharing a story about a high school summer working the straightest job he could think of—dairy hand. The milk-sodden, muck-covered disaster that ensued. No one had ever done this kindness for me: when Mike left the U-Haul pulled out of their driveway, and I just folded the feeling down like a used napkin until it was small enough to carry.

When I finally cracked the door wearing Gail's zip-up robe, I found Paul sitting on the floor in the hall, nursing one of her crystal highball glasses, the Hermès box I'd needed to show him still in his hand. "Had to break into the Glenlivet, forgive me." He clinked the remaining cubes. "You need a silk turban for that outfit, Zsa Zsa."

I smiled, lifting the heavy hem to join him.

He paused me. "I know you're on death's door, but let's do this on a couch. My ass isn't as young as yours."

"Sorry, yes. Of course." I reached down and tugged him up as the doorbell rung.

"I called Ronald." Handing me the box, he walked to the entry-way. "I thought maybe that would help."

"Thank you," I murmured, making myself put it down.

"Oh my God." Rachelle marched in, unlooping her long scarf. "Jamie." Seating me on the couch, she took my hands in hers. "What happened?"

"Jean did it for him."

"He had his *sixty-five-year-old secretary* do it for him?!" Her outrage was so gratifying. "That's the worst thing I've ever heard. What did you say?"

"Nothing. I mean, what *could* I say?"

Paul spoke softly to the carpet. "You have a small penis, I never really loved you, you're doing me a favor, you fart in your sleep . . ." He helped himself to a refill. "To your dignity." He lifted his glass for a toast before taking a swig.

"He's forcing himself to do this, you know that," she said. I did, but not for the reasons Rachelle assumed. "He's totally going to regret it," she declared with absolute certainty, unpeeling her coat.

"Really?"

"Yes! You handled it perfectly. Perfectly."

"You left him something to miss." Paul sat heavily in the club chair opposite us.

"It just pisses me off so much!" Rachelle fumed, pounding her fist into the cushion. "Rutland got what he wanted and here you are, gut-wrenched. It makes me literally ill."

"Men suck." Extending his legs, Paul rested the glass on his chest.

"But why now? Why all of a sudden?" She turned to me.

I couldn't tell them what I feared, that finding out about Mike had revealed me to be too broken to be loveable, which was the first time I ever admitted to myself that might be what Mike had done—broken me. My brain slammed shut against the revelation like a cellar door facing a cyclone. I took a girding breath. "Paul, what did happen with Brianne?"

Paul's eyes swerved to Rachelle.

"She's not going to tell. Am I just another—am I that stupid?"

"You're not stupid. And you're not just another. Not that I know of. Not for years as far as I've heard." I was simultaneously heartened and heartsick. I squeezed my fingers over my eyes as the tears returned.

"Fuck this." Rachelle shook her head. "He owes you."

"What?" Distracted by the pain slashing my chest, I couldn't follow her logic.

"A job," she stated.

"At the least," Paul agreed. "If not for him you would've had a paying position at the White House, instead of playing Dungeons and Dragons over at the Department of Bullshit Hysteria—"

"I don't care about that. I just need to crash for awhile and—"

"No!" Rachelle pounded the couch cushion. "Nonono. We're writing a letter."

"A letter?" I asked.

"Telling him he owes you. Remind him so he can't ignore it."

"Yes!" Paul slammed his empty glass on the coffee table. "Stand up for yourself. Somebody should fucking stand up for themselves in this cesspool of a town where everyone just gets to do whatever the fuck they want—fuck the moral consequences, fuck decency."

Rachelle touched his hand. "Okay, first we'll write Greg, then we write Tom."

I threw on some clothes and then stared at my laptop while they stared at me. "This is pathetic. If Greg wanted to help me, he would. What he wants is for me to go away. I have to face that."

"You talk, I type." Rachelle bumped me over and pulled the computer onto her lap. " 'Dear Smoothie King.' "

"Just 'Greg.' "

"Dear Mr. President," Paul dictated from the bar. "I'm writing to you because you said I should reach out to you if I ever needed anything—"

"He didn't say that."

Rachelle folded a Twizzler in her mouth. "Could he think he said that? Is it close enough?"

"I guess so, maybe."

"While I respect your decision," Paul continued as she typed, "our situation notwithstanding, I am now stranded as a DOHS intern, far from my career path. Working at the White House was supposed to be a stepping-stone to a larger professional stage."

"Furthermore," Rachelle picked up, "I had been accepted into a position on my own merit and then was summarily transferred. We both know why that happened. I am relying on your sense of honor to rectify this wrong."

"A little strident, isn't it?" I asked.

"You think Chancellor Merkel calls him and pussyfoots around?"

"Or his *wife?*" Rachelle went there.

I winced. "So much happened today. I just need to—"

"You'll psych yourself out," Paul said firmly.

"I'm hitting 'Print,' " Rachelle informed us. "And then we're gonna messenger that shit."

"Like I have a messenger."

"We can use my work account—it's the least they can do." She called it in while I made a pot of coffee for Paul.

"I'm going outside for a cigarette." My parka was still sopping, so I grabbed my wool coat from the closet.

"You've got a little . . ." Paul gestured at his own chest.

I looked down at the smattering of white flecks.

"What?" Rachelle asked me. "You just went other-side-of-the-aisle red."

"It's—it's." I couldn't say.

"Shit!" Rachelle lunged, her face practically planting against my boob. "Holy fuck, it is!" She pulled back. "What, did you not even have time to disrobe?"

"It wasn't like that." It was. "Let me get a damp paper towel."

"Are you kidding? You should frame it," Rachelle quipped. "Or make a throw pillow. They do that on Etsy—"

"Give it to me." Paul stepped in front of her.

"Give it to you?" Rachelle repeated.

"It should be destroyed." He swerved for a second, extending a steadying hand to the wall.

"She doesn't need to give it to you," Rachelle said, her protective edge surprising us. She hung the coat back in the closet.

Paul took us both in. "Yes, right. Well, I think I should get home. Shall I take the envelope down?"

"We've got it," Rachelle said. "Thanks."

"Paul, thank you." I turned to him.

"It's nothing."

"No, really, thank you," I threw my arms around him. "No one's ever done for me what you did today. I just—really appreciate it."

He looked awkward, embarrassed and, for a moment, deflated. "Appreciation," he snorted to himself as he pulled on his duffel. "A rare and wondrous thing."

Not three hours later my phone rang. It was the secretary to Lewis Franklin, entrepreneur, CEO, who sat on the board of the Shoah Foundation and multiple others, was a major Super PAC funder for Greg in both elections, and who personally wanted to meet me in his midtown Manhattan office the next morning.

Rachelle lent me her MK bag, I steamed my good suit in the shower and boarded a predawn Amtrak.

The skyscraper had been designed to be the corporate equivalent of the White House, humbling all who entered. Passing through the cavernous lobby, riding in his private elevator, and crossing an office bigger than Gail's apartment to lay my paltry résumé on his desk left me feeling like some circa-1900s urchin by the time I shook Mr. Franklin's hand.

He was distinguished the way Greg was, but where Greg's eyes were warm, his were wary. "Please, have a seat." I didn't know what he knew.

"Thank you so much for meeting me."

"Greg tells me you're looking for a job." He slipped on his wire-rims to peruse my résumé, the snow-bleached skyline stretching behind him.

"Yes."

"You apparently made quite an impression during the furlough." He said it straight.

"Well," I answered quickly, "we all worked very hard."

"And now he's recommending you for a job in our New York office."

I swallowed. Of course New York. Greg would not be summoning me next Sunday. "Yes, that would be amazing. I'm not looking for special favors." His eyebrow shot up. "I mean, this is a recommendation, a commendation. But I don't expect anything. I'm just hoping for an opportunity where I can prove myself. I'm a hard worker. There were eighty interns and only two were offered permanent positions." Again the eyebrow. "That had nothing to do with Gr—with the President."

He continued to read while I stared out the fiftieth-story window at the vertiginous drop. He seemed to hold the page for longer than it should have taken. "It was helpful to meet you in person." He stood. "I will pass this along."

"Thank you. I can't tell you how much I appreciate it."

He walked me the yards to his tiger-maple door in silence. I had zero sense of where I stood.

"And I'm just glad we can all be adults about this," I preemptively tossed out—and instantly regretted it. If our indiscretion was going to come up, I'd wanted to control it.

He paused, his hand not yet on the knob. "Yes," he said to the carpet that looked like the hair of an Irish setter. Then he opened the door and let me pass through.

People on the sidewalk moved briskly through their lunch hours, collars held secure with gloved hands against the bracing cold. Fearful that I'd flubbed this, demeaned myself in Lewis's eyes, and confirmed to Greg that I couldn't be trusted, I scurried down Madison, hunting for the perfect gesture to cement my appreciation. Not just for the job, but for the relationship, to let Greg know I would always be in his corner. Where I would shut the fuck up. I stopped in Brooks Brothers, but I didn't know his shirt size, and he didn't need a key chain since he didn't carry keys, nor would he probably ever again, and nothing else I looked at felt quite personal enough. I walked blocks out of my way, through heavy revolving doors, looping through the heat and then back out into the freeze. Cold, hot. Cold, hot. I was almost late for the train, my toes blistering in my boots, when I spotted the antique shaving kit.

I held it in my lap on the ride back, surrounded by businessmen and women typing on their laptops. I kept picturing the open view from Lewis's office as the gray landscape chugged by. I'd get a room in some share with people who watched *Mad Men*. I'd ride the subway. Go to things—openings—walk the High Line. Let myself be kissed and kiss back. With a dry prickle of hurt in my throat, I vowed to be fully and completely there without waiting for his call.

I texted Gail: *"Good news: job and departure imminent. Thank you again."*

To my surprise, she texted back immediately: *"No, please stay. There's no need to rush."* Had Lena made her change her mind?

When we arrived at Union Station I stepped onto the platform, into the crush of dress coats jockeying to dinners and receptions. I realized that I recognized the guy stepping off a few cars ahead of me. "Paul!" I called as the train on the opposite side of the platform started to pull out, its engine hissing. "Paul!" I tried again, but he couldn't hear me. Inside the shuffle slowed to a standstill and I saw that people were clustered under the televisions.

". . . no date set as of yet, but sources say the prosecutor will be moving swiftly, with depositions expected to begin almost immediately." Wolf Blitzer held everyone's attention. "We'll be talking in just a moment to our correspondent, who's standing by on the steps of the Supreme Court. Again the ruling has come down. President Rutland *will* now stand trial for the civil suit brought by Brianne Rice. The first time in history that a sitting President has been tried for an action allegedly committed before taking oath. Let's go to Jeremy."

People in the murmuring crowd whipped out their phones. Stunned, I craned to look for Paul—but he was gone.

Chapter Nine

January 28

I spent the weekend alone, filling Rachelle's voicemail while she was stuck at home with food poisoning. Between the pending trial, what the anxiety must have been doing to Greg, my gaffe with Lewis, and the fact that there was nothing I could do about any of it, I was nearly as sick.

Brianne's legal team blanketed the news, as if their mandate was to say "Here is a President who has *lied* to the American people" as many times as possible. In retrospect it must have reminded Greg, Amar, and Lewis what I could have been capable of doing, had I been like Brianne. But I wasn't—and Greg had to know that.

I wanted him to help me with a job because he loved me and wished me to succeed. Not because he was nervous.

At three a.m. all I could see was the ceiling of the Oval Office as I lay nestled beside Greg by the Christmas tree. All I could feel were his fingers stroking my bare back. How his chest vibrated under me as he spoke of needing to take me to Europe, to be with me the first time I saw Venice, to introduce me to a little restaurant behind the Guggenheim that he loved. He kissed the top of my head as I told him I could imagine finally holing up with him in some hotel, getting to be completely naked on an actual bed. He squeezed me so tight I had to breathe in sips. As if he were afraid none of that would ever happen.

Monday morning Paul hesitated for a second when he saw me waiting at his desk. I'd been worried about him as well, knowing that this thing he'd been dreading was actually in process. And he looked worthy of my concern: his shirt collar was only half-tucked under his coat, and the gray tweed matched his pallor. He ducked his head under the strap of his bag before dropping it on the floor. "Did you get my voicemails? Are you okay?" I asked. He looked at me blankly. "About the trial?"

"Oh—that. Yes, well, it'll still be months before they even get around to subpoenaing me. I just have some stuff going on—family stuff," he hastened to add, and I realized that was the exact excuse I'd given him on my first day.

"I'm so sorry."

"I'll manage."

"If there's anything I can do."

"I'm good, thanks."

"Okay. Well . . . I didn't want to bother you, but I might have a job."

He cocked his head, surprised.

"I had an interview with Lewis Franklin on Friday." I lifted my eyebrows to underscore the enormity and waited for his response as he pulled off his coat.

"Lewis Franklin," he confirmed.

I nodded, biting the side of my mouth. "The letter worked."

"So the man's best friend just called and made you his VP?"

"His office called and I went to Manhattan for an interview. I saw you, actually, on the train back—"

"So it's an interview, not a job," he cut me off.

"Right, but I'm praying nonstop." I raised crossed fingers at the fluorescents, anxious bees breaking loose from the hive below my ribs.

Paul shook his head. "He could have pulled a favor *anywhere*."

"I know. It's big. But I'll work my ass off—"

"I have a relationship, an honest-to-God *relationship*, with a joint lease and everything, and I'm fucking shunned like my nose fell off, but you blow a guy and step in shit." Blood rushed to my face.

"I thought you wanted me to stand up for myself."

"I said a lot of things. Half a bottle of Glenlivet will do that." He picked up his satchel and withdrew a new bottle. "Here. For your landlord."

"Did you have a good trip at least?" I tried with a smile as I took it.

"What?"

"Were you in New York, too?"

"Just a meeting. Did you get the spreadsheet finished?"

"Almost—"

"I can't go into the meeting without reviewing it."

"I just need another—"

"In my hands by two o'clock. Can we please just concentrate on that?"

"Yes—"

"Great," he said to his desk, and then, dismissal issued, picked up his phone.

"That's so assaholic—it's not your fault he got dumped," Rachelle said as she sat across from me that night in her tiny kitchen, dinner still untouched between us on the plastic patio table. "And why are we even spending time on Paul when you're so out of there. Lewis. Franklin." Her short bronze nails lifted to cup her cheeks. "I'm *so* jealous. That place is iconic. They did a challenge on *Celebrity Apprentice* there and it was *so* beneath him. You could tell his publicist had to *beg* him to do it. Did he say which company, which division? Are you going into marketing now?"

"Over full-time dog-walking, um, yes. Wouldn't you?"

Her hands flung over her heart. "*I* would never have left his office. *I* would have been, like, 'I'll just curl up around this potted fern and occasionally spit into it to earn my keep, thank you.'"

"It was hard to leave," I admitted. "Especially without any more information than when I got there." I glanced at the photo on her refrigerator of the two of us pretending to hold up the Washington Monument, the tourist bit she insisted we indulge in because it would "make us really happy when we're really old." "I don't want to leave here. I mean, *here* I could live without, but not you. And honestly, Paul has left me feeling a little, I don't know, uncomfortable with the whole thing."

"Jamie." Rachelle gripped my forearms. "They want me to assist filming some power plant in Niagara Falls. Buffalo. In *April*. With *Geoffrey*. I'm going to cease to exist altogether and become some bodiless hand carrying his half-eaten fruit around the tundra."

"I'm sorry—"

"No. Don't say that. That's the whole point! Jamie, everyone our age is slogging up a steep incline of shit, which seriously seems like it might just go on for, like, ever. Shit economy. Shit employment numbers. Shit opportunity. Yet miraculously—"

I opened my mouth but she pointedly continued.

"*Miraculously*, in the middle of all that a hand reached down to pull one of us out and it's you. It's you, Jamie. A once-in-a-lifetime opportunity. And if you don't fucking make the most of it, then I will seriously never forgive you." Her brown eyes bored into mine. "Okay? *Okay?*"

"Yes," I said softly, and she released me. She was right. Paul was bitter and it was coloring everything he said. Why would I let him take this away from me—from us? "As long as you promise to come join me soon, because I looked at Craigslist for five minutes today and it scared me. What does 'European-friendly' mean?"

She exhaled and reached for her Diet Coke. "That you're cool with people walking around naked. P.S.: You are not. My brother squinted at that detail in Tucson and the guy walked right on into the shower with him. Plus, you need a studio for when *he* calls you."

"That is *not* going to happen," I said, trying to get used to what letting go would sound like.

"Jamie, he's setting you up to be his girlfriend, I just really think so. I mean, it's his best friend getting you a job. He wants you to be taken care of and within reach until he finishes out his term."

"Really?" I curled around her vision like she would around Lewis's plant. "Paul made it sound so pathetic."

"Jamie," she said sternly.

"Sorry, fuck Paul."

She shook her head. "You need to nix talking to him, like, full stop. You can't afford for his toxic shit to mess with you right now."

"I can't stop talking to him, Rachelle. He's my boss."

Her lips twisted to the side as she weighed this fact. "Fine," she conceded. "But you have to remember that he's just totally jealous."

Paul didn't come in to work the next morning. It was just as well, as I suddenly had three back-to-back Skype interviews that necessitated my squatting in the stairwell, while selling myself at a hundred miles per second to a tiny black circle in the frame of my laptop. Nobody referenced how Lewis Franklin came to recommend me, and I was excited to hear that the position was on the community development team. It wasn't urban planning, but it was urban outreach, and I tried not to let myself be sidetracked by the realization that Greg had been listening all that time.

And then, two days later, when Jean summoned me with her usual pleasant obtuseness, I knew it. I didn't get the job, and he was having the decency to tell me in person. But the prospect of getting rejected by Greg on yet another front was too much. I seriously played through not going.

But then I went. Of course I went.

I know jumping every time he called makes me seem like, at best, a lapdog, and at worst, a call girl, but given the nature of our placement in the world it could never have been the other way around, so I didn't dwell there. It was like when people in Freshman English got worked up about Shakespeare using male actors to play female parts. That was British law—so it was impossible to claim it reflected anything about his lack of feminist principles. Similarly, I reasoned, our circumstances didn't reflect how Greg felt about me. He couldn't show up at my apartment. Or send flowers. It was risky to have even bought me those gifts. He could only call. And if I went, there was always that chance—maybe this would be the time I stumbled upon the phrase or action that unlocked our future together. How could I live with forgoing that?

When I was ushered into the room, he didn't walk over from behind his desk. He stood there in his pinstripe pants, red tie slightly loosened. The veins at his temples were visible and his fingers pushed against the leather blotter, the tips going from white to purple like candy corn. There was no acknowledgment of any kind. Of my arrival. Of the fact that I'd sat astride him in that leather chair. That he had broken my heart. Leaving the door ajar as always, I crossed to the other side of his desk. He put his fist into his hand as if it were a ball in a glove. "I got a call from Lewis."

"Yes." I nodded, nails taking position against the flesh of my palm. *Crying will only make you seem more—whatever it is he decided you are. Cry at home.*

"They're going to call—will be, um, calling you, I'm sure—this evening. But I wanted to be the one to—"

"Well, I appreciate your trying to help." *Look him in the eyes, show him you can—*

"No—you got the job."

My fingers opened. "I did?"

"You did."

"Thank you!"

"No need to thank me. They loved you. You got raves all the way around. Not that I'm surprised."

"And it's not really an unpaid internship wearing an Elmo costume in Times Square?"

He let out a short laugh. "You'd make a great Elmo. But no."

"Well, I really appreciate you making the call. Wow. *Wow.*"

"So you're on your way, then." His left hand recupped his right.

"That's what you—" I faltered when he looked at me—hopefully. And suddenly everything—paid-off loans, a secure roof over my head—seemed worthless by comparison. In that second, given the option, I would have lived the rest of my life suspended in the revelation that he still wanted me. His hands hovered at his sides, as they had that first time, and it was evident that this was there for me—if only until he was called to his next emergency.

He quickly rounded the desk. "I need to show you something."

"Greg," I begged off.

He continued to the hallway. "Seriously, I want you to see this." I suddenly wondered if I had misinterpreted Jean's phone call about not moving forward. Or if perhaps she had made it of her own volition. Maybe Rachelle was right, and he was setting me up to take this to the next level when he was finally able to get away. He turned back to me, his gaze hard, telegraphing a current of need more anxious than lust. "Please," he repeated, and I saw a bead of sweat on his forehead. I followed him, right up until he stepped out of the way of the darkened bathroom doorway and motioned for me to go in.

To my surprise, I couldn't. And it wasn't a ploy. The pain outweighed the desire. "I can't."

"I'll stand out here then. Fuck, Jamie. Please. Just look in the bathroom."

I tipped my head in and saw, in the light from the hall, the silver shaving kit sitting beside the sink on the black marble. He leaned in around me and picked up the brush. "I've been using it."

"Really?"

"The highlight of my day."

"Shaving?" I asked, reaching for levity.

"Don't you believe me?" He stepped closer and I looked up at him.

"How are you hanging in there with all this?" I asked.

He gripped the silver handle. "Today is . . . my brother was killed today. At least that's when we found out."

"I'm so sorry."

He stared at me a long moment, inches away, finally still.

"Greg, whatever I said or did to make you think I couldn't or wasn't—"

"I keep thinking about how you smell." He looked down at the brush, running his thumb back and forth over the bristles. "And how you hunch when you laugh. Do you think about me?"

"Yes."

"What do you think?" He looked up. "That I'm pathetic?" I watched his eyes dart back and forth like he was trying to scan my face into his brain.

"Honestly?"

"Please."

"I try to get myself to accept that I'm never going to know what it's like to have you inside me."

His knuckles whitened.

"Is this over?" I asked.

"I'm just going to kiss you."

"Over forever? Are you never going to find me again?"

"Just once. Okay?"

My lips were trembling. He took my jaw in his free hand, and my arms wrapped around his neck. He lifted me onto the vanity, my skirt pushing up, my thighs meeting the cold stone. His eyes flashed in the darkness as he tugged down my panties. My hand went for his belt, our arms mashing as we both tried to find the other's wetness. It was desperate. I kissed his lips, his jaw, his neck, running my tongue over the prickle of stubble he would shave, thinking of me. And all at once he was right there, where he had never been, warm and solidly insistent. Shaking, he sunk his forehead against mine, gripping my ribs. I thrust, tilting my hips, but suddenly he bucked away, stumbling back, his face stricken.

I felt my chest cave as hot tears broke. Twisting to the wall, I lifted my hand to shield me. He enclosed me in his arms. "You get to leave," he said into my ear, his lips landing hot and then roving to my mouth. The salt of tears—mine—his?—blurred with our tongues. Then all at once I felt the cold handle of the brush slipping inside me. My eyes flew open and he was staring into me, kissing me. "Remember me," he murmured like an incantation until I bit down into his shoulder, squeezing my quivering thighs around his wrist while he shuddered against me, warm liquid seeping through the thin wool of his trousers.

It was suddenly still. I could hear the faint tick of the grandfather clock in his office. His breath was shallow as he leaned against the wall, spent. He looked stunned and suddenly very far away. I hopped down, one heel clicking against the tile, then the other. I tugged at my skirt. He touched his hand to his pants, with a mixture of surprise and shame.

"I'll change," he said. "Could you?" He jerked his head at the hall. I stepped outside as he slipped into the spare suit that hung behind the door. Then he joined me, pulling it shut with finality. He slid his arms though the blazer sleeves without meeting my eyes. "I won't be able to see you now," he said weakly.

My skin was still static. "Because you're done with me," I asked, no clearer.

"Because of the trial."

"Are you worried they'll find out about—"

"No. No. We're the only two people here." His presidential absoluteness resurfaced as he buttoned his blazer. "Don't get sucked into the hysteria. You're too smart for that." This was it. The last few moments. Questions swarmed, batting each other out of the way like desperate exiles trying to board the last boat. Was this different from Brianne? Was this real? Do you care about me? Should I wait for you? Instead I asked . . .

"You told me to call you Greg when we first—met. Even Amar doesn't call you Greg. Why?"

He paused for a second and I expected yet another evasion. "Because of the way I felt at that moment," he said quietly, the answer not easy for him. "The way I feel at those moments," he added, acknowledging the ongoing grip of his anxiety. "That isn't the office. That's me. No one but you has ever seen me like that."

"Not even Susan?" It was the end. I could say it.

"Susan doesn't see me."

"Sir?" Jean called pointedly from her desk. "Your next appointment just checked in at the gate."

"Yes, thanks!" he projected out to her, his booming voice at odds with his expression, wasted from what had passed between us. "This was—I shouldn't have called you in." His hair flopped down and we both went to push it away, his warm fingers enclosing mine for a last second.

"I'm glad you did. Always do—if you ever find yourself unencumbered . . ."

He smiled so sadly, the creases around his eyes deepening. "Jamie, in three years I'll be able to rethink a lot of things. But by then—" His voice caught. "You'll be conquering the world, clubbing every night."

"Clubbing." I smiled back. "You're dating yourself," I said, repeating my quip from our first phone call as panic surged. "I love you."

He suddenly crushed me against him. "I love you, too." Just as quickly, he turned away, his back to me, but I'm certain he said, "This isn't goodbye," before the door shut.

I returned to the DOHS as if there were a tow-truck hook sunk into my back, its steel cable stretching farther and farther across the city. At security I stared into my purse for my ID, startling when a man said my name. "Yes?"

He slapped an envelope into my hand. "You've been served."

The guard looked me over as the man hustled away. My heart sounded like a field of startled birds taking flight. *Go to your desk.* I walked through the scanner and into the lobby—the guard had to chase me down to return my ID. *Call—who? Who do I call?*

Paul was watching as I stood, coat on, envelope in hand. I saw the Edith Wharton tile atop some papers and, not knowing what else to do, put it in my bag. My line rang and I picked it up, but couldn't speak.

"You okay?"

I looked over and saw that it was Paul.

He hung up and came quickly over as I started to hyperventilate. Guiding me by my forearm, he led me back out to the hall. I choked out about being subpoenaed, about Amar Singh, how he must have given me up during his deposition. He was the one that wanted me out of the White House. He'd wanted Paul out, too, hadn't he?

Paul tugged me into a hug as a trio of suits from the next office passed, pressing my face into his chest to muffle my questions. "You cannot do this here," he said sternly. As their footsteps grew faint, he took the envelope from my shaking hand and put it into my bag. "Go home."

My knees started to cave. "What do I—"

"Get in a cab." He took out his wallet, tugged out twenty dollars, and put it in my hand. "That's all I can do."

—

Lewis Franklin was the one to get back to me. The phone rang within minutes of my incoherent call to Jean. He told me to meet him at the Hay-Adams the next afternoon.

After a sleepless night on Rachelle's futon, I wove on unsteady feet between the empty tables to where he half-stood to greet me. "Do you want anything?" he asked, about to signal the bartender, who was stocking nuts for the imminent cocktail crowd.

"No, thank you. I need to keep my mind clear."

He nodded.

"I'm sorry to be seeing you under these circumstances," I said earnestly. "I can't tell you how much I'm looking forward to working—"

"Can you make that louder?" he asked the bartender, interrupting me.

The bartender nodded and pointed a remote at the screen. I waited for Lewis to catch whatever he needed on C-SPAN, but instead he leaned in. "Somebody has gone out of their way to put you on the OIC's radar. We think it was Gail Robinson."

I was stunned. "No, that's not possible," I said more forcefully than I had a right to. "I know she's with the RNC, but I'm close to her family. I saved her daughter's life." The truth suddenly sounded absurdly dramatic.

"Could she know about your friendship with the President?"

"Yes, but—"

"Did you tell her, or did she figure it out?"

"Jean called—on Gail's landline—on New Year's Day."

This paused him, checking his obvious desire for the blame to fall entirely on me. He drummed his fingers on the side of his glass before asking, "So who else could it be?"

"The Chief of Staff. He didn't like me."

He shook his head emphatically. "Singh wouldn't do that to him."

"Would he have a choice? If they asked him if there were any other . . . friendships. He saw me once outside the Oval—the day I got the job in the scheduling department, I ran up to tell the President and he overheard me. Greg said he was the one who suggested I be moved out of the building."

"Out of D.C. would've been more productive," he muttered. "Look, a list of items has been requested by the prosecutor. It includes a receipt and corresponding explanation for an unaccounted-for Hermès purchase in August. The President did not disclose this purchase to anyone." My stomach turned to worms. *Brooke.* It *was* all my fault. She had seen it because I couldn't wait to get it home. And now Greg thought I couldn't be trusted.

"It was a birthday present."

"I really don't need the details." He glanced at a couple of men in cashmere overcoats walking to the bar.

"It was one of the other interns. She saw me coming out of the ladies' room where I opened it. I'm so sorry. But she doesn't know anything for certain. There's no other corroborating—" But I realized it wasn't true. She was there the first night, outside the President's dining room.

"I'm not saying this as a future employer or in any professional regard. I'm saying this as a friend. I have a lawyer I advise you to see." He didn't lean forward, continuing as if about to recommend a golf pro. "Wallace Whitborn, excellent guy."

"That would be amazing—"

"It is his opinion that you should file a preemptive affidavit. Not expose yourself to the myriad variables created by a deposition. It will be with your doorman within the hour. You should get it to him by nine a.m. tomorrow morning so that it can be filed." His focus went back to the door, where people were trickling in. "And then you should get your things together and take a noon train to New York. Call my assistant when you arrive."

"So a preemptive affidavit would . . ."

"State that your interaction with the Oval Office was on a professional level. All interactions that occurred in the White House were on the up-and-up."

I stared at him.

"That's the scope of this," he stated, waiting expectantly for my confirmation.

"Yes. That is all that happened."

He rotated a cuff link. "Greg is adamant that you're trustworthy. It's not my place to doubt him. But it's necessary to ask—if there is anyone else who could have gotten a mistaken impression about your friendship, you need to tell us."

"Of course." But I was afraid and embarrassed, and I stupidly prayed that no one would ever have to know how I had slipped.

"And you'll call Gail and correct her misperceptions."

"Yes," I answered, though I had no earthly idea how to do that to one of the shrewdest women I'd ever met.

Then he lifted his folded paper and tapped it on the table before standing. "I have a benefit at the Met tonight."

"How will you get back so fast?" I asked.

"Chopper."

"Right." The option that wouldn't have occurred to me. But then everything that was happening now was the option that hadn't occurred to me. "I promise this will be the last you hear about anything like this. I feel like I have so much to offer your—"

"Do what you have to do to get this behind us. Onward and upward." His voice returned to a normal pitch as he walked me out. "Say hi to your aunt for me. Sweet of you to stop by for her." He patted me on the back and we parted ways.

No sooner had I left the bar than Jean called to ask that I bring any "mementoes of my internship" to her house for safekeeping. Like I'd taken a pen and those red, white, and blue M&M's.

"Fucking Brooke," Rachelle fumed over the phone as I dragged out the box from under my bed an hour later. We agreed it *had* to be Brooke. That Gail couldn't possibly have done this. And yet she did ask me to stay just as the Supreme Court decision came down—at a moment, according to the fears Lena had voiced months prior, she should have wanted me gone more than ever. "I can't believe that monogrammed washcloth would have the chutzpah."

"I can't believe that monogrammed washcloth could hate me this much." I emptied the box's contents into Gail's Families for America tote, the tile distorting the canvas. "She had to go out and *find* somebody to tell." I climbed back to my feet, overheating in my parka. "She obviously wasn't on the subpoena list." I grabbed the glass by my bed and chugged the mouthful of water that was left. "I have to talk to her, find out exactly what she said."

"Unless she's going to make *more* of a story out of your talking to her," Rachelle said fearfully. "Oh my God, would she? Like, blog about it or something? Is she even still in D.C.? I don't know, Jamie. I don't know if you should throw gas on her fire."

I looked longingly into the bag. "I'll just keep the book, okay?"

"That's it. I'm coming over."

"No! I can't show up at Jean's with you." I flicked off the light. "I have to go alone."

"Then I'm tracking down the beige bitch. We'll garrote her with pearls. Call me as soon as you unload the goods."

"And what do I do about this affidavit they've drafted?" I asked, opening the front door.

"Read it to me."

"It's not here yet. I was thinking of calling Paul—he's going through this—he could tell me—"

"He *sent you home.*"

"But he'd know—"

"That you signed a false affidavit," she said pointedly.

"I haven't signed it yet."

"You will. He's jealous and drunk half the time and being so, so weird. You cannot trust him. Full stop."

The buzzer rang and the doorman informed me that an envelope from the lawyer's office had arrived. I stood in the vestibule.

"Jamie?" Rachelle's concerned voice eeked from my speakerphone.

"Yes?"

"Go."

It was dark as I hurried along the suburban Maryland block, gripping the bag. I saw Greg picking each item out for me, the consideration, the intention to please. On my shoulder, the one-page document smoldered through my purse. I had started to read it on the train, then had to stuff it back in its innocuous manila folder, given the magnitude of the lie. A description of a relationship that would see me still working at the White House, maybe in a share with Rachelle, Donkey as my boyfriend—an alternate path in which I never wrapped my thighs around the wrist of a man whose political calling made divorce, and therefore us, impossible.

I passed glowing living-room lights, caught glimpses of dinners being prepared, homework being slogged through. I heard piano being practiced. I tried to convince myself to call Gail and lie to her. I knew Lena must have fully told her, but I couldn't conceive of what Lewis said Gail had done with that information.

I suddenly remembered an early spring night outside a Poughkeepsie bar with Lena, our friend Angie, and Angie's shit boyfriend, Justin, a local who owned the sub shop. They were so much drunker than we were. One minute we were stumbling back to campus talking about pizza bagels and the next Angie was on the sidewalk, holding her bleeding face.

Justin ran off. Angie locked herself in her room. I remember feeling like we were playing at being grown-ups and that any second some guidance counselor was going to call "scene." Instead, Lena and I huddled on the dorm roof, working our way through a pack of Marlboros and every possible course of action. Something had to be done, there was no maybe about it. We had seen it and it could not be explained away, much as Angie would try. By dawn, sitting shoulder to shoulder under Lena's purple duvet, fervently wishing we could go back to before it happened, it felt as if we were the only two people alive.

If Gail had done what Lewis said she had, that would be the real end of us. But what can you do about facts or the magical wish that they aren't? It would be like trying to get Angie to report Justin. Only I would be Angie, swearing I had tripped and that what Lena saw, she didn't see. In the final steps to Jean's door, I actually longed for the affidavit to be true.

"It's beautiful out here," I said as I stepped inside her toile entryway.

"Yes, I love that green is never altogether gone in this region." She clutched the top of her cardigan closed as she pulled the door shut behind me.

"Smells delicious."

"Just roasting a chicken."

"I didn't get the impression you were ever allowed home long enough to enjoy a whole chicken." I mimicked Rachelle's social ease while debating asking for Jean's guidance. Between us were the assignations she'd scheduled. The times I'd departed by way of her desk, kissed into a flushed frenzy. Her accepting nods at my full cans of soda concluding the ritual we were now conspiring to conceal. And I sensed that beyond legal constraints, she might actually be incapable of speaking about Greg as he really was.

"I'd love to ask you to stay," she said, less with regret than with insistence, her only acknowledgment that this was already a sort of trespassing.

"So, um, here it is." I reluctantly lifted the bag to my chest and realized I was giving it a little hug. She reached for it. For a second I still felt the weight, and then my arm was lighter as I registered the start of a knot in my neck, my eyes wetting. "Thanks for being so kind to me. I wish this wasn't happening like this. Or, you know, at all."

"It was a pleasure to meet you, dear." She offered me a tissue. Then I was back out in the cold.

As the train back into the city rumbled above the streetlamps, a stream of texts came in from Rachelle.

"Brooke now working for aunt's real estate company in Boston."

"Living with boyfriend in family apartment. Beacon Hill."

"Adopting Boxer puppy from Texas breeder."

"Naming it Farrell."

"Poor Farrell."

What Columbo could have achieved with Facebook.

The train barreled into the tunnel. Hunkered in a corner seat, I stared at the affidavit:

> *I did not have a sexual relationship with the President. He did not offer me employment or any other benefits in exchange for a sexual relationship. After I left my employment at the White House, I only saw him at formal political functions in relation to*

my job and other people were always present in the room. I declare
under the penalty of perjury that the aforementioned is true and
correct.

When the doors slid open, I was the first person out.

It took three long presses of Paul's bell for him to crack his door.
"Jamie." Two syllables carried to me on a plume of scotch fumes.

"Please," I begged as I shivered, the cul-de-sac of town homes
doing nothing to block the wind off the Potomac. "Please let me in."

"This isn't a good idea."

"We're so far past that. *Please*, Paul."

"Jesus." He tugged me inside and locked the door behind us.

"They've prepared an affidavit for me—"

" 'They'?"

"Lewis got me a lawyer." I reached into my bag for the envelope
and he reluctantly pointed me into a once-elegant living room that
was now glaringly missing half its furnishings—a packed bookshelf
stood next to one starkly empty, side tables sat beside spaces where
chairs once held the people who might have put down a drink.
In all these months he'd made no effort to encroach on Tom's ab-
sence.

He returned with a glass in his hand and a bottle under his arm. I
put the envelope on the coffee table as he poured me a generous por-
tion, then refilled his own glass. "They want me to sign it tonight."

"I'm sure *they* want you to do all kinds of things." He pushed my
glass toward me.

"Please read it. It says there was no relationship."

"How do they know about you?" he asked, standing back by the
fading embers of the fireplace. "Have they told you that?"

"This girl I interned with."

"I thought you said the Chief of Staff."

"No, I'm sure it was her." I lifted the glass, but the smell made my
empty stomach lurch. "I'm supposed to stay clearheaded." I placed it
back on the table.

"Overrated." Above him was the dust outline of a departed picture, the portrait lamp casting his face in long shadows. "Water, then."

"Please."

He turned back in the doorway. "You know you can't sign that thing. It's a lie." He went to the kitchen, taking with him the pretense of complexity and leaving me with the truth. I texted Rachelle that he had helped me, that I didn't think I could do it.

I pulled off my parka, my knee knocking the table and sloshing the scotch. Looking around, I saw a Kleenex box on the nearby desk. Reaching for it, I realized that amidst the scribbled notes and circled calendars, I was staring at a timeline of my life the last few months. The date I arrived at the DOHS. When I saw Greg on Halloween. When he dumped me—oh God.

"Here." Paul appeared, putting the glass in front of my face.

"I thought you were subpoenaed about Brianne," I said, stepping back, my voice shaking. "That was years ago."

He saw what I was staring at. "Your phone keeps buzzing like some relentless bug."

"Hello?" I fumbled for it.

"Please hold for Mr. Franklin."

"Oh, I can't—"

"Jamie."

"Sorry, can I call you back in a few—"

"No," Lewis commanded. "You need to call Wallace Whitborn. Your direct manager is on the goddamn witness list."

"I know—I'm sorry—"

"He's already being deposed. Out of all the witnesses, Brianne's lawyers called him first. Does this man know?"

Paul's eyes bored into me.

"Yes."

Lewis hung up.

Rachelle's text came through. *"GET OUT NOW."*

I pushed around him for my jacket. "You're right," I said quickly, barely any air under my words. "I shouldn't have come. I shouldn't have ever talked to you." I darted to the door.

"You'd better remember that I didn't ask for any of this. I was just doing my job, trying to scrape my life back together." He was right behind me as I fumbled with the lock. "And then *you* dragged me back into this heaping fuck-mess, you know that, right? I was just trying to be a decent fucking guy!"

He lunged forward and I ran out to the street. I ran for two blocks before I realized he wasn't following me.

Rachelle was waiting in my lobby, shaking with worry. I fell into her arms. "I'm going to help you pack and then," she said into my hair, before pulling back, "we're going to get really drunk, you're going to sign that affidavit, and this will be over."

"I can't."

"It's the only way to protect yourself and finish this. And you'll *get* Greg."

"I won't—"

"You'll get his gratitude and keep his love. Paul's looking out for Paul. Wallace Whitborn isn't. Trust me, Jamie." I wanted everything she said to be true.

In the morning we wrenched ourselves apart. She swore she would join me in New York—soon—and we'd live a life so much cooler than anything Lena and I had ever imagined. Rachelle would settle for nothing less than every day being an adventure. As I scurried around the apartment to gather the last of my things, my cell rang and I let it go to voicemail. "Hey, James, it's Mike. I *really* need to talk to you. It's urgent. Call me back. Please. At work. Let me give you the number." I erased it.

I loaded my three cartons onto the brass cart for the UPS pickup, courtesy of Lewis Franklin's corporate account, and closed the door on Gail's apartment for what I thought was the last time. I had no idea what I was supposed to do when I arrived in Manhattan, but at this point I was ready to walk there. Just as I was stepping into the Metro, a number I didn't recognize came up on my phone, and after a moment's hesitation, I answered it.

"It's Paul."

"Hi." I stopped.

"We need to talk."

"Why?"

"They're closing in on everything. I don't know when we'll be able to talk again."

"I'm leaving."

"Meet me first."

"That's my other line," I lied. "I'll call you right back. At this number?"

"Yes. It's a pay phone. Hurry."

I texted Rachelle.

"Shitshitshit," she wrote back. *"Tell him he has to backtrack with Brianne's lawyers and he's an asshole if he doesn't. Make sure you drop off your affidavit first. Go somewhere loud. At the station."*

He agreed to meet me there.

As I walked through the glass doors, I spotted Paul waiting next to a window display of sherbet-colored socks. He looked even more wretched, if that was possible. Unshaven, unslept, his hands shoved deep into his trench pockets. We walked toward the restaurant.

"I have a battering headache, so I'll be quick," he said. "You need to get your own lawyer. Stop doing everything he tells you or tells you through others."

"Paul, I signed it. I just dropped it off. I'm getting on a train."

"Fuck."

"Paul, I thought you were my friend. Please, I'm begging you to help me. Please. *Please.*"

"I'm *trying* to help you."

"I've sworn there was no relationship! Promise your testimony won't contradict me." I grabbed him, seeking confirmation. "Please, Paul, *please.*"

But he suddenly looked like a faded copy of himself, peering over my shoulder as if the building were crumbling behind me. I turned, following his gaze to two men in dark suits walking briskly toward us.

"Jamie McAlister?"

"Paul?" I attempted to ask, but nothing came out.

"We're with the Federal Bureau of Investigation. You need to come with us now."

"Paul?"

His eyes drifted closed and my legs gave way as if the skeletal support were being ripped from them.

I was on my own.

Part III

Chapter Ten

February 5

You think you know what's next. This is the part where my story—where *I*—became public. It's possible, if you own a TV or laptop or tablet, that you've regrettably heard me speak in my own words about my time with Greg, about everything that led up to that moment. But I have never, officially or unofficially, spoken about what was done to me. So you don't know.

As the elevator lifted me inside the Phoenix Park Hotel, my senses penetrated the static that had descended while I was escorted out of the train station and across the street. My first thought was that I had gotten away from Paul. These agents were here at Greg's request; they weren't FBI but Secret Service, and this was their cover. Lewis sent them to make sure I boarded safely. When I obviously couldn't, they changed plans. I was being harbored. "Is he upstairs?"

One agent exchanged a glance with the other. Of course they couldn't say anything. "This way, ma'am."

Halfway down the corridor, the door to Room 1608 opened. I walked in ahead, assuming the agents would stop at the door and that Greg would be waiting to pull me protectively against him. Instead, I found five suited men squeezed around two pristine queen-sized beds, their expressions making it sickeningly clear—this was not a rescue mission.

I spun back, but the agent barring the door lifted his blazer to show me his gun. I realized my chest was puffing in rapid bursts.

"Ben, grab her a paper bag."

I fell in the desk chair, waving it away. Instead I dropped my head between my knees, letting the rushing sound in my ears, like dialysis, drown out the room for a second. The door opened and closed again. "Ms. McAlister." I squinted up at a man in a different cut of suit, a hard cast to his face suggesting his day, and maybe his life, wasn't going how he wanted. "I'm Scott Riddick, legal deputy for the Office of Independent Counsel. We've been sanctioned by the U.S. Attorney General to investigate crimes committed in relation to the Brianne Rice case. You're in severe trouble, Jamie."

I moistened my mouth enough to speak. "Crimes?"

"We are prepared to charge you with perjury, obstruction of justice, subornation of perjury, witness tampering, and conspiracy, which adds up to twenty-seven years in jail."

Heat blew up from my gut. Whether or not he loved me and left her, whether or not we were meant to be, I was going to miss it— marriage, children, all of it. I couldn't even repeat the charges. I knew I needed someone there, someone to protect me, to understand what was happening—to protect me. "Aren't we going in to your office?" I didn't know the term—station? Bureau?

"Not yet," he answered. "Not if we don't have to. It's up to you." I couldn't grasp how our location was up to me. "This is time sensitive."

"Why?" I mustered.

But he just stared, leaving me to try to fill it in—my brain thrashing like snakes dropped into setting cement—because I'm leaving? Because—I gripped the bottom of my chair—

Because Greg was scheduled to file his deposition the next day. There was no way for him to know that Paul's testimony contradicted ours.

"Ms. McAlister, I am giving you an opportunity." Agent Riddick leaned on the edge of the desk, close enough for me to grab his legs. "I'm trying to be helpful. If you *want* to be helped, you can follow my colleagues into the next room, where they'll take a statement regarding the nature of your relationship with the President. You will tell the *whole* truth. Then, once they're satisfied you've cooperated, you'll make some phone calls for corroboration, which we'll record. To Jean

Hargrove, Lewis Franklin, and the President." You know how when someone suggests something—"Do you want to have lunch?"—you automatically envision it—the restaurant, what you'll order, or what you'll wear? But I was blank, the words conjuring nothing.

"I've filed my affidavit with Wallace Whitborn." I struggled to fill my voice above a whisper. "That's my statement in its entirety."

Scott nodded to one of his agents, who passed over an iPad. Scott touched the screen.

"Was Brianne the first?" I heard my own voice. *"She's not going to tell. Am I just another—am I that stupid?"*

"You're not stupid." It was Paul. *"No, you're not just another. Not that I know of. Not for years as far as I've heard, not since Brianne."*

"So." Scott turned it off while I sucked in my lips against what was coming. "Anything you'd like to add?"

I lunged for the wastepaper basket. Stomach empty, I wiped my mouth with the back of my hand.

"Okay, then, Ms. McAlister," Scott resumed as one of the agents removed the basket. "If you cooperate *immediately,* I can reduce your sentence from twenty-seven years to five."

Immediately. More thrashing snakes. More cement. "Can I call my lawyer?"

"We don't want this discussed over the phone."

"Could I take a cab there? If you came with me?"

He looked to one of the other officers. Something passed between them. "Our concern is that he'll contact Lewis Franklin."

"I—I'm confused. I thought you just said you wanted me to call Lewis Franklin."

"That would be a very different kind of conversation. One in which you ask him to corroborate certain statements."

"What statements?" I grasped for information.

"Did Lewis Franklin offer to get you a job in exchange for lying under oath?"

"No! That's not at all what—is *that* why I'm here?" There was no answer. "I have to speak with Wallace Whitborn."

"Wallace Whitborn can't help you because he's a civil lawyer." (He wasn't. He had over twenty years of criminal law experience. But there was no way for me to know that Agent Riddick had been told to lie to me.)

My mind raced. "Could he recommend someone?"

"If you called right now asking him the name of a criminal specialist, that would make him suspicious." He tilted his head. "You might lose your window to cooperate."

The room was rapidly overheating with the seven of us crammed in. I felt light-headed. "Can I call his partner? Maybe he could recommend someone? I don't have to say who I am."

"We'd prefer it if you didn't call anybody."

No one knew where I was.

I glanced at the clock and realized it had been over an hour. "Can I use the bathroom?"

"Empty your pockets."

"What?" I scanned the impassive faces.

"Give us your phone." I thought of the texts to Rachelle, the emails, the internet searches—for homeopathic bladder infection remedies, lingerie flash sales, Greg's childhood, Brianne. Every little thing that I'd hit a button on in the last few months. How any moment of insecurity or longing was recorded there and could be—

"We're not going to turn it on—we don't have a warrant. We just need you to leave it on the desk." One of the agents stepped into the bathroom, we heard a snap, a cracking, and he walked out with the wall phone. I took in the crude plaster scar on the wallpaper before locking the door and immediately sliding to the stone. People describe leaving their bodies and it always sounded to me like a floating, but this was a draining. I seeped out through the floor. Gone.

I could hear the room's door open and Scott talking to someone in the hall. I saw the reflection of the Phoenix Park matches on the vanity. *Could I start a fire? Would they leave me locked in with it?* Which makes no sense, I know, but I was that afraid.

After a few minutes there was a knock. "Ms. McAlister!"

"Coming," I said weakly, managing to pull myself up. When I opened the door Scott was standing with his arms crossed, popping a new idea to the forefront of my mind. "My mom will be worried. I'm moving to New York today."

"We know."

"I should be on the train right now. I would have called her when we pulled out."

"You don't need your mommy," he said cuttingly.

I hadn't called her that in years, but hearing the word, I began sobbing and sunk on the bed, past trying to handle this well, let alone to impress or endear. I don't know how long they let me cry.

I felt the mattress sink and squeezed my eyes open to see Scott sitting beside me. He lowered his voice. "Jamie, just go in the next room and let us record a couple of quick conversations. You don't owe these assholes anything."

But the idea that I could make Greg feel the way I now felt about Paul was untenable. I shook my head no, wiping my face on the back of my arm.

"What now?" An agent addressed Scott.

"We wait."

"I need some air. Please."

"Agent Cuellar here can escort you to the hallway."

"The hallway?" I repeated stupidly.

"You're free to walk up and down, think about our offer. You only have a few hours left to save yourself."

I stood as Agent Cuellar unbolted the door and I followed him into the hall, which was measurably cooler than the room. He rested against the ivory wallpaper and checked his email while I moved toward the window at the end, the square of sunlight, wondering if it unlocked, wondering if I had it in me to jump.

I didn't.

The elevator opened and I whipped around. A woman in sweatpants pushed a stroller with a small cloth sheep clipped to its shade. The bellboy wheeled ahead, a car seat piled atop her luggage. Agent Cuellar watched me. Could I say something to her? Ask her to call Greg? To warn him?

She looked up and caught my eye for a brief second—I smiled. Her child started to whimper and she went to soothe him. We'd made contact. I could smuggle a pen into the bathroom, write a note on the toilet paper, then use another walk to slip it under her door—

"Jamie?" Following Agent Cuellar's outstretched arm, I reentered, hit by the oppressive fug, like the air in a locker room. I took the seat by the desk.

"Well?" Scott asked, pulling up a seat across from me.

"I need to call my friends."

"That's a new one," he scoffed, twisting in his chair to share a laugh with the agents. "You want to Facebook this?"

"I was supposed to be getting into New York now," I answered, trying to keep my voice steady. "They're waiting for me on the platform. And I'm not there." Surely by this hour, Lewis's assistant would realize I hadn't called in that I'd arrived. They had to be looking for me.

His smile dropped. "Send them a text." He picked up my phone. "Tell me who, and what to say."

I gave him Rachelle's number as my mind spun, trying to invent a code, something that could mean *warn the President.* "Sorry, unexpected delay, missed my train," I dictated.

Scott shook his head, redacting me. " 'Missed my train.' "

My head throbbed. Rachelle would have to know that the only reason I wouldn't get on that train was that something had stopped me. And she would have to think it weird that I didn't elaborate. He hit Send, and the incongruous sound, like a tiny happy ball getting squeezed through a happy tube, confirmed the message's enviable departure. Would she get my intention?

He turned the phone off. "Anyone else hungry?" he asked. While we waited for their room service, the agents asked me small-talk questions. Were they bored—or trying to disarm me? Did they think that if we chatted about the Chicago Blackhawks' season, I'd follow them blindly next door?

I picked at the food while they shoveled in burgers. I slipped a pen off the desk and played with it for an hour until no one noticed it anymore. I asked to use the bathroom. With trembling hands, I scribbled a note for the woman across the hall on a shower cap box I quickly unfolded. It was barely legible, but still I offered to wheel the cart back out so I could slip it under her door.

Scott looked at the clock. He said sure. "Don't make a run for it," he chuckled. "Anyone you talk to becomes legally involved."

Picturing the little swinging sheep, the small life it belonged to being dragged into this, I rolled the cart onto the red and gold carpeting—and reentered the room, the cardboard still in my pocket.

How much longer could they hold me? Not through tomorrow, could they? Greg's deposition was scheduled for nine. I thought for sure I'd be able to get a message to him by then. I had to. Rachelle would help me. Scott's phone rang and he took it into the hall. "Now they *want* her to call someone?! . . . Right, right, fuck. No, not Whitborn, I'll think of someone. . . . I don't know!" he shouted. "No, I explained it all *very* clearly. She seems to fucking want to go to jail, I don't know what to fucking tell you!"

"I can call someone?" I asked when he returned.

"No."

"But I thought—"

"No."

At sunset, someone turned on a lamp. More hours passed. It felt like when I was young, when Erica and I shared a room and our parents would discover evidence of her poorly concealed delinquency well past bedtime—a crudely glued vase, or missing money—and, unable to contain themselves, they'd throw open our door and start screaming at her. I'd lie beneath the covers, trying to breathe like I was sleeping. I'd focus on my sleep breathing until I wasn't there anymore.

"Agent Riddick is expecting me." The voice in the hall was firm, authoritative. The wrong voice. The door unlocked.

"Hi," I said, inhaling the word.

"Hi."

"What're you doing here?" I asked.

"I was instructed to call your parents," Agent Riddick answered for her.

"And they sent me." Erica turned to Scott, with the same steely confidence she'd used against Dad. "What's going on?"

Riddick rubbed his stubbling face, trying to wake himself up. "Your sister is facing twenty-seven years if she doesn't cooperate with our investigation into crimes committed by the President of the United States in conjunction with the Brianne Rice case."

Erica didn't ask what it had to do with me. She set her camel-hair coat and bag on the bed. I'd never seen her in a suit before. "So you're arresting her?"

"We're giving her an opportunity." Riddick slipped his thumbs into his waistband, his elbows widening the space he took up in the room.

"Have you spoken to a lawyer?" she asked me.

"This is time sensitive," Riddick repeated. "If Jamie cooperates, we will mitigate her sentence."

"Her charges, you mean." Erica squinted. "Mitigating her sentence isn't up to you."

"Right."

I could tell that she'd picked up on something, something I was too overwhelmed to see. "What do you want Jamie to do?" she asked.

"Allow us to record her talking to the President and a few other people."

Erica looked me fully in the face and I shook my head.

"Criminal charges *will* be filed," he pushed. "She *has* to do this."

"Okay," Erica answered evenly. "Then we'll call our lawyer, so you can repeat your promise to someone other than us."

Riddick smiled. "You want it in writing?"

"Um, actually, yes, we do."

We could see it on his face, in the ripple that went around the beds, like when they replay candidates' gaffes during a campaign. "I don't have a typewriter."

"Or, I'm presuming, a gramophone." Erica pressed her advantage. "Handwrite it."

Riddick looked unsure of himself for the first time in almost twelve hours.

"We're calling our lawyer." Erica pulled out her phone, twisting away from them. "I got her name from Peter—she's big-time," she said under her breath to me as it rang. I braced for Riddick to jump on her for talking to Peter, but he weirdly didn't. "She's expecting to hear from me tonight—Elaine?" she said on speaker.

"Yes."

"It's Erica McAlister. I'm here with my sister and—" She held the phone out. Riddick introduced himself and took her through the charges. They started going back and forth about my legal options, Erica holding the phone out like a tape recorder. *Oh.* I was so stupid. I realized how Paul had done it. As easy as keeping the voice memo running on his iPhone.

"If she cooperates, Ms. Schiller, we're prepared to offer transactional immunity."

"I see," Elaine mused. "That's interesting."

"As I explained to Ms. McAlister," Riddick continued with increased urgency, "this is time sensitive. I'm sure you'll advise your client we're being generous."

"Thank you, Mr. Riddick. Erica, please take me off speaker." Erica lifted the phone to her ear and I stepped close enough to listen while Riddick exchanged tense looks with the agents. "Leave."

"What?" I asked Elaine.

"You haven't been charged with anything yet and he's not authorized to offer immunity. Just walk out. I'm on the next train and I'll meet you first thing tomorrow morning. Who was representing you for the affidavit?"

"Wallace Whitborn."

"Okay. Don't talk to anyone tonight." She hung up.

Erica put the phone back in her purse. "We're leaving."

"Ms. McAlister—"

"We're leaving." Taking hold of my arm, she grabbed her things and moved me toward the exit. In the hallway she jammed her finger into the Down button as I fully expected a hand to land on my shoulder—to get thrown against the wall and cuffed.

But they let us get on. And they let the door close.

The hotel's doorman got us a taxi, just as if we were any other guests. He asked if we'd enjoyed our stay.

We got in, he shut our door, and we pulled into the street.

And somehow I didn't crumple. Or ask questions. Because I didn't know if he was a real cab driver.

At Gail's building the doorman welcomed us, registering alarm when he saw my swollen face. But he didn't say anything. Had he always worked there? It wasn't until the elevator closed that I finally spoke, "I have to warn Greg."

"What?"

"He's testifying tomorrow." I whispered furtively. "He needs to know—they'll catch him in the lie. I have to go to Jean's house."

"You're not going *anywhere*," she whispered back. "They could be sitting across the street waiting to arrest you."

"I have to do *something*."

We turned on only the overhead in the vestibule, didn't even take off our coats. Erica led me to the bathroom, where she twisted on the sinks and showers. We huddled on the bath mat over her cell phone. "Hello?"

"Elaine, sorry, did we wake you?" Erica sounded smaller—whatever she'd drawn upon to get me out of that hotel room was rapidly diminishing.

"I'm already en route. Where are you calling from?"

"Gail Robinson's apartment."

"I see."

"Is it not safe?" Erica asked.

"I don't know yet."

"Where should we go?" I asked.

"It isn't advisable to make any sudden moves right now. I just got off the phone with Whitborn. They knew your affidavit was left with him this morning, but affidavits aren't filed until five p.m."

"What does that mean?" I asked.

"To catch you the FBI and the Office of the Independent Counsel had to wait for Whitborn to file your false statement. If you'd spoken with him today, he'd never have filed it, and they'd have nothing to hang over you now—"

Erica interrupted her. "I just can't follow this. What does a civil lawsuit against the President have to do with the FBI or the OIC?"

"It shouldn't. We're in Narnia right now. Someone tipped them off about you, and gave them enough information that they could go to the Attorney General and make you getting a job in exchange for silence a government investigation." *A government investigation.*

"Elaine, I need to get a message to Greg tonight."

"No," her voice cut down the line. "You don't. And that is the end of what's discussed about this case on the phone—or in that apartment. Are we clear?"

"Yes," we answered, our foreheads almost touching.

"You are both under legal quarantine."

"Both? What does that mean?" Erica asked.

"An-y-one you speak to—and I don't just mean your parents; your boyfriends, friends, colleagues, the fucking barista at Starbucks—can be subpoenaed. And that will cost them each around two hundred thousand dollars in legal bills."

Erica swallowed. "What should we be prepared this is going to cost?"

"Five hundred thousand if I can keep it from going to trial. Two million or more if I can't. And Erica, you should expect to be subpoenaed by end of day tomorrow at the latest."

"We can't talk to our parents?" I asked, as if I could bear to. My face burned like I was in a sandstorm.

"Not until you have immunity. Look, we're not out of the woods yet. We haven't even *entered* the fucking woods. Try to get some sleep."

"Thank you, Elaine," I mustered, because I realized Erica had started trembling. I disconnected the call as she slipped to the tile.

"I can't see," she said, gripping my hand. "Get me to the couch."

I turned off the faucets, opened the door, and walked her to the living room.

"Fill a bowl with ice," she whispered as she folded onto the cushions. "Put a washcloth on my forehead."

I slid her head onto my lap and placed the terry cloth across her pulsing temples. In the lone light from the vestibule, her skin was the bluish white of skim milk. "Colder," she whispered when she needed me to re-wet the cloth. I watched the stars disappear over the Capitol.

So passed the first night.

Chapter Eleven

February 6

With the sun rising aggressively at my back the next morning, I squinted as it banked off the mirror lining Gail's bar, gauging whether I should dump the bottles before Erica awoke. But I could never afford to restock it. Even the decanters housed irreplaceable vintages. And what would I do with the empty bottles? Were they going through my trash? My stomach found an extra millimeter to constrict as Erica's phone rang with Elaine's number. I jumped to answer before it roused her.

"Did you sleep?" she asked abruptly.

"Not really," I said quietly as I stepped into the kitchen. Eyeing the light fixture for signs of a camera, I placed a shielding hand over my mouth.

"Any public spaces in your building where we can meet?"

"There's a gym on the roof."

"That'll work."

"What happens next?" Lena's words had been frantically repeating in my mind—*that's the government government—these are the people who can drop you down a well.* "How do I stay out of jail?"

"I don't know yet. I'm on my way in to the OIC. You need immunity or you won't see daylight until your forties."

She was brusque. But after actively tugging the grenade that was Paul into the foxhole with me, I was incapable of trusting anything warmer. I gave her my address and, hearing Erica stir, wiped my eyes. "How are you feeling?" I asked, going back to the living room.

She pushed herself to sit. "I can see," she said drolly, her voice raspy. "So that's something." She looked out the glass doors as I waited to learn which Erica I would be getting that morning—the one who would let me in or the one who would cut me off. "I thought it'd be like with my sponsees—knock the drugs out of your hand, stay the night, get you support, be back at work by sunup." She spoke as her thoughts came, as if I weren't there.

"Well, Elaine's headed to the OIC. So we should know more soon—including how long you're stuck here. With me."

She nodded, her shoulders rising back from the defenseless position they'd been in last night. "I need coffee."

"Or course. What else?"

"I'll need to borrow clothes."

"Everything's with the doorman for UPS," I remembered.

"I'll buzz down." She crossed to the intercom while I busied myself with straightening the couch.

"Erica," I tentatively broached as she hung up with the lobby. "If Riddick called Mom, why didn't they come?"

She dropped her head for a second, as if already exhausted by the conversation we hadn't started.

"Erica?"

"He was too drunk to fly." We stared at each other.

"Because he's ashamed of me."

"Because he's an alcoholic," she answered sharply, going to unpack her purse on the table. "He's tried to control it rubbing a fucking rabbit's foot, but he can't handle stress. He can't handle anything. Great. Lip gloss, a rubber band, and two Tampax. I'm set." She shoved the leather sack aside in frustration.

"I can lend you things, really. And God knows Gail has things." Limoges, Baccarat, possible recording devices.

"Things—great." Her storm cloud started to spin, sucking what little air I'd found before she woke.

"Well, maybe Mom can tag you out," I suggested.

Her expression set into the familiar rage. "Yeah, she's up for that. Are you making coffee or not?"

She stalked to the bathroom, tugging the door shut. God, why did they send her? It would have been better to be trapped alone.

As the shower turned on my phone pinged with a text. I threw a dish towel over it, uncertain whether it violated the quarantine. But, unable to control my curiosity, I stood directly over it and discreetly lifted a corner of the terry cloth. It was from Jean. *"Family emergency—please call."* I dropped the towel—I had no idea what to do. I wanted desperately to help Greg, to see through what I had done by signing that affidavit.

Less than a mile away, his testimony would be starting within the hour.

Another text. I quickly lifted the towel's corner again. From Lewis this time. *"Good news—please call."* Fuck. *Fuckfuckfuck!*

Jean re-sent her text.

Lewis re-sent his.

"Turn it off!" Erica shouted from the doorway, zipping up Gail's bathrobe.

"What?"

She lunged for the phone, powering it down.

"Erica!"

"The only reason I'm not throwing it in the fucking garbage disposal is I think that would be tampering." She grabbed her laptop from her bag. "What's the Wi-Fi password?"

"Elephant." She bent over the dining table, typing and scrolling while I watched. I flashed to when we were kids and I'd sit next to her playing video games for hours, never wanting to take the controls myself, to risk being up against her. I just liked how she was when she succeeded, suddenly generous, kind. "What are you doing?"

"Googling you . . . it's just that article from the *Tribune* about your sixth-grade science fair prize."

"That's on there?"

"Shit. And this." She swung it around so I could read the Drudge Report. A rumor "going around Washington" pertaining to the President and a "certain White House intern." "That's why they're texting you," she said, swiveling the computer back. "Every outlet will be covering this in minutes."

We turned on the news. She was right.

Erica returned to her laptop. "I need to email work and tell them I'm not coming in. Tersely. Then I need to email Peter and tell him

I'm not coming home. Tersely." She looked down at her sizable engagement ring.

"What about Mom and Dad?"

"Elaine will have to be our go-between."

"We don't have any food," I said, because other than making coffee, cooking was the only manageable task I could think of.

"Are you hungry?" She didn't look up as she typed.

"No."

"When we are, we'll order in online."

"I can't afford that," I answered from a mind stuck in a day ago.

"Next to the five hundred thousand we have to come up with, I think we can swing a bagel."

"What are Mom and Dad gonna do?" I asked.

"Empty Mom's 401(k), wipe out their savings, sell the house. Then there's *my* savings."

"Yours?" I was stunned.

"We don't have a choice. I already asked Peter."

"When?"

"On the way to the shuttle. Obviously Elaine was going to need a retainer."

"How do you know all this?" I asked.

"*I* live in the real world," she leveled at me.

"Seriously?" I glared, throwing my hand at the television. "How much realer could my world get right now?"

"Oh my God, Jamie, being the President's girlfriend doesn't make you a grown-up—it makes him a child."

"Fuck you."

"You already have! I'm your goddamned prisoner!"

"I didn't ask you to come!"

"But I had to anyway, didn't I? But if you're expecting me to sit here and braid your hair, Jamie, it's not going to fucking happen."

"As you never fail to make abundantly clear, Erica. I got it."

While Elaine's oxblood suit was out of place in the gym, her intensity and focus put the lunch-hour lifters behind us to shame. Her nose, cheekbones, and short blond haircut were all equally sharp, reminding me of an angry hen, and I wondered about women like Elaine. Would Brooke become an Elaine? Would Erica? Or had Elaine once been more like me, blurry, unsure? I doubted it. She sat us at the lone table in the corner intended for diagnostic sessions. If she was aware of the palpable wall between Erica and me, sitting as far from each other as the Formica allowed, she didn't let on.

"Wouldn't it be better to be in the apartment?" I asked, eyeing the guys on the treadmills twenty feet away.

"No." Elaine pulled a yellow pad from her briefcase. "I made it clear to the OIC that I will fight any misuse of the Patriot Act. Any evidence acquired through wiretapping, et cetera. I pointedly let them know we would be up here. If they want to debug Gail's place they can."

"So what does Jamie need to do?" Erica asked.

Elaine looked squarely at me. "*If* you wear a wire, the special prosecutor is prepared to offer full immunity. That offer's for real."

"No."

"Jamie." She looked at me plainly. "This isn't the moment to start having integrity."

"Start?" However deserved, it smarted.

"He's married. You talked. You *need* to cooperate." But how could I? And in the same breath, how could I keep Erica trapped and bankrupt our family?

I looked up at the screens over the treadmills. Greg was about to start his press conference on the clean energy bill. He approached the podium while the commentator shared that the President had just come from giving his sworn testimony that he did not have a sexual relationship with Brianne or anyone else other than his wife—

In my tie.

The one with the little raccoons—he hadn't declared it. He was standing there on national television, still trying to communicate that we were a team.

"What are you willing to tell them?" Elaine asked.

I watched him at the podium, my heart aching that I'd put him in jeopardy. I should *never* have told a single person. I should have had

EMMA McLAUGHLIN AND NICOLA KRAUS

the strength. He trusted me to handle it and I gave him away. "Nothing." It was the right thing to do.

"Nothing?"

"Regardless of what Paul recorded me saying—"

"Paul?" Elaine asked.

"Paul Hoff—he made the recording Agent Riddick played for me at the hotel, I think—unless the apartment *is* bugged and this was all Gail and Brooke . . ." My head throbbed from trying to parse it. I couldn't make myself hold the truth of the extent of Paul's betrayal. It kept sliding off, like a coat you're trying to hang up when you're drunk.

Elaine flipped through her pages. "They didn't mention anyone named Paul Hoff—"

Suddenly the two middle-aged guys on the treadmills both stumbled, their earbuds flying out.

"Give me the remote!" Elaine rushed to the screens. "What did he say?"

"Who the fuck is Jamie McAlister?"

It was as if someone had smashed my head between two cinder blocks.

"He's gay?" The other guy looked puzzled.

"Well." Elaine grabbed up her things. "That's the end of your wire deal. I need to find out if you still have value."

"Value?" Erica asked.

"Jamie, I cannot impress this upon you hard enough—you're *only* safe from prosecution so long as you're useful."

Within minutes the networks had my picture. Within hours they were on my parents' lawn. By dinnertime a blonde in a pink coat was reporting live from Vassar, talking to some guy I'd never met who apparently recalled me as "always up for a good time." I remembered too late that one of my old classmates from high school was an intern at Fox. My Facebook photos went national, what felt like endless images of me drunk at parties. A narrative of my promiscuity emerged faster than I could change the channels, a handful of guys multiplying like gremlins into an imaginary horde.

Erica's phone rang until she shut it off. She unplugged her laptop. I caught her eyes darting to Gail's bar.

Elaine called us back up to the gym. I sat with Gail's Lakers hat pulled low.

"They want you to swear, under oath, that you were given the job in New York in exchange for your silence."

"But that's just not true."

"Jamie, they have your letter to Rutland."

"What?" Lewis Franklin hadn't mentioned that.

"They have a letter you messengered the President demanding a job."

"How?"

"Someone gave them the messenger company records and they subpoenaed it."

I had to shut my eyes for a second as I remembered how Paul had egged me on. I was a sucker; a tourist in Times Square duped at a card game, a retiree bilked out of her savings, an easy mark. Twenty-two and needing to be liked.

"That letter isn't an admission of anything. I know what it sounded like"—crude and mercenary. "But it wasn't like that at all between us." Greg smiled when he told me I got the job. He wanted me to be happy. If he couldn't be with me, he wanted to at least send me off to success. "This whole thing is insane. Brianne Rice brought a sexual harassment case against him," I clarified. "I am not charging anyone with anything. If I fit their criteria it would mean the President propositioned me for sex, I turned him down and lost my job. I said yes and still lost my job."

Elaine was momentarily silent for the first time since we'd met. "Let me be extremely clear, because you seem to be missing the scope." She put her palms together and tapped the edge of her hands against the table as she spoke. "The Office of the Independent Counsel wants the President impeached. He lied under oath about having sexual relations with you. And they will come for you with everything they have until you confirm it."

My mind reeled at what that meant. "But he didn't offer me that job for silence. He was helping me because he—"

"Don't say it," Erica said to her lap.

"He likes me," I finished.

"Sleep on it." Elaine stood. "And give me the right fucking answer in the morning."

"FBI! Open up!" Erica and I looked at each other, momentarily bridging our animosity because, without cooking meth or running guns, we had somehow crossed over into a world where this shit was actually happening.

My laptop and cell were seized. Followed by the computers and phones of everyone I'd emailed or texted since June ninth. Erica. Our parents. Lena. Gail. My friends from college. That asshole from the jazz concert on the lawn. But except for Lena and Gail, none of my high school or college friends had known about Greg.

They did now.

Elaine returned to repeat the OIC's demands, but I clung to my last directive.

"I stand by my affidavit. He'll stand by his testimony. When I texted Lena or Rachelle, I never used his name. That audiotape is inadmissible, right?"

"Technically, yes."

"Then it's our word against theirs. They have nothing." I stood firm, my arms crossed. A President behind me.

The next morning, Erica shook me awake from the last tendrils of Ambien. "They have something," she said, already returning to the living room.

"Who?" I asked, immediately up and following. On the TV was a coffee commercial—happy people excited to greet their day in fisherman sweaters, walking big dogs. Then the camera panned the *Today Show* crowd.

"They said coming up we were going to hear you talking about Greg."

Confused, I shook my head as suddenly we heard sobbing incongruously layered over Savannah Guthrie's listening face. My sobs. Then, "I d-don't think I can take it anymore, I really don't. But how could I have refused him? Pushed him away? God, it hurts so f—ing much." That was bleeped.

"Oh my God." It hit me when I'd said that—and to whom.

"What—what is it?" she asked as my hands flapped in front of my face like panicked butterflies. "Jamie, what is it—you're scaring me."

"They got to Rachelle."

"What?"

"Paul wasn't with us."

"But they were bugging the apartment—"

"We weren't *in* the apartment—she was helping me pack and we ran out for cigarettes. Rachelle went on about my being brave and I just broke down, sobbing in CVS like a crazy person." I thought of those hours in the Phoenix Park Hotel, sick at the thought of what the FBI must have done to her to press her to do this—what they must have threatened her with.

"I'm calling Elaine." Erica reached for the landline.

I clicked over to *Morning Joe* to hear myself slur, "No one's ever made me come like that, you know, that—hard. Like there's no plateau—I just slam over the edge." *If I live to be a thousand—if everyone on the planet dies—on that day I will be lifted up to abject humiliation from where I am now.*

"Paul Hoff wants to see you," Elaine said as she answered the phone.

I couldn't even respond.

"He knows about the legal quarantine, right?" Erica verified.

"He knows he's a fucking asshole who got the OIC to use Rachelle against me, right?" My voice was raspy with tears.

"He said he needs to talk to you—in person. Obviously it's out of the question."

"So, Rachelle?" Erica prompted Elaine.

"Yes," she confirmed, "she's officially cooperating with the special prosecutor."

"How do I get a message to her?" I asked. "To apologize for dragging her into this."

"You don't."

Erica started sleeping during the day and spending nights in the gym to avoid me. Sometimes I'd go up and watch as she moved through the circuit, running mile after mile, her eyes on the televisions, as if daring herself to sprint toward the onslaught.

I couldn't go out on the balcony because everyone with a view into our apartment had rented their windows to paparazzi. I kept thinking if I could just pull back the drapes and stare, really stare at the curved edifice lit in the moonlight, then Greg would know that I was holding out, through the humiliation, the financial tsunami, the threat of jail—I was not wearing down.

Erica's emails from her personal account went public first. Where she referred to clients as gullible morons. Her bank immediately distanced themselves from her and she learned she'd been fired from Anderson Cooper. I knew she must have been frantic to connect with Peter, but there was no way at that point for us to talk about it, or really to talk at all.

I don't know how to convey to you what this period was like. As citizens, we turn on our TVs or Twitter to find out about what's going on in the world—to keep informed so we can join in on the conversation. We don't, in the course of a normal life—not that I will ever know firsthand what that is—hang on Wolf Blitzer's every word because we're waiting to see how our day will go. To find out if we have upended the life of one more person we love.

Lena. The girl I shared a bunk bed with—whose fingertips I could reach up and tap when one of us had an anxiety dream—was now a two-dimensional emblem of my shame presented in HD. Seeing her carried into the courthouse like pasta floating on a boiling surface made me loathe myself for ignoring her advice, for costing her so much money, and privacy, and things I wouldn't even know about for months to come. As our emails and texts were made public, I knew she must have lost her job. And I realized that, despite the bravado that had kept me from reaching out all these months, like a toddler with an exaggerated sense of independence pushing her parent away, I missed her so fucking much. I couldn't believe she was somewhere there in the city and I couldn't even get to her.

"What if I said I made the whole thing up?" I asked Elaine, desperate for a solution that would let everyone get back to what was left of their lives, without impeaching the President. *Impeaching the President.*

By way of an answer, Elaine headed for the door. "Your parents will be here tomorrow."

I woke to the doorman buzzing up. Everything I'd done to prepare myself for seeing them melted—they'd each easily lost twenty pounds, faces hollowed out like cored apples.

Mom enveloped me in her arms and started to sob. Dad walked right past us and turned on the TV. "Jim, shut that fucking thing off."

Erica's eyes met mine.

But he didn't listen. He sat down and stared hard at the screen.

"There's no new information since we boarded the plane," Mom said, wiping her face.

"You don't know that."

"Have you heard from Peter?" Erica asked anxiously.

Mom shook her head. "He hasn't returned our calls for a week or so. How are you?"

"Okay."

I realized that, despite the hug, I hadn't actually been asked the same.

"Can you get to a meeting?" She put a hand on Erica's arm.

"Oh yeah, they love paparazzi at AA."

"Honey, you do what you need to do to take care of yourself."

"Um, how about change my name?"

"Has Elaine been keeping you guys up to date?" I asked.

"I have," she said, arriving behind them.

"What's the plan?" Dad watched the television as my friend Ashley entered the Justice Department building to be deposed.

"There's no admissible proof," I reminded them—and myself. "We just have to survive this, let it be our word against theirs."

"Ours?" Dad asked.

"Mine and Greg's."

Erica snorted.

My father looked at me, incredulous. "Sean Hannity says you're going to jail."

Elaine stepped in. "We have to get the reins on public perception—get them to back down by making it look like they're clubbing a baby seal. Now that you're here," she addressed Mom, "I want to remind America this is a wholesome girl from a wholesome family." We all glanced at Dad, who had that sour, gray look he did when he was drinking. "I've made an appointment tonight at a salon in the Four Seasons. We'll go out through the garage here, straight into their garage. I have a crisis management team waiting to make you over."

After the weeks of confinement, the cold air whistling down into the garage felt like defibrillator paddles. We pulled above ground in our SUV and I didn't make out the shape huddled in the darkness on the sidewalk until it rose like a Mummenschanz character. Our driver was blinded as the paparazzi ran forward, lenses clicking. We instinctively covered our faces.

"Jamie, Jamie!" They chased the car, hitting the back window, hurling questions. One rose clearly above the din, "Who's the brunette?"

We turned to each other in the car. We had no idea.

The three of us sat dumbly in the row of beige leather swivel seats, like animals being shorn, while Elaine paced and made calls, trying to find out what the paparazzi were talking about. Was there someone else? Another intern?

My mother, sister, and I were, I suspected, thinking the same thing: it should have been fun. A makeover. A girls' night out in the kind of place we never could have sprung for. Instead, we sat in queasy silence as the team asked each other how to make us seem "likeable," as if it were an insurmountable challenge. The stylist held up the mint-green Lands' End twin set she kept enthusiastically extolling would make me look "sexless." Everything about the experience highlighted our collective abject misery.

"I'm sorry," I said quietly to my mother as they foiled her hair. "I'm just trying to do the right thing."

"I know you are," she replied flatly.

"You're shitting me!" Elaine dropped her phone in her Birkin, covered her face, then said into her hands, "Can someone turn a TV to NBC?"

We spun our chairs to the flat screen as the colorist grabbed a remote.

"Tonight," Brian Williams was saying, "Rachelle Rubin is breaking her silence. Many of you know her as Jamie McAlister's best friend and confidante. In our exclusive interview she'll explain why she breached that confidence and take us behind the scenes of Jamie McAlister's alleged relationship with the President of the United States." I reached across the space and clutched Mom's cold hand. Over a series of pictures starting with her teen years, Brian introduced Rachelle, describing how she survived her parents' bitter divorce, her father's remarriage to the stripper he supported while still with Rachelle's mom, his subsequent bankruptcy—so much she'd never shared with me. And I realized that during all our hours together, despite the confessional nature of her monologues, she was as skilled at selective disclosure as I'd been with Lena.

The montage ended with us holding up the Washington Monument. Then at once there she was, seated across from Brian Williams in some hotel suite, which was all beige silk and plumped pillows and bowls of tulips.

She looked amazing. First I felt a fleeting pang of missing her—then relief that this hadn't broken and drained her as it had me. While the salon owner was figuring out if anything could be done for the red web of broken capillaries from my lashes to my hairline, Rachelle looked—radiant. Her hair was pin-straight and shiny, and someone had changed the shape of her eyebrows.

"So, Rachelle," Brian said, shifting to get comfortable as if he'd dropped into the seat seconds before. "I have to start by asking you the question America's wondering—why did you do it?"

"Which part, Brian?"

"Why did you record your friend's conversations?"

"To protect her. She couldn't see clearly. She was in love. She was. And I didn't know—I'm not saying the President, but those around him—I didn't know what they were capable of. Someone needed to make a record."

"This is good," I said, on the edge of the chair. "She's going to make this better." *Thank God*, I thought. *Thank God for Rachelle.* She'd somehow found a way to defend me. She was so poised. Like she'd been having this conversation every Friday night of her life.

"That might be understandable," Brian continued. "But then you went to the Office of the Independent Counsel of your own volition. You handed them these recordings—"

"She went to the OIC?" Mom gasped.

"Shh!" Erica hissed.

I remember feeling as though the lights of the salon had been turned all the way up to burn and there was no window to open. I had to close my eyes.

She sounded indignant. "He was getting away with it—"

"Getting away with what?"

I struggled to keep listening. Truthfully, what I'm about to recount I had to learn from rewatching online later. Much later.

"He took away her job at the White House. Her student loans had come due. And he wasn't doing *anything* to help her and it was all his fault—"

"The President?"

"Yes, the President. We called him Greg." That would become a Republican punch line. "Guys think they can just get away with making empty promises. I thought the OIC could help Jamie, protect her, make him do the right thing." But anyone who had been in the

OIC's presence would find that laughable. And then I knew, and wished that I didn't, that this was not just her spin to the public, but to herself. I shakily stood and went up to the screen. She was as righteous as ever.

"In the blogosphere, people are saying this was a heinous violation of your friend's trust."

There was a half-beat of sadness before she regained her composure. "I know. And I hope she can forgive me someday. But I never imagined those recordings would *ever* be made public. We're still not sure how they leaked. They're not part of the formal investigation. They were just supposed to be her insurance policy. So he couldn't hurt her."

"So *he* couldn't hurt me?" I breathed.

"Oh, Jamie," my mother murmured.

"What do you say to the allegations from the White House that you both made this up?" For the first time, she looked thrown. "That you were just two young girls who fabricated those recordings to corroborate a fantasy," he pressed her. "Aren't you shopping a book deal?"

"How did you—no—well, yes," she stuttered. Everything started to swerve.

"And talking to producers about selling your story for film?"

"But that's not why I—no, I'm telling you the truth."

"But you have no proof. Jamie McAlister is still refusing to testify under oath, the President *has* testified—"

"He's a liar."

"Excuse me?"

She was the only one, however fucked up her motives. She was the only one calling him on it. I needed her to keep going. I needed her to *shut up*.

"He lied about bringing her back to the White House. He strung her along. And she waited and was patient and did what she was told."

"So you say."

Her face flash-boiled. "He came on her coat. And she was so sweet and trusting she wanted to clean it, but I made sure she—" I didn't hear the rest of what she said, because Elaine sprung up and out in every direction like a cat thrown in water.

"Is she telling the truth?" Elaine demanded.

"Yes."

"Jesus, Jamie!" Erica spat.

"Where is it?" Elaine was already dialing.

"The apartment," I whispered. "In those unpacked boxes in my room. But they couldn't—"

"They have the search warrant," Elaine explained while it rang. "Yeah, it's me. . . . Good. Don't stop for red lights, and call me when you get it."

"Dad's there!" Erica rattled off his number.

"Can he destroy it? Is that legal?" I asked as Elaine dialed him.

"He might get a fine, but it'll be better if you have a coat with a bleach spot than if they actually get their hands on—he isn't answering."

We left with hair half-cut, half-wet. Elaine tried Dad repeatedly as we raced back.

But the FBI was already parked outside the building.

We got off the elevator as Agent Cuellar was leaving with the coat in a plastic evidence bag, his hands still in blue latex gloves. We found Dad dazed and drunk in the vestibule, holding his phone in bewilderment.

I hated Rachelle. I hated her with every molecule.

Within an hour, CNN was reporting that a garment of mine had been taken into custody potentially with the President's DNA on it. Testing forthcoming. Stay tuned.

Deniability was over.

The President would have to come forward, apologize to the American people, and beg forgiveness for his weakness. I imagined him saying it just like that because the implication—that I made him weak—still thrilled that stunted part of me. It would be done— I wouldn't have to take the stand against him, and someday we still could be . . . I know. It's cringe-inducing. But I'd been alone for weeks with nothing but a television amplifying every terrible thought I'd ever had about myself. There was a paucity of perspective.

And so I waited for his statement.

By the next night every comedian in America—and probably around the world—was guessing how his semen got on the coat. Did I try to swallow—and fail? Did I spit? Was I just bad at it? Here's who'd made jokes at my expense by that point: Gretchen Carlson, Joe Scarborough, Sarah Palin, Bill Maher, David Letterman, Jimmy Fallon, Jimmy Kimmel, Jon Stewart (those ones still sting—doesn't he have a daughter?), and Michael Moore. I was "hippy." I was "flaunting my breasts in his face." Yet also "flat-chested" (Ann Coulter). Jay Leno compared my hair to tumbleweeds. One of the housewives did a whole bit with Andy Cohen about introducing me to the man of my dreams, John Frieda. I wanted to take the mike just to tell people that my hair was soft and D.C. was humid.

I sat next to my parents on the couch and watched, none of us able to pull ourselves away, needing to stand by the side of the road and watch our own car burn to a charred husk. As though we could somehow control it if we just knew *every* single horrible thing people were saying. Or, better, finally found the thing that actually killed me, took the pain and humiliation to a place that ended this. So maybe we manifested what happened next.

The following evening, at Mom's insistence, we changed the channel to a sitcom. But none of us were really paying attention until the show was interrupted for a live press conference. I stood up. "Here we go. He's going to apologize," I said, expecting to see Greg at the podium in front of the blue curtain.

"I don't understand," Mom said, equally baffled. "Why's that guy from the library on TV? Is he going to say something nice? It's about time somebody defended Jamie. Why is his wife with him?"

He did that little coughing thing he does when he's nervous, a split-level house floodlit behind them. "Hi. My name is Mike Harnet and this is my wife, Patty. I'm coming forward now because I feel it's my duty and responsibility to tell the American people I knew Jamie

McAlister a few years ago. She pursued me just like she pursued the President. She's an unstable girl, a predator who stalked me with no respect for—"

"Off!" Dad shouted.

Erica fumbled with the remote.

"—her aggressive agenda and she told me she was going to the White House for one reason only—"

"Turn it off!" He flung his foot forward, smashing the flat screen back on its console, the glass shattering.

We were frozen in the loud silence that followed, tiny droplets of blood starting to drip from his ankle. "Jamie, what was he saying?" Mom finally asked through gulping tears. "That's crazy—why would he do this? You were a kid when you knew him."

Being his girlfriend doesn't make you a grown-up—it makes him a child. Worse than a child.

"A predator," Dad breathed.

"Why, how?" Mom's voice came in little rasps.

Erica's eyes were dropped, her face awash in something I couldn't place. No one rushed to comfort me.

I thought for a long minute, finally landing at the truth of it. "Because he paid attention to me." I got up and walked to my room, shutting the door. On the other side, I heard my father throw up. I would have given anything, *anything*, to talk to Greg at that moment. I wanted to fling open the window and scream *I need you!* Only he would understand.

I lay on the bed, pressing the pillows around me until I could pretend it was Greg holding me, his arms strong and reassuring. The safest place in the world.

Elaine arrived in the morning with her iPad loaded to the tabloid sites. All of which were covering the story of Mike Harnet, the innocent librarian who stoically suffered my relentless advances. And they seemed to have been talking to the same "White House insider" saying that I was a contender for a *Fatal Attraction* remake.

"The OIC got their evidence—they want her to testify—how does making her seem crazy help their case?" Mom asked. Dad was still in bed.

"It doesn't. That's the White House's strategy," Elaine retorted.

"Greg would *never* allow it," I said, pushing the tablet's crocodile case away.

Elaine flipped it shut. "Who do you think plucked Mike Harnet out of obscurity?"

I shook my head against the preposterousness. "Mike came forward because he's—he's jealous and just—I don't know—a fucked-up person."

"Jamie." She leaned forward, her fingertips tented on the dining table. "I spoke to my contacts at ABC this morning. Mike is repped by a powerful D.C. publicist. Who found *him*. Somebody put them on the trail and is footing the bill. Did Rachelle know about Mike?"

"No."

I'd only ever told one person about Mike. One.

Part IV

peering up through the veil of a rimmed hat. There should have been rich rays of sun slanting across the room as lawyers made grand speeches. But there were no speeches. There was a flat gray March light, all but gone by the time we broke each day. And I was sitting in my once perfect suit, which now hung off me, my fingernails searching out a spot of remaining sensation in the callusing flesh of my palms.

I was not pleading for anything. I was merely a means to an end, present so I could prove the President had lied in his deposition when he said he did not have a sexual relationship with me. More specifically, that he did not touch me with the "intent to arouse or gratify." I felt like that delinquent tied to the chair in *A Clockwork Orange* with his eyes pinned open before the traumatizing footage—only I was also the footage.

"How?"

"How did he kiss me?"

"Answer the question, please."

"He . . . leaned down and put his mouth on mine."

"For how long?"

"Um, a couple of seconds?" How does one know?

"Did he use his tongue?"

"Yes." I wanted to take off my shoes, shuffle my feet. I kept searching for a mental automatic pilot that would allow me to slip back to the part of my mind frenetic for solutions—how to wound him, get to him, unlock this so I could get out—but the prosecutor kept forcing me into the past.

"And where were his hands?"

"Um, on my blouse?" The jurors looked at me as if I were the ceaseless television in a waiting room, some programs calling their interest more than others. I focused on the variation in their listening expressions. At one end of the box was a woman with a predilection for jaunty vests who smiled a little too broadly, as if afraid. On the other, an elderly man whose mouth moved as if he was mimicking what I was saying, but on a two-second delay.

"His hands were on your blouse or inside?"

"On top and then inside."

"Were they rubbing you?"

"They were still." Warm. Curious.

"Were they making contact with your nipples?"

"Yes."

"And did he put his hands on your vagina or buttocks?"

"No." Not that time. The prosecutor would get to that time when my father was in the courtroom. He slipped in on the third day and sat in the back row in his one blazer, hands clasped, staring into the middle distance the way he did at church.

"How long was his hand on your breast?"

"I don't know."

"Longer or shorter than five minutes?"

"I don't know, shorter. The same amount of time he was kissing me, I guess."

"Was he visibly aroused?"

Dad was pale but expressionless. "No." I was trying to come to terms with the fact that the technical execution of our affair would be foisted on everyone. I thought about Greg's children. Where would they be when this information intruded? Beside a friend who could help them by cursing me? I hoped they wouldn't be as alone as my dad looked, that the friend would be vicious and equipped with a relieving sense of humor. That they wouldn't be in the halls, attempting a normal day, backpacks over their shoulders, only to see it trending on Twitter.

"Did you feel that he had an erection?"

"Yes." And I thought about Susan. Susan, whose pain I will never be able to bear fully examining. I'd seen her on television the night before, standing beside him, her face a mask of anguish. He stepped aside for her to reaffirm her commitment to him and ask us to do the same. But when she leaned toward the mike, the words stuck, and she only heaved with sobs until she was escorted off the stage by Abigail. I had made myself watch to confront the humiliation and disappointment I'd enabled, only to be stunned that what I witnessed was simply heartbreak. Acute and final.

"Did you make contact with it?"

"Sorry?"

"Did you make contact with his erection?"

"No, not directly, no."

"Indirectly, then."

I slid my nail along my cuticle, slicing into it. "I guess."

"With your vagina?"

"No."

"With your hands?"

"I just, um, felt it."

"His erection was making contact with your body."

"Yes."

"Please point to where."

I did. There was no feeling where my hand landed on my abdomen. And I wondered if that had been true for Susan as well—after Brianne. If it hadn't been safe to be present with him anymore, like she was an animal hibernating from the risk that he would do it again. If she had left the surface of herself.

"Did he attempt to penetrate you?"

"No." Not then.

"And what did he say?"

"He didn't say anything." They wouldn't ask me about the over seventy times he called until later, as if it were an afterthought. That he had kept me on the phone for two-to-three-hour conversations was incidental to their mission. They weren't interested in a court-ship.

"So the last thing he said was . . . 'please'?"

"Yes."

"What did he mean?"

Elaine protested. The question was dropped. But I wanted us to go back; I wanted to ask everyone in the room.

"Where else did he put his hands?"

"On my stomach, my face. My, um, torso." What *did* he mean?

"For how long?"

"I really don't know." What had he wanted?

"Do you need to take a few minutes to remember?"

"No." What could he *possibly* have hoped for? "To be honest, I wasn't counting."

≡

On the fifth day the questions no longer followed a timeline. Surrendering, I revealed every image that came to mind, admitting even to the shaving brush, which "manually masturbated me" as if it could have done so of its own volition. Rachelle's ambition spared me nothing. I was blank, a talking vessel. Yes. No. My left breast. My right hip. His penis in my hand. *Hurt him. Get to him. Get over him. Hurt him. Get to him. Get over him* . . .

"It's still unclear how you came to be 'alone' with the President." The prosecutor, flipping through one of his densely inked yellow pads, gave a slanting look of skepticism that occasionally appears in my dreams to this day. "Your testimony is that on the first occasion of your sexual contact he did not send for you. Please explain, then, how it occurred." His eyebrows were badly in need of a trim, angled like two sides of a roof.

"He didn't. Send for me, I mean."

"You 'ran into each other' in the private dining room." The hairy incline steepened.

"I was instructed to deliver urgent papers to Amar Singh. I was looking for him and instead found the President."

"At which point he just—" The prosecutor cruelly flipped his hand at the implausibility, the cool kid's taunt in front of the entire party—I thought of Brooke. "—kissed you."

"Yes."

"Did he proposition you first?"

"No."

"Imply he could help you out?"

"No."

"He made no mention of any potential career advancement," he chided.

"No."

"But he's the President of the United States—it's implied."

"Objection."

"Sustained."

"Withdrawn. So you propositioned him. You wanted this kiss?"

I'd wanted so many things. I didn't expect someone to step out from the Macy's window and *give* me the gown. "No, I didn't proposition him. I didn't invite it—explicitly—"

"Implicitly, then. You physically enticed him. You used your body to communicate nonverbally that you were available for—"

"It wasn't like that. It was spontaneous. You're making it sound like I—"

"You can't expect us to believe the man holding the country's highest office wasn't at the very least *implying* he could offer—"

"He was in no position to offer me anything. He was losing it; he could barely breathe—"

" 'Losing it,' " the prosecutor repeated. Everyone in the room, drowsy from the radiators, was shifting to attention. "Granted the federal government was suspended, but presumably the President is accustomed to *breathing* under such circumstances. Tell us then, Jamie, why was the President *losing it?*"

Elaine bolted to cry conjecture, squinting for a half-second as she sat down, telegraphing this was bad—it was. An anemone of dark intention unfurled, prickling my numb abdomen. It was bad and it was finally, *finally* something I wielded.

The question was excitedly rephrased. "Ms. McAlister, what *exactly* did you observe about the state of the President in the minutes before he kissed you?"

"Like you said, it was the furlough. Greg was—" Disdain swept their faces. They'd managed to reconcile my fellating him, but my ease with his Christian name was palpably offensive. "The President was—"

Elaine shot up, making an excuse to extricate me. I was marched back to the break room. Elaine whipped around, holding the doorknob shut at her back. "What've we stepped in here, Jamie?"

"I'm just answering the question."

"Volunteer your observations of him as a person or a President, *especially* where the two overlap, and we'll be here for the rest of your life."

"But that night he was—"

She halted me and then continued carefully. "They're looking for evidence of a sexual relationship, which you have given them. *That* is the extent of what we've agreed to. Don't stray outside the lines." There was a knock on the door and she cracked it open to my father. "Good." He stepped inside. "Talk to her. Four more minutes of recess, less than sixty of testimony, and you can put this thing behind you." She left us.

"This thing," I muttered to the table, its Formica maple veneer cracked to reveal actual wood chips. I heard the rustling as Dad reached into his breast pocket. He slid a pack of gum to me as if there were a jail key inside. I waved it off. "No thanks."

"Now I had to go to three newsstands to find the real thing, not that sugarless crap. Chew a piece of gum."

I glanced at its school-bus-yellow wrapping, the same brand he carried when we were little. He'd chewed it ceaselessly while getting sober the first time. The second time it was spearmint Life Savers. We'd come across wispy foil strips as if our house was slowly, steadily shredding. What was getting him through now? "Greg's terrified," I told him.

"I'm sure."

"I mean, that first night, *that's* how we started. He was shaking with terror. He suffers panic attacks, severe ones." Dad looked at me questioningly. "Even if most people say I made it up as retaliation, he still won't be able to shake it. Republicans'll have a field day. He'll be second-guessed on *everything*."

Dad nodded. But if I'd expected him to rally as he'd done countless times for his team, I got the opposite. He barely moved. "I mean, I'm not just going to take it—I'm supposed to fight."

He fidgeted with the gum wrapper before slipping it in his pocket. "You know you have our support." He fell back on that catchall with its conflicted undertone, as if describing other people he kind of hoped would take over.

"Thanks." I was annoyed at myself for having expected anything different.

"Okay, then." He nodded and turned to the door.

"That's it?"

"Jamie," he said tightly, his fingers on the handle. "What do you want me to say?"

"I don't know." I lifted my hands. " 'Make the fucker sorry'?"

He looked over his shoulder at the table between us. "I'm the one who passed out and let them get the coat."

"Dad." I dropped my voice, aware that the coat was the least of what we were talking about. "It's not that simple."

"You deserved a hell of a lot stronger father than you got—is that what you're after?" And there we were. Same as always. Dad flagellating himself, me expected to say something to exonerate him. *It's okay. I'm okay.* But for the first time I couldn't.

"I don't care about what I deserved. I just want you to *be* with me without this—this *thing* sitting between us." I knew what I had to say—what my mom somehow couldn't and Erica didn't in a way he could hear. "Dad, you have to get help. You have to."

"I don't deserve it," he said miserably.

"So you're just going to hate yourself." He looked up. "Forever?" I could see the pain he was in, see his struggle to reach me through the darkness we'd coddled him in. "Ask yourself, *what* does that get us, Dad? The people who just fucking love you? What?"

He stared at me for the first time without a rejoinder.

Elaine rapped on the door. "You're up."

When I returned to take my place the bullet was weighing on my tongue, heavy and smooth. It was the last lap and the prosecutor's entourage jockeyed to cement their careers, feeding him note after torn note while he relentlessly stabbed after my omissions. I was at last poised to show Greg what it felt like.

"So." The prosecutor stared me down, brow glistening, out of yellow pages to flip. "*The reason* the President kissed you is that he was really upset about the furlough. That's your testimony."

My father dropped his head, closed his eyes. It was my turn to speak. To punish Greg for not being the man I deserved.

"My testimony . . ." I wanted saying it to solve—correct—*add up* to something—other than simply making me capable of being what Greg had exposed himself to be. At best, weak; at worst, cruel. I stared at my father's bent head, his hair thinning at the crown. I'd loved two men who mistakenly believed they didn't deserve help, who locked themselves away when the fears became too strong. And I knew that whatever pain punched Greg so hard it knocked his breath out had to be worse than anything I could do to him then and there. "Is that I don't believe reason was present. And that's all I have to say."

I remember that the juror with the vests waved goodbye as if we'd shared a harrowing plane ride. How violently Dad and I were jostled as we tried to make it down the courthouse stairs through the flashing cameras and shouting reporters, spittle flecking our faces. The possibility that we might trip and be trampled. And that for a moment, I prayed for my knees to buckle so it could happen and I wouldn't have to face that my only window to free myself had closed.

That evening as we said goodbye in the foyer Dad confirmed he would call the sponsor Erica had hooked him up with. There was a softness in its infancy between Dad and us. But as soon as he left for the airport, the tense silence resumed. After being trapped for so many weeks by the law, Erica and I were now trapped by the paparazzi. We'd been eating, sleeping, and breathing this captivity for so long that we hadn't the slightest idea what to do next. So Erica made sandwiches.

The silence was punctured by a knock.

"Don't," Erica said through a peanut-butter mouth as I got up.

"I'm only looking through the peephole."

"Jamie," she warned, at my heels.

I saw a young guy in an Urban Delivery T-shirt, the lobby cart behind him laden with grocery boxes. "Can I help you?" I called out.

"A friend sent me," he said furtively. "To help you leave. I have a truck in the garage and I can sneak you out."

I undid the lock and wedged the door open. "To where?"

"I can't tell you any details. I'm sorry." He looked really nervous and maybe all of seventeen. "In case we fail, this person can't be associated with this."

"Well," Erica muttered. "That narrows it down to everyone."

"Ma'am, these deliveries take about fifteen minutes and I just made one to a lady upstairs. If you want to leave, you need to get in a box now. Seriously, we need to go."

Erica crossed her arms. "You can't even be considering this. Nobody will know where we are. How stupid can you be?"

"Erica." The apartment was filled with so much unresolved anguish it seemed to drip from the ceiling like stalactites. Anything had to feel better than there. "Here's what we know. When the government comes for you they send ten men with guns—they don't send Urban Delivery." I let him roll the cart inside before running to my room to grab my bag. But what was there even to take? My perfectly cut suit? The makeup I wore to the witness box? I picked up my wallet and phone, tugged on my hooded sweater, and ran back. "Fuck," Erica said when she saw that I meant it.

"How do we do this?" He lifted the top grocery-box flap to reveal that a stack of six boxes had been glued together and gutted to make the space for two people. Giving a perfunctory hug of Erica's rigid frame, I climbed over and in with a pounding heart.

"Fuck, wait." She ran for her bag. "I texted our attorney," she threatened as she returned. "So if you're thinking of killing us, don't." She climbed in beside me.

My knees in my chest, I stared out the dime-sized air holes cut into the cardboard. Then there was the tangy aroma of the garbage room as the cart was pulled into the service elevator and then under the blowing fans of the basement garage. We tilted up an incline and then, with a grunt, slid into a penetrating cold. "Once the truck is moving you can get out," the kid whispered, followed by the rolling slam of the truck door enclosing us in darkness.

I listened to myself breathing, the air getting denser. The vehicle revved to life and the fluorescent bulb flickered on outside the holes. I inched open the top of our enclosure with shaking hands. We were surrounded by boxes of groceries yet to be delivered, errant salad greens sticking to the floor. I climbed out, almost falling as the truck turned, and I sat hard on a plastic-wrapped stack of water bottles. Erica made her way to the door like a tightrope walker straining to stay steady and tried to lift it.

"It's locked. We're locked in!" She ballasted herself with the wall. "Can I leave this shit-mess with my heart still beating—could you maybe manage that?"

"I'm sorry! They're trying to get us out of here."

"They who!?"

"Maybe it's Elaine? Did she text back?"

"Why wouldn't she just tell us she was sending help? And out of here to *where*? *Where* do you think we're going that this isn't going to follow us? You fucked the President of the United States, which pretty much rules out, you know, fifty of them!"

"I asked for your help," I leveled, gripping the bottles as the truck made another curve and picked up speed—on the highway? "Back in New York, on my birthday. I told you this was happening and you flat-out refused."

"You know *I* have never asked *you* for anything," she said with pent-up venom as she flailed over to the crate opposite.

"Well you could've! You're my sister, for fuck's sake!"

"As everyone now knows. Lucky fucking me."

"Erica, why do you hate me so much?" I asked the question I'd never been brave enough to hear the answer to. "Now, I've given you every reason. But it's always been like this and I just need to know: what did I do?"

"I don't—" She went to dismiss me, and then her face went slack.

"Yes, you do." The answer sat between us in the feet of empty space smattered in grubby neon stock stickers.

"Not you, just . . ." She shook her head. "The contrast you pro-vided."

"Contrast?"

"When you started school it was effortless."

I went to protest.

"It *seemed* effortless. To me. I couldn't make sense out of anything. You were so little, but your letters followed right along on the dotted lines and I—I couldn't even see which end was up. So yeah, I hated you. How you made me feel. Defective. Broken. I guess I wanted you to feel broken, too. That's why I was always so—"

"Mean."

She turned away and blew out, her breath visible in the cold. "So I told you there was no Santa. And that Dad got fired."

I nodded.

"I wanted to be the one—to see the look on your face. And when Mike dropped you off that one time—"

"What?"

She got so quiet I had to lean forward to hear her. "He looked at you like you were some kind of doll, like you weren't even real."

"You knew?"

"The hate seemed so valid by then, Jamie, and I was so fucked up—it's not like Dad and Mom would've taken anything I said seriously. So I talked myself out of doing something about—" She let out a pained breath. "What I guess was, in fact, happening to you."

The truck pulled to a stop and the engine cut. To my surprise, Erica stepped in front of me, protectively squaring herself. I watched over her shoulder as the door rose open to reveal that we were in a parking lot.

Behind our driver, who was motioning us out, it was still and dark. Normal.

"Is that Nordstrom?" Erica pointed to the building lit up in the distance. He turned.

"Yes, ma'am, it is."

"Where are we?"

"This would be the Montgomery Mall, Bethesda."

Erica picked up her bag before walking tentatively to the trailer's edge. He helped her and then me to the pavement.

"I've been instructed to give keys to each of you." He dug in his pocket, then handed them off. He pointed us to where two cars were parked nearby in the sparsely populated section of the vast lot. "You got a week. You just have to return them to an Avis counter at an airport. I'm supposed to remind you to drive careful because they're not in your names." He pulled two envelopes from his back pocket and passed one to each of us. There was a thousand dollars cash inside each.

"But who sent you?" I asked.

He turned to face the edge of the lot where a sedan parked by the retention pond flicked on its floods. Erica grabbed my arm.

"Who is that?" I asked, my heart leaping maddeningly.

"I can't say, ma'am, I'm sorry. But your sister has to go right away. Okay?"

"No," Erica answered. "Not remotely okay."

"Erica."

"It could be God knows what—Susan Rutland on a revenge spree. The RNC demanding a pelvic. A sicko looking to expand his basement collection—"

"Or answers." I stared at the car, trying to make out the driver, obscured by the headlights.

"It's not him," she said sternly, but her face betrayed an uncertainty. He'd come to apologize, to cry and tell me he hated himself for what he had done, to let me hit him.

The kid backed up to the cab. "I have to get the rest of my deliveries done or I'm in trouble."

"Wait!" I tugged one of the hundred-dollar bills from the envelope. "Please. Is it? Is it him?"

He lifted his hands to deflect my gesture. "I couldn't." He hopped up and the truck pulled out, maneuvering back onto the highway.

"I'm not going anywhere," Erica's voice was uncharacteristically small as we peered into the blinding lights. "There's nothing stopping you from driving off with me right now—"

"If I don't call you in ten minutes, call the police," I instructed, squinting. "85G3RU7. 85G3RU7. That's the license plate. Say it back to me." I turned to see she was crying. I went to touch her arm and she jerked it back with that same look Dad had, like she was undeserving of the comfort. I nonetheless took her hand and held it. She gazed down at my grasp, her rigid fingers relaxing. Crying harder, she placed her other hand gently over mine, enclosing it in both of hers. "Let me do this."

"I can't."

"Erica, this isn't like before. I'm not asking you for anything."

"But I don't want it to be that way." She sucked in air. "I don't want to make you feel like that."

"I believe you. But this isn't coded. I'm telling you to leave. Say it back to me. 85G3RU7."

Her bottom lip quivered. The rhythmic woosh of the nearby high-way sounded like waves. The brisk air had a hint of dampness, of fir trees, of gasoline, of someone's fireplace. "85G3RU7."

"Now go."

"Jamie."

"I will call you in ten minutes."

With the same fierceness with which she'd kissed my forehead in her apartment all those months ago, she pulled me into a tight hug. "Please don't die," she said into my ear.

"And miss our next act?" I clung to her, we clung to each other, and for once that hard force that had always kept our torsos from touching disintegrated.

"Ten minutes, Jamie. I'm starting the clock right now."

As soon as she drove out to the highway, the sedan started and the lights approached. I thought what I must have looked like, and I ran a flattening hand over my hair. Wiped under my eyes. The car pulled to a quick stop beside me, the window rolling down—

"I'm sorry, I know you were expecting him."

My mouth hung open. It was the furthest thing.

"Could you get in for a few minutes? Quickly, and then we both should be going. I just can't risk getting out with you here, okay?" Her blond hair tucked under a baseball cap, her face free of its TV-makeup mask, Brianne Rice leaned over to push open the pas-senger door for me.

"*You* sent the truck?"

"My nephew works for Urban Delivery. It was all I could think up that didn't involve anyone else. I wanted to give you the best shot. Please, Jamie. Our time is so limited. Please get in."

I did and she turned off the ignition, cut the lights. She fidgeted with her keys, her French-tips fingering the ring as she seemed to gather her courage. "I'm sorry I can't give you more money. I know it seems like I'm rolling in it, but none of that's actually mine."

"I . . . I didn't expect . . . anything from you."

"I could never have imagined they'd drag another girl into this. I mean, I *wondered* if there were others, you always do. It's not like he had a reputation when we met. But watching these last few weeks— I mean, I was thirty-two when he started flirting with me and God knows my world went upside down. But only twenty-one." She shook her head, her eyes wide with concern. "I can't imagine."

"So you did have an affair." I wanted to know—I didn't—I felt like I was finding out exactly when and how I would die.

"No. No. Nothing like what you—you've described."

I sucked in my lips, reddening. Surprised I still could.

"There was a connection between us. It was . . . potent. He asked for me all the time. Suddenly I was tagging along for everything. It went on for months, growing, but I was too scared to risk it. Not as a single mom." She steadied the photo of the boy and his soccer ball dangling from the rearview, her thumb caressing his face before her hands dropped into her lap. "Not that I didn't want to—I mean, you know, God, I wanted to. It feels good to admit that." A smile flickered across her tense features. "But then . . . well, Greg had been on the rise since we met, but after his convention speech he was deemed the second coming—and I was fired." She snapped her fingers, startling me. "Just like that. And his team, you know, they made sure I wouldn't get another job that chanced having me cross his path again. It was like he wanted to just erase the temptation. I filed a complaint and thought that would be that. When the RNC showed up I was working retail, no health insurance, going into foreclosure." Her face wrung itself and then she exhaled. "They're covering my family and friends' legal bills, paying for my son to go to a good school. I had no idea it would ever get to be this—I'm sorry."

My stomach clenched. "I don't know what to say."

"Nothing. You don't have to say anything. Listen, Jamie, I don't mean to be dramatic, but you have maybe until dawn to do *whatever* you need to do before the press is back on you. A waitress or some gas station guy, someone will call TMZ. It's going to be a lot for a long time—"

"How long?"

She looked at me, her brow rising. "I had to leave my house in a friend's trunk to get here."

"Right."

"Make the most of tonight, okay?"

"Okay. Thank you." I went to open the door and get out. I was struck with the memory of the one time, toward the end, when Mike was closing down a library fundraiser car wash, my parents had forgotten to pick me up, and Patty drove me home in silence, almost saying something as I got out of the car, but then only bidding me good night. I bent back down to Brianne. "Have you ever heard from him?"

She gazed past the steering wheel. "Nope."

I steeled myself—she was the only other person who could tell me. "Did he do it—or was it his people?"

Her face shifted into a sad smile. "I've had kind of a ridiculous amount of time to think about that."

"And?"

"I guess what it comes down to is . . . does it matter?"

I called Erica and told her I would text her when I got wherever it was that I was going. Checking the time, I pulled up to the service road exit. The traffic light blinked red. One night, or what was left of it. One night to do what I had to. Rolling down the window, I turned up the radio and found my way to the highway that would take me north.

Shockingly, he was still listed at whitepages.com. Redburn Street. Garbage cans were pulled to the end of driveways. Bikes leaned against garages. Easter decorations peppered the dark lawns.

I thought of the girls who were growing up there around him. The ones who came from houses like mine, a little too much chaos, a little too little attention. Sleeping now, or still staring up at glow-in-the-dark stars, trying to make sense of their day. In the morning they'd climb onto their buses, their lives teetering between unpredictable and diminishing, always on the lookout—yearning—for something to define them. Stupidly, tragically open.

Then I was leaning on my horn in his driveway, leaning with my whole weight until a light went on in an upstairs window. A curtain parted and there he was. I stepped out so he could see me. He jerked back and another light went on as I stormed up their walk. The front door opened. A soft paunch drooped over his boxers as he crossed his arms against his bare chest. His thinning hair was tossed from sleeping. *"Jamie, are you insane?"*

"You should get your wife."

"What?" He squinted at me.

"Patty?" I tossed my head back and yelled. "Patty?!"

Lights went on in the houses around us.

He grabbed my arm, but I yanked it free. "I've been led enough for a fucking lifetime, thank you." The door whipped open behind him and she stuck her head out.

"What's going on?"

"Now you want to know? I've finally piqued your attention?"

"Jamie, whatever you think you're—"

"It wasn't 'puppy love,' Patty." Their neighbors' porches illuminated as they peered out of their doors. "I was lonely and he knew it. He's found a girl in every town. And he's convinced her it's something other than his illness that he's roping her into."

"Jamie." Mike tried for his librarian voice but it slipped. "Come inside."

"You will never. *Never.* Tell me what to do again. Never suggest it, or desire it or manipulate it. As disgusting as the two hundred pages of my testimony are, I gave them. And Susan and Adam and Alison and I have to live with the consequences. The whole fucking country does. But I've owned it. I've accepted responsibility. *That's* being a grown-up. *Everything* you've said to the American people and to her are a lie. And you and your family have to live with that."

"I'm going to call the cops." Mike turned to go in, but Patty didn't move for him.

"You're trespassing," Patty murmured to me, pale as her nightshirt.

"Fucking call them," I growled, squaring my shoulders. "I've spent the last two months going toe-to-toe with the FBI. Call the police. I've got a story to tell and, thanks to both of you, I couldn't be more warmed up."

She took a step back into their front hall and we both heard the dead bolt click. Mike looked stunned. He tried the handle, called her name, pounded the door. The porch light went off and then the light in the vestibule. Neighbors watched as he became frantic, trying to get back inside what he'd spent God knows how many years defiling.

I left him there.

It was only a few hours before dawn. I know driving through the night from Maryland to New Jersey and on to Pennsylvania conjures a Tarantino-esque image of me gripping the wheel, a samurai sword on the seat beside me. I had thought wounding Greg required the public. But there was no driving up on that lawn. That lawn wasn't even his. He didn't have a cell phone. His mail was opened by others and always would be. Even after he left there, he would have a Secret Service detail until his last breath. I had to get him alone.

Two hours later the sun was orange on the horizon of the abutting fields as I slowed in front of a sagging barn, the only building within proximity of the white clapboard house a ways down the road. A fallow field separated the two structures and there was an inky wood lining the periphery of the property. I got out into the biting air, pulling my hood up and tucking my hands into my sleeves. There were no signs of life from the house, but the government-issue sedan parked across from the drive told me that she still resided there. I locked my car and, hearing a flutter, spun as a fat crow flapped into the sky. I began to walk the frozen crags of mud, stepping over the remains of cornstalks that had been struck down. I watched the house, maybe a hundred yards away, as I made my way diagonally through the field, my heels cracking into the iced water pooled between the trenches. The home was plainly landscaped, a large satellite dish incongruously revealed as the back came into view. That never made it into the photographs of the President's childhood home.

Mud caked into my treads, making my feet feel weighted. Arriving at the tree line, I tried to kick the mud off on a fallen elm before stepping into the leaves. The trees were slippery and dark around me. I could see my breath in silvery puffs. As I climbed over rocks and pushed back extending branches, I began to panic. It had been decades; what if this didn't work? What would it leave me to do? Sink into this mud and atrophy here? If this worked, what was I even planning to say?

That I had loved him. It may have come from some senseless place, but I had loved him. And that was real and mine and nothing could take that from me, not even the revelation of who he really was.

And that I hated him. It burned me from sleep and paralyzed my lungs, and I was so scared I would never be able to let it go.

Then I saw it—flat architectural planes among all that organic decay. I hurried over to the crude wood steps at the base of the tree. A few feet up there was a makeshift platform, overly nailed with rusting heads. And farther up, stretching out from the bare branches, a thick wire. I imagined him there, happy. Flying over the ground in summers that must have surrounded that white house with golden light and cicadas and whispering clouds.

I dropped to my knees, the dampness sinking through my jeans. I bent to reach under the steps, pulling out a clog of wet leaves to feel around in the freezing mud before my hand landed on a tin. I tugged it out and pried off the top. Most of its contents had been eroded by time; musty tear-outs from a *Playboy*, what remained of a crumbling pack of Marlboro Reds. But the small Coke bottle with its cut-down cork was intact. I carefully tapped out the rolled yellowed paper, tugging my pen from my pocket.

Greggy,

I'll be on the bus when you find this. I put a lock on your door, so use it. Keep getting her to church, it seems to help. One way or another I can't ever come back here. I wouldn't do this to you if I didn't

think you could handle it. I know you can. Be good. Get out how-
ever you can.

Love,
Sam.

I know you can handle it.

I imagined a boy's hands clutching this note, the child left ques-
tioning if he could survive, the doubt itself shaming him—a paradox
capable of strangling his windpipe to that day.

I stared over the brown earth as the legend of the doting mother
who raised him all on her own mummified and blew away. Now I
knew what had happened after Sam left. Greg was not her answer; he
was her disappointment. So he was driven, as grandly and historically
as he had worked in the opposite direction, to be all of ours. I finally
knew his secret, too. And, thinking of his last words to me, there was
only one thing to say.

"Goodbye." I wrote it on a sheet of notepaper and then I signed
my name, as I had done on my application, and his Christmas card,
and my affidavit. I rolled it back into the bottle with his brother's
note. And I sat on that sloping child's step, once the only means to
flight, until I knew that a new day had begun.

Epilogue

I wasn't the first young woman to have an affair with a President. And in the context of the scandals that have broken since—Strauss-Kahn, Berlusconi, Kennedy, Spitzer, Weiner, that senator who was soliciting gay sex in airport bathrooms, the congressional leader who was pressing his male pages for a grope—it all makes my story almost quaint. I know that.

And as sure as each election brings fresh opportunities for these media cycles, the talking heads will toss out my name as a shorthand, a universal stand-in for orally servicing a man in power. She gave him a McAlister. And now more frequently—he gave him a McAlister. More often than not, the picture of Greg hugging me on the rope line that stultifying July Fourth will flash on the screen, my lip gloss and haircut now almost back in style. The same photo always serves as filler in the tabloids when they have no images of the latest story to run. The same question is then always raised—where did I end up, anyway?

I apologize that in this whole long tale, my location is the one thing I'm going to withhold. Suffice it to say I found a nice community far enough off the beaten path that it would be a waste of a paparazzo's day to come all this way just to shoot me running errands.

People in town were, of course, stunned to find me in their midst. But I was determined. I just kept going to the store, dropping off my dry cleaning, volunteering to help plant bulbs in the little meridian over on Main until people had, if not accepted, then gotten used to me.

The advantage of the virtual age is that I run my web design business online from home. My clients have only ever heard my voice on the phone—the last name doesn't ring any bells.

Before we go any further, I need to address this absurd idea that I cashed in when I collaborated with that biographer. Yes, I'm talking to you, Ann Coulter. I sit here at my West Elm desk and laugh that you could posit this all was an elaborate get-rich-quick scheme. I was confronted, at twenty-two, with a *seven-figure* debt and *I* was the only collateral. Rehash some already well-known facts or pose for *Playboy*—those were my choices. From Lena to Ashley to Brooke, *anyone* who was subpoenaed or deposed because of their relationship with me—I've repaid their legal fees. Every dime.

Of course that could never come close to wiping out the balance of what I owe my parents. Even if I could have bought their house back, they still would have left Naperville. My mom's boss was kind and managed a transfer to Omaha. It's cold and flat, and the locals are at a complete loss as to what to make of Dad's Irish humor. But at least kids don't spray "slut" across their front door.

They know Erica and I are ready to get them down to Florida when they say the word, but each time Mom reads about the Burmese python epidemic they put it off another year. "Nine hundred eggs *at a time*," she shudders at us over Skype. "We know, Mom, we know." It's nice that Erica and I can laugh at Mom together now—at both of them—the things that once grated us shrunken to quirks, mostly endearing.

Peter covered Erica's legal expenses, which she characterized— accurately, it sounded—as paying her to go away. It was amazing to hear about her transformation in those first few months: she moved to San Francisco and got certified to teach yoga while she figured out her next move. Then, in a you-can't-outrun-your-fate kind of way, she met a ridiculously successful financier in AA. Now she lives in South America and has thrown herself into being the perfect expat wife and mother in a community just complicated enough for her to stay excited. She frequently says running carpool on the Upper East Side would have bored her back to drinking—but shuttling her kids to school in an *armored car* is an adventure. I never thought I'd see her with laugh lines. Or splattered in freckles. Or happy.

From what I've pieced together, Paul Hoff left Washington long ago, another expat. Apparently one of the journalists fruitlessly in pursuit of his story ended up taking him to a coffee that became a marriage, according to the *New York Times* Vows article. They had a ceremony at an inn in Vermont, and Paul looked so much brighter that at first I didn't recognize him.

I thought about Paul a lot when I passed the age he was when this all went down. It's getting harder to gauge what twenty-one-year-olds look like, to pick them out at the mall. I see girls I think are in grade school and it turns out they're high schoolers. I can't imagine how alone Paul must have felt, already heartbroken, trying to ballast against the sideswipe of Brianne compounded by my graceless entrance. I send him a Christmas card via his husband's address at the London *Times* every year. "I'm sorry," I write. "I'm sorry. I'm sorry." I don't know if he gets them.

So it was Rachelle. Entirely Rachelle. Driven, I've come to see, by the same desperate fear that led me to follow Greg into that darkened warren in the first place. Fear fueled by the recent memory of imperfect childhoods, compounded by the dawning reality of having to navigate our lives in a world of people busy navigating their own. Would we ever get it right, be seen, be loved? It made us clumsy and desperate. Both of us. We thought life only gives you one "it." So I went to a married man and she went to the OIC. I still don't know the exact date, but it was shortly after election night. I've learned they coached her on how to encourage me to take steps that would escalate my situation from the immoral to the illegal.

Her book came and went. I never read it. But she got that reality show off it, or really the media around it. Remember? It was the one where she made over college seniors. I watched it once. She was certainly a girl you wanted to hang out with; that never changed.

Now you know her for her preternatural tan and ability to occasionally hold her own as Ryan Seacrest's sidekick. She's interchangeable with the other smiles hosting red-carpet shows and entertainment extras. Her boobs are no longer hers, but for the most part the rest is. I'd like to be able to say it doesn't, but it hurts to come across her on TV, just for a second. Then I find myself staring at her bleached teeth telling quick jokes, wondering if she outran the fear, if it was worth it, if she's loved.

Disgusted by both parties, Gail left political fundraising after the whole ordeal and now she's helping UCLA Medical Center expand its oncology department. She sold her apartment at three times what she paid for it and lives in L.A. full time so she can be on call for her grandkids. Their mother, now running her own boutique firm, will tell you with a smile that she knows every fucking thing there is to know about me and would love to forget half of it.

I have just hung up with her now, in fact. Lena, in the back of a town car inching through city traffic; me, standing at my kitchen counter. And yet she's still my girl. It's so silly, the things you think will matter at twenty-two. And so earth-shattering, the things you think won't.

Which brings me to Greg. I read about him all the time, of course; I'd be lying to say otherwise. His hair never really did go gray, but retains a Robert Redford–like fullness and luster that has everyone convinced there's a portrait in a closet somewhere of a bald, wizened ex-President. There he is at Davos. There he is addressing the DNC. On the board of this. Consulting that. He gets two hundred thousand dollars to speak for forty-five minutes. His thousand-page book, in which I warranted only a small paragraph that included the word "unfortunate" twice, brought him an eight-million-dollar advance and stayed at number one for weeks.

Susan is remarried to a retired obstetrician she and Greg went to college with. Her path not chosen. Adam is still working in a lab— which I always think is such a windowless existence for such a sunny person. Maybe he's looking for the cure to something. Alison's lesbian phase at college was cynically seen as a political move, but I imagine that would have been a welcome change from boys whose words seemed as fabricated as her father's.

He never remarried.

I have had a lot of time to pore back over our every encounter, although the time between those intruding memories stretches for greater and greater lengths. And I have wondered—why me? Why was I worth risking so much for? I look at the old pictures and see that while I was objectively nowhere near as lovely as Susan, I had a freshness. A naiveté. But I don't think now that he wanted to be with me, ultimately, as much as he wanted to be twenty-one again himself. The pressure of his responsibilities and his crippling self-doubt made him want to create a space to hide—a zip line in the woods, a place to stash a letter in a soda bottle. I was a secret *and* a haven. His brother abandoned him to handle something he could never handle. In a way, he did the same to me.

I stare out the window at the dusting of snow on the backyard. It's not that it's unseasonal, just unusual for this region. Elsewhere, February means down coats. You will probably be surprised to know that those same back channels that tracked me down at Gail's have served Greg faithfully. The first time he found me, the phone ringing out of the ether, I went numb.

The caller ID is always blocked. He says my name and then we both wait for the next word, but it doesn't come. He breathes, waiting for me to speak. I'm always the first to hang up.

Today is an anniversary of sorts. Of Sam's death, or his hearing of it. The phone has not rung, as it sometimes does on this date. But I knew it wouldn't after the itinerary arrived in my mail a few weeks ago. There, mixed in with some bills and a Pottery Barn catalog, was a thick envelope from an elite travel agency in Manhattan. Inside, written in black and white, was his name beside mine, for the first time in nearly twenty years, in service of us alone.

A trip to Venice.

I don't know if he just isn't aware of anything about my life since, or if he's willfully ignoring what and whom I'd have to juggle or hurt to join him. Or perhaps he doesn't care. Avoiding collateral damage was never his priority. He assumes, hopes. Determined to have been right that last time we were together. Like his calls, the gesture was to speak for itself. I sense it is his final attempt.

As I stand here, hands on the counter, he sits in a first-class seat in an airport I would have made a connecting flight to by now. He stares at the open bulkhead door and anticipates.

The minutes pass on the oven clock behind me. I watch the flakes drift, cling to the grass. He wills my arrival, imagines my fingers entwined in his when the plane lowers over the water, my wonder as we touch down on land where there shouldn't, organically, be any. How he'll burst with pride that he's about to make good.

He is finally taking me, he thinks. That little place behind the Guggenheim.

In a few seconds the flight bridge will pull away.

He doesn't know—will never know—that I've already been.

ACKNOWLEDGMENTS

We wish to thank our phenomenal editor, Greer Hendricks; her spectacular assistant, Sarah Cantin; and everyone at Atria Books under Judith Curr, who makes the publishing experiencing such a joy. Suzanne Gluck, and everyone at WME, thank you for ten great years. Pilar Queen, for stepping in with style at the zero hour. Our fierce and fabulous lawyers, Ken Weinrib and Eric Brown. Stephanie Jones, Kirby Alison, and the team at Jonesworks, without whom we'd be shouting in a well. Tiffany Bartok, we really don't like to leave the house without you. The brilliant Katie Brandi, who for over thirteen years has been telling us what's what. Kelly Grace Gibson, for being our favorite insider. Kathy Stone, Kristi Ising-Wilson, Lennie Ross, Rebecca A. Little, Amanda Scherger, and all our fabulous fans and followers on Facebook and Twitter who rock our worlds every single day. Thank you.

Emma thanks her parents, Joan, John and Janet, and Joel and Nora, whose wisdom, humor, and generosity gave her a home while hers was under renovation. Shannon, Sara, Sarah, and Kira: who make her want to be lounging in the unforgiving plastic chairs of the cafeteria. Jordana, for being there at word one and blessing her with g'nights from too many miles away. Heather, for flying the flag through the move. Sophia, without whose perfect care of our family, half this book couldn't have been written. Joel, for still giving her the thrill of an illicit crush. And Theo, for being.

Nicki thanks Auntie Olivia, chauffeur, nanny, disciplinarian, fashion coordinator, and all-around star member of Team Sophie. And David. Please always make sure your bike helmet light is working because she couldn't live without you.